THE GUNNER FACED NOT A MAN, BUT A DERVISH.

A creature too fast to be human tossed the gun into the wall, where it embedded itself, then grabbed the commando by the hair and began slashing him with a knife, but the knife moved too fast to see.

The commando's battle harness, his handgun holster, his black suit and white gloves and mask—all of it seemed to disintegrate from his body like water flowing off him.

The commando found himself standing stark naked in the judge's chambers.

Remo snatched at the several thunks that resulted from his quick disrobing of the gunner. He came up with a handgun, a knife, a magazine for the rifle and a walkie-talkie. He twisted the gun, dismantled the radio and snapped the knife. No explosives.

"Where's the suicide charges?" he demanded.

For the naked commando, this was one too many bizarre facts to cram into his brain. His brain choked and he said, "Uh."

"Very helpful."

CREATED BY MURPHY & SAPIR

THE

DESTROYER

POLITICAL PRESSURE

A GOLD EAGLE BOOK FROM

WORLDWIDE®

TORONTO • NEW YORK • LONDON
AMSTERDAM • PARIS • SYDNEY • HAMBURG
STOCKHOLM • ATHENS • TOKYO • MILAN
MADRID • WARSAW • BUDAPEST • AUCKLAND

First edition April 2004

ISBN 0-373-63250-9

Special thanks and acknowledgment to Tim Somheil
for his contribution to this work.

POLITICAL PRESSURE

And for the Glorious House of Sinanju,
sinanjucentral@hotmail.com

Frank Krauser had already received his fifteen minutes of fame. Tomorrow he would be famous again, but he wouldn't live to see it. Frank Krauser was on his way out, about to meet his Maker. He was eating his proverbial final doughnut.

Doughnuts were what got Frank Krauser in trouble in the first place. He ate a lot of them, and he spaced them out throughout the course of the day. The problem was that he never left the Dunk-A-Donut shop in between doughnuts—even while he was on the clock for the Chicago Streets and Sanitation Department.

Somebody at Channel 8 News did some hard-core investigative reporting, which involved sitting in a car on the street and aiming a video camera at the front of the Dunk-A-Donuts, turning the camera on and letting it roll. The place was all windows; the camera saw everything that happened, clear as day. Channel 8 came back with six hard-hitting hours of video of Frank Krauser sitting in the corner booth at the doughnut shop, reading the *Chicago Sun-Times,* talking to cops and other city workers, chatting with the locals and the staff, reading the *Chicago Tribune,* reading the back of the sugar packets and generally not performing his duties as an employee of Streets and San.

At the end of six hours, Frank pushed himself to his feet, spent a good ten minutes making his farewells to the staff and he walked down the street to the work site, where the crew he was supervising was cleaning up after its day of street repairs.

Channel 8 didn't show all six hours, but it did broadcast forty-five seconds of it during a sweeps piece called "Slackers at Streets and Sanitation." The mayor held a news conference in his rumpled suit and promised an investigation and immediate reforms. Frank Krauser was suspended.

The Committee for a Cleaner Streets and Sanitation Department roamed the city of Chicago for days, then public interest waned. The committee turned in its official Report, which was actually the same report turned in years ago by a similar committee made up of the same committee members. They did go to the effort of changing the dates in the margin and, unlike the 1999 report, they ran the spell check. So you could say it was a new report.

Frank Krauser's suspension was lifted, which really irritated him. Unknown to Channel 8 News, it had been a paid suspension. Krauser was getting paid for doing nothing and found he really enjoyed it. Now he'd have to drive all the way out to the work site, every single day.

"It's inconvenient," he told his cousin, who was one of the top dogs at Streets and San. "What kind of a sham investigation did they do, anyway? You can't tell me they did a complete job in only two weeks."

"It was very thorough," his cousin said defensively. "I keep telling you to throw your back out or something, Frank. Go on disability. You can milk it until retirement."

"Easy for you to say," Frank said. "They only pay you like seventy percent of your salary."

"You'll save that much buying your doughnuts by the box at the grocery store, Frank."

Frank slammed the phone. His cousin was a moron. Supermarket doughnuts—he hated supermarket doughnuts!

So, unhappily, Frank went back on the job. Instead of getting his own four-block zone of the city, his cousin insisted on putting Frank's crew on a rotating schedule of work sites, so Frank always had to be looking for a new doughnut shop. Sometimes, after arriving at a new work site, he'd find himself without a doughnut shop within a mile or more! He was *not* walking that far!

So nowadays he had the crew drop him off first thing in the morning—he never even went to the work site.

Even worse, not every doughnut shop was the same. Even among Dunk-A-Donut franchise outlets there was a noticeable inconsistency in the quality of the product. Sometimes there would be no franchise, just a local bakery-type place, where they frowned on his hours of loitering even though he bought doughnuts one after another all day long.

On the very last day of his life, Frank Krauser discovered Krunchy Kreme Do-Nuts.

He'd heard about Krunchy Kreme. Who hadn't heard about Krunchy Kreme, the doughnut chain from the Deep South? People said eating a Krunchy Kreme doughnut was like taking a bite out of heaven. You could watch them being made! You could watch the doughnut move through a waterfall of doughnut glaze! Frank watched the news about the first Krunchy Kreme opening in the Chicago suburbs. Lines of patrons gathered outside at four in the morning—and the shop didn't even open until six! The first customers came out munching doughnuts and beaming for the news reporters. "Delicious! Scrumptious! The best doughnuts I have ever eaten!"

"Oh, give me a break!" Frank said to Officer Raymond O'Farrell. Ray and Frank often shared coffee and French Delights about midmorning—when Frank was working anywhere near Ray's beat.

Ray shrugged. "I hear they're good."

"Maybe good, but how much better can it get? I mean, you believe these idiots?"

But Frank Krauser's interest was piqued. Krunchy Kreme shops started opening inside the Chicago city limits. Finally the day came when Frank Krauser's crew was transferred to a new work site within two blocks of Krunchy Kreme.

"Drop me there," he told his assistant supervisor. "I'm gonna see if these damn things are as good as everybody says."

The morning rush was over, but the place was still pretty packed. Frank bought a couple of Krunchy Kremes and a big coffee, then paused for a moment to gaze at the famous doughnut factory through the windows.

Dough was extruded in rings onto the stainless-steel conveyor, which carried them down into a vat of hot oil. They bubbled and bobbed before emerging golden brown. Up the little roller coaster they moved, cooling for a twenty seconds or so, and then they reached the famous waterfall of glaze.

The rich-looking glaze spilled thick and gooey over the hot doughnuts, drenching them in sugary goodness. Frank Krauser had to admit, it looked delicious.

Then came a series of gleaming steel dispensing machines, which coated the doughnuts with a shower of multicolor sprinkles or toasted coconut or crushed nuts, or drenched them yet again, with chocolate or white frosting. A select few doughnuts were penetrated by a rapid-fire cream-filling machine, whose nozzle dripped cream between thrusts.

Frank Krauser felt himself becoming aroused.

"All for show," he told himself as he broke away and took the only empty booth in the place.

It was a nice enough place. Clean. Polite people behind the counter. Coffee smelled good. But none of that mattered if the doughnut failed the Frank Krauser quality test.

At 9:18 a.m. on that momentous Monday morning, Frank Krauser bit into his first Krunchy Kreme.

At 11:56 a.m. on that same morning, he bit into his eighteenth.

"So, they as good as they all say, Frank?" asked Officer Ray, who stopped in about two that afternoon.

"Better believe it!" Frank leaned back in his chair and pulled tight on the bottom of his T-shirt. "They gave me this."

"'Krunchy Kreme Konvert,'" Ray read aloud from the front of the shirt.

"And proud of it. I ain't never eatin' no other doughnuts!" Frank didn't know how prophetic his words were.

When Ray went back to work, Frank noticed the Ford SUV parked across the street. He was sure he had noticed it before. Like an hour ago. He could see the silhouettes of two men sitting inside. Frank got worried. If he got busted again on Channel 8 News, it might not blow over so fast. He might be forced to take unpaid leave.

At four o'clock the SUV was still there, and Frank knew it was another damn news camera in there, violating his privacy. His assistant supervisor showed up at five.

By then Frank had a brilliant plan. "Listen, Paul, I'm staying here. You go back and have Margie mark me as off today. Say it's a personal day."

"How you gonna get home, Frank?"

"I'll take a cab. Later."

Paul left. Frank chuckled with self-satisfaction. Let them film him all day. He wasn't officially working today, so he really wasn't doing anything wrong. As an added bonus, Frank had a good excuse for staying right there at Krunchy Kreme Do-Nuts. He could eat doughnuts and egg on the idiots from Channel 8.

When Frank Krauser finally headed home to his south-side town house, he strolled past the site where his crew had been yanking out sidewalks all day. A cement truck was parked there, its huge drum turning, keeping the concrete mixed inside. Must have a night shift coming to pour it overnight so the new concrete could set before the morning vandals came along with the bright idea to write their names in it.

A vehicle roared up the street and swerved, coming to a halt with a chirp of tires right in front of him. It was the Ford SUV from the doughnut shop.

"What the fuck?"

The doors opened, front and back, and the four men who emerged wore tight black outfits that covered them completely except for their hands and heads. Those were covered in white gloves and white ski masks.

"Who are you clowns?"

Then he noticed that the masked men were carrying small plastic devices, each with a pair of metal probes at the front. They also had machine guns dangling from shoulder straps.

"You ain't from Channel 8!" Frank exclaimed, protectively pulling his big sack of Krunchy Kremes to his chest.

The biggest of the gunmen approached Frank silently and swiftly, his eyes blazing behind his mask. Frank turned to run and found that one of the black-and-white clowns was right behind him, holding one of the little plastic things at him. Sparks of blue electricity sizzled out from the twin metal studs.

"Hey, assho—"

Frank's flabby arms were locked behind him in a pair of arms that felt more like steel clamps. "Hey! Lemme go, you piece of shit!"

Frank leaned forward and swung his great girth from side to side, the dangling sack of doughnuts flying all over the place. Frank lifted his assailant right off the ground—but the lock on Frank's arms didn't weaken.

Another one of the black-and-whites came right up to Frank and stuck the zapper in his neck. Frank couldn't get his feet moving, and he felt a painful jolt that stiffened his wobbly limbs.

The next thing he knew, Frank Krauser was being carried. There were grunts and curses, and it seemed he was being hoisted high off the ground before being dumped on a cold metal platform. A loud rumble nearby came to a stop.

"He'll never fit!" somebody complained.

"We'll make him fit."

Frank was able to shift his head enough to see the back end of the cement mixer just a few feet away, and watched with growing horror as the black-and-white clowns attached a big screw clamp to the opening and cranked it, forcing it apart. The steel ripped. Soon the entrance into the cement mixer was widened enough for—

"No. No way," Frank croaked.

"Yes way," said the great big black-and-white. Behind the white mask the hulk was grinning.

"Why?"

"You are corrupt," said the unemotional voice of another man.

"I ain't!"

"These are a symbol of your corruption." The man lifted the bag of Krunchy Kremes that Frank still clenched in his frozen fist. Frank jerked the bag away.

"Guess you need another dose of cooperation," the smaller man said, and put the stun device to Frank's throat again. Frank jerked and went limp. Lightning flashes obscured his vision, but he felt himself being lifted again. It took all four of them to get him up, cursing and screaming.

Where were the cops? This was the city of Chicago. There were four million people. Hadn't anybody called the cops?

They had his upper body inside the drum when they paused to gather their strength. Frank could feel his legs dangling outside. His vision cleared enough for him to see, by the light of the street lamp, the mass of wet concrete that waited below to swallow him. He forced his body to work, to move. He pushed against the slimy insides of the drum and lost his grip on the doughnut sack, which slid down, down, down into the concrete, where it rested on the surface. Frank sobbed.

"Come on, let's finish this," said one of his assailants.

Frank felt their hands on his legs and he started kicking, feebly. They grabbed his ankles anyway and pushed all of him inside the mixer.

He whimpered and tried making his arms work, tried to get himself turned, and only managed to move sideways before he slid into the concrete. His head landed on the sack of doughnuts and forced them into the wet mess. Frank felt the cold mass embracing him and he tried to shout. The gritty, heavy stuff filled his mouth and covered his eyes.

With a last surge of adrenaline, Frank crawled upright and thrust his body out of the concrete. He opened his eyes and saw the light outside the mixer for a moment. He cried out and reached for the light, but then the junk blotted it out for the final time. He clawed for purchase, unable to see, unable to hear.

But he did feel the rumble of the engine. He felt his world begin to turn.

NONE OF THE MEDIA OUTLETS really knew how to handle the event. Channel 8, the news station that had vilified Frank Krauser the previous year, wouldn't touch it. A few of the other stations tried to come up with a Frank-Krauser-as-victim angle but gave up. Most of the coverage was limited to anecdotal blurbs in the papers and a twenty-second brief on the morning news show. The police never could decide if Krauser was murdered or not, so they conveniently decided on "not" and forgot about him. In fact, before very long, almost everybody had forgotten about Frank Krauser.

He had simply not been a very important person.

That morning, though, one man who read about Frank Krauser's death in the online newspapers had been searching for just this kind of thing. What he read made his lemony face pucker with concern.

2

His name was Remo and he would have made a lousy used-car salesman.

"You don't exactly have a face a man can trust," said the sailor with the shotgun.

"That's actually one of the nicer things anyone has said about my face," Remo replied. "You fire that gun and you'll put a big hole in your sails."

"The first big hole will be in you. You're the killer, aren't you, eh? You killed Rudy from the *Queen Bee*, didn't you?"

"I didn't kill Rudy, and I didn't kill the captain of the *Turnbleu*."

The man with the shotgun stood up straighter, his face narrowing. The frigid wind tossed his long, greasy brown hair, and the icy droplets of rain collected on his yellow rubber waders, forming rivulets that trickled all the way down his body to the deck. "The *Turnbleu* was Finster's boat. Finster's dead?"

"Yes."

"They find the body?"

"No, just a lot of red stuff that used to be inside of it."

"Why you telling me this?" the sailor demanded. "You proud of killing innocent men?"

"I didn't kill those sailors, but whoever did is working his way down the winner's list, and you're next."

The narrow-faced man looked more stricken. "Finster was leading the pack after Rudy disappeared. If Finster died, then I'm in the lead."

"And in first place on some bad apple's to-do list," Remo added.

"Which is you," said the narrow-faced man, raising his gun.

Lee Clark dropped the shotgun and cursed his clumsiness, stooping to grab it back. He didn't see it on the deck. Come to think of it, he hadn't heard the clatter when it hit the deck. And how come it just left his hands like that?

"Here," Remo said. He was still standing in the same spot on the other side of the deck hatch but now, somehow, he was holding Clark's shotgun.

"How'd you do that?"

"Did you notice I am not murdering you at the moment, even though I have the gun?" Remo asked.

"Yes." Clark's tone made it clear he didn't expect his luck to continue long.

"Good. Your next unexpected visitor isn't going to show you that courtesy, if my hunch is correct," Remo said as he removed the shell from the shotgun and tossed it to Clark. The sailor looked at it as if he'd never seen it before.

"I helped myself to this, too." Remo was holding up a short, thick chunk of cable with heavy screw clamps on either end. Clark knew it looked familiar, but it took him a few seconds to place it.

"That's a battery cable."

"I'll put it back when I'm done," Remo assured him. "Your generator and batteries will be useless without it, and I could stop you before you could rig up a replacement for this. I don't want you calling for help."

Clark laughed sourly. "So what are you up to if you aren't the killer, eh?"

"I'm the killer *catcher*," Remo explained. "You're my bait, whether you like it or not."

Clark felt his hopes sink as the man in the summer clothes tossed the shotgun over his shoulder, and he had to have tossed it harder than it seemed because it took a long time for the weapon to rise, vanish against the slate-gray sky, then appear again, falling butt first and straight as a spear. It slid into a rising wave.

The frigid water was cresting at twenty-five feet that morning on the Drake Passage. The sky was the same color as the sea, like dirty bathwater.

Lee Clark never felt more helpless.

"YOU HAVE TO CALL IN on the emergency radio if you have a communications breakdown. That's in the rules."

"Yes. That's right," Clark said.

"We'll do it together," Remo said. He accompanied Clark belowdecks, into a cramped helm behind a narrow window.

"Not much room to stretch your legs," Remo commented.

"After eight, nine weeks at sea you get used to it," Clark said.

"Eight weeks? That explains the smell."

Clark raised an eyebrow. "What smell?"

Remo pointed at the emergency radio, in a tiny, water-resistant plastic case mounted near the ceiling. Clark opened it and turned it on. The unit fed off the sailboat's generator power, so the batteries were always fully charged. It didn't take long to get a reply to his hail. Remo had already warned Clark of unspecified consequences if he strayed from the script.

"What's your situation, Lee? We got mighty worried when we saw your data feed go down."

"I'm fine, base. Just a generator problem. One of my cable clamps busted and it just fell right off. I'll have another put on soon enough. Meanwhile, I'll leave the emergency unit on to receive."

"Good to hear it."

Clark signed off and looked expectantly at Remo.

"I told you I am not the killer."

"Where's your boat?"

"I jumped in."

"You parachuted onto a sailboat going eighteen knots

in twenty-five-foot seas? Without me noticing? You expect me to believe that?"

"You ask too many questions."

"And in that getup?" Clark gestured at Remo's attire.

Well, Remo had to admit he wasn't dressed for the climate by most standards, but he had found that, under most circumstances, his uniform did just fine. The Italian, hand-sewn leather shoes were comfortable, pliant and tough enough to stand up to days of abuse before going into the trash. Usually the Chinos and T-shirt were warm enough and gave him freedom of movement. There were times when Remo needed freedom of movement.

"I was wearing a windbreaker when I jumped," he admitted. "It got soaked so I scrapped it."

"Uh-huh. So what now?" Clark demanded.

"Nothing. Go about your business. The next move is the killer's."

"AREN'T YOU COLD?" Clark shouted across the windswept deck. He was retying one of his ropes. The GPS on his watch told him he was still on course, but the wicked wind had him using his smallest sails and he was hard-pressed to keep his sailboat, the lovely *Traverser*, from heading into the rocky mess of Chilean islands that made up the southernmost point on the Americas.

The wicked wind drove the drizzle under your clothing no matter how tightly you tied your sleeves and collar. The wind and the water could suck the life out of you in no time if you weren't careful. Clark's captor—

or protector, he wasn't yet sure which—was not being careful. He had refused the spare coat Clark offered him and come outside in just his blue T-shirt. The T-shirt was wet again.

Clark and Remo were inside for less than a half hour, but Remo's shirt and pants were bone dry by then. Clark couldn't help but notice. Now, how had that happened?

At least this Remo was a skilled seaman. He strolled around the heaving deck without apparently noticing the abrupt rises and the sudden plummets. Even Clark didn't get used to oceans like this, and he made dang sure he wore his safety cable when he was on deck. All it would take was one slip. If he lost his footing during one of those big risers and got dumped in the icy waters of the Drake Passage, he was as good as dead. The *Traverser* would be out of his reach in seconds and there would no hope of rescue.

Remo didn't seem too worried about the danger. Lee Clark almost hoped the man *would* get dumped in the water.

Hell, killer or not, Clark knew he would go back and rescue the guy. It was just the kind of man Lee Clark was.

Remo was cocking his head again, concentrating.

"Are you trying to hear something, is that what you're doing?" Clark asked.

"Killer's boat," Remo explained.

Clark shook his head. "Son, there could be a Fourth of July parade marching alongside us and we wouldn't hear it in all this weather."

Remo just cocked his head.

"You don't expect somebody to come from one of the other racers to get us, do you?" Clark probed.

"Don't know."

"There's more than fifty boats in this race, right, Remo? Most of 'em are the Class IIs and they're way back. But everybody is way back now. There isn't anybody close enough to ride up from behind and catch this boat, even with a quick dinghy."

"Not necessarily."

"I tell you they'd have to have a quick dinghy. We're going twenty-two miles per hour land speed. How they going to catch up to us without a quick dinghy?"

"If you don't stop saying 'quick dinghy' I might have to kill you after all," Remo growled.

"Remo, are you steamin'?" Clark asked incredulously when they were inside again.

Remo didn't answer, but Clark didn't need an answer. He could see the steam rising off Remo's T-shirt.

"You some sort of a cyborg? You know, you got heating elements under your skin, like them little wires that get all orange in the toaster?"

"Yes," Remo said. "That's it exactly. Mum's the word."

Clark's eyes grew wide. "You a secret agent from the government? How much did you cost? More than six million dollars. Steve Austin cost six million dollars."

"That was the 1970s. Human amplification technology is way more expensive these days," Remo explained. He had recently picked up the term "human amplification" from an airplane magazine article and was pretty pleased to have the chance of actually using it in a sentence. It made him sound downright credible.

"You really are with the government, eh?" Clark mused. "So why you keeping me prisoner like this?"

"I told you, Lee, I need bait. You're it. I couldn't have you doing anything out of the ordinary that might warn off the killers."

Having come to terms with the fact that Remo, last name not clearly enunciated, was not the killer, Clark now had to accept that another party, which was the killer, was likely to be joining them.

"How soon until them murdering sons of bitches make their move?" Clark asked.

"Soon, I hope, before I pass out from the smell," Remo said.

"What smell?"

THE SEA CALMED as they moved north, and after a night that seemed like days the wind dropped, too, the waves settling to a more reasonable five feet. That was when Remo became even more alert and went up on deck. The sky was less dreary than the day before, but the sun was still no more than a bright spot in the gloomy cloud cover. The precipitation was gone and the air was scrubbed clean, giving them a view to the horizon.

Clark had bundled up and tromped out after Remo, only to find the expensive bionic CIA operative standing there doing the listening thing again. Clark examined the ear too closely.

"You're violating my personal space, Lee."

"It's a superear like Jamie Sommers, eh? You know, Steve Austin's girlfriend?"

"If I told you I would have to kill you," Remo replied and moved a few paces away from the man who had lived for nearly two months on a sailboat that had no shower.

Remo's sense of hearing was well beyond the range of most humans, but there were no electronics stuck in there. Remo Williams had the highly tuned hearing of one trained in the arts of Sinanju.

There was more to Sinanju than hearing, and in fact all Remo's senses were magnified to an uncanny degree. His sense of balance came not from years at sea but from Sinanju, as well. He controlled his body to a degree far beyond that of everyday men and women. Staying warm in inclement weather and the ability to dry his clothes— these came simply from manipulating his body heat.

But even that was just the beginning of what Sinanju was, and Remo was the Reigning Master of Sinanju. The only other living Master, the Master Emeritus, was back home in Connecticut watching Spanish language soap operas.

Soaps or no soaps, Remo would have preferred the Connecticut duplex to this fume-filled toy boat. When would the killers come?

And how would they come? Not by air. The spy satellites would spot them for sure. After the first mysterious murder many electronic eyes had started monitoring the Around the World All by Yourself sailboat race. Still, another sailor had been murdered, out in the middle of nowhere, and the electronic eyes never saw a thing. Not on radar, not on thermal, not on visual.

A boat? The spy sats knew how to look for the wake of any boat that was fast enough to catch up to a racing sailboat.

So if it wasn't above the water or on the water, it could only be below the water. Remo had spent hours listening for the sound of a surfacing submarine, or any anomalous noise resonating through the *Traverser's* hull. There was nothing.

"What if the killers don't come, Agent Remo?" Clark asked. "The government gonna send out a boat to pick you up?"

"I think that would not be appreciated by my superiors in the agency," Remo commented. "I'll walk home if I have to."

"'Cause I got to tell you," Clark added, "it don't look like they're coming."

Remo nodded. Then he heard the sound. "Well, look, Lee, here they are now."

Clark spun like a top and looked northeast, where the horizon hid the Chilean shore. He saw nothing at first, then a pinprick resolved against the waves. "Coming fast!" he muttered. "What the hell is it?"

"Not a submarine," Remo said.

"I know, but what?"

"A water wing or a wind-effect craft or whatever they're called."

"A ground-effect craft, you mean?" Clark said. "Well, that explains it."

Yeah, Remo thought. That explained it. He had taken a ride on such a craft before. This was a smaller version of the heavy-lift craft he once rode across the Atlantic. This vehicle had a wingspan no bigger than that of a twin-engine aircraft, with broad, canopied wings that took it only a few feet off the surface of the water. The propellers out front powered it and air pressure built up between the wings and the water's surface to keep her airborne at all but the slowest speeds. Without the drag of the water, the craft could go as fast as a speedboat. This one looked souped up to go much faster.

In under a minute the winged craft had closed in on the bobbing *Traverser*, and it banked to reduce speed quickly, then landed hard on the water's surface, her speed propelling her directly at the sailboat as if to impale her on its sharp nose.

By then Remo had sent Lee Clark belowdecks. Remo was now in a plastic yellow rain jacket. He felt stupid wearing it with his hand-sewn leather shoes, but he wouldn't wear it long anyway.

The ground-effect craft was black and shiny, polished to help it slip through the air, and there was a sheen of water covering wings. Remo had noticed that the thin steel rods that jutted like fingers from the wings and the nose were configured to penetrate the ocean's surface, even when the craft was airborne, and channel water over the top surface of the wings in a constant trickle. Remo understood that. It was controlling its temperature to hide it from the thermal-imaging satellites looking for hot spots. No wake and a skin color the same as the ocean made it visually undetectable. A perfect way to sneak up on a speeding sailboat. And the thing was fast.

"You guys are in a big hurry, eh?" Remo called down to the men in tight-fitting outfits that jumped out of the side door of the craft just after tossing out their preinflated life raft. The inflatable's electric motor came to life with a high-pitched whine. Only a few yards separated the strange craft from the sailboat, but the raft closed the distance in a flash.

"That's a pretty cool motor you boys got on that little blow-up there, eh? Where's the fire, eh?"

The strangers never even slowed, just grabbed onto the *Traverser's* deck rails and yanked themselves over, landing on the deck in the same instant.

"Pretty neat moves," Remo said. "You guys ought to be in a water show. You know, a year don't go by that the wife and I don't get out to Wisconsin Dells for the *Tommy Bartlett Show*. Now, you guy's ain't *that* good, eh, but—"

"Shut up!" barked one of the men. Their thermal suits included hoods that exposed only their faces.

Remo found he could only tell them apart by nose size. Even their automatic rifles were identical.

"Hey, there, now, Big Nose, we don't allow no guns on board, eh."

"I said shut up! Put your damn hands in the air!"

"Don't appreciate the unfriendly tone of voice," Remo replied.

"He's lost it," said the second man, waving his blackened rifle at Remo Williams. "He was out here too long and he snapped."

"Well, my wife always says I'm crazy," Remo said happily. "She says I'm as loopy as a loon. 'Remo,' she says, 'you're as loopy as a loon!'"

"Remo? I thought your name was Lee," the first gunner said. "Lee Clark."

"Don't tell me we got the wrong boat."

"Right boat, Bigger Nose," Remo said, all the friendliness gone from his voice. "Wrong sailor."

"Shit, they made us!" Big Nose exclaimed.

"Let's kill him and go!" Bigger Nose added.

They agreed on this course of action without further discussion and began firing their weapons.

Their quick, controlled bursts of automatic gunfire should have been sufficient to wipe out a large crew, but for some reason this one sailor went untouched. He was moving, shifting, almost dancing this way and that, even as he was coming at them with slippery speed. Surely he wasn't dodging the bullets?

He got to them before their magazines were used up,

snatched the rifles out of their hands with a brisk movement and twisted the barrels together like wire.

They were both trained soldiers, and they both instinctively went for backup weapons sheathed, strapped and holstered about their bodies, but then they froze, paralyzed by pain.

Remo held each of them by the wrist and pushed a thumb into their flesh, in just the right spot.

"Who talks and who dies, eh?" Remo asked.

"He'll kill us!" one of them croaked, his eyeballs craning to the side. He was referring to the ground-effect craft.

Remo could hear the rapid movement of the pilot inside. Going for a gun, Remo assumed. These guys took their security seriously if they were willing to waste their own men.

"Let's go," Remo said, jerking the attackers across the deck, where the pilot couldn't target them.

Remo took only two steps before he felt something strange, a tiny surge of an electrical current that passed through each attacker's body. Then he sensed the activation of a minute electromechanical switch somewhere on the torso of each man.

Remo moved fast, spinning himself in place and dragging both the attackers with him, then he released them. One of them flew down from the rail, directly into the sea and exploded just as he hit, blasting the *Traverser* and Remo Williams with a wall of water.

But the second attacker was airborne over the deck

of the sailboat when the explosives strapped to his body detonated. Remo had put all his skill and strength into launching his attackers, and there wasn't time to dodge the blast, but he had expelled the air from his lungs and allowed his body to ride out the crushing cushions of air that slammed him from two sides.

It was over in an instant, and Remo inhaled deeply as the sailboat bobbed wildly. The *Traverser*'s deck was cratered where the second attacker had blown up, and the deck was littered with gore and body parts.

The ground-effect craft revved her engines and gathered speed, her hull rising high in the water. Once she was released from the friction of the sea, her speed would increase rapidly.

Remo glanced around and found the twisted rifles, pushed to the aft end of the deck by the explosion. He lifted the awkward, heavy contortion of metal and tested its weight in his hand. The escaping craft skimmed a high wave and lifted free, humming props accelerating her to raceboat speeds.

Remo flung the twisted metal and watched it wobble through the air as he heard Lee Clark emerge. Clark took in the bizarre, morbid scene and followed the long flight of the twisted metal.

The conjoined rifles seemed to hover high above the accelerating ground-effect craft, then floated down, down, inserting themselves into the right prop just about the time the craft reached sixty-five miles per hour. The prop disintegrated, the right side lurched and the wing penetrated the water while the left side kept going forward. The result was a spectacular cartwheel of fiberglass and metal parts and spraying water. The frameless body and wings were designed to withstand extreme forces, but this was way beyond their design limits. The craft separated into two large wing pieces, the passenger compartment and many smaller parts.

"Aw, crap," Remo said, and jumped over the rail into the inflatable landing raft that the attackers had used. The little motor had died once the attackers left it, but it buzzed angrily to life when Remo pushed the button.

Remo had faster ways of reaching to the crash, but not of getting there and bringing back a seriously wounded pilot. He arrived just as the steel cage of the cockpit, floating in a jagged bowl of broken fiberglass, leaned into the Pacific Ocean, filled with water and submerged. Remo leaped from the inflatable and hit the water in a dive so sharp he barely rippled the surface or the floating debris.

He caught up to the pilot cage about twenty-five feet down, reached inside and dragged out the pilot.

The pilot stared at Remo Williams all the way back to the surface, and all the way back to the sailboat. The pilot wasn't going to be answering any questions, but at least he was a corpse that might be identified.

Back on the *Traverser*, around-the-world sailor Lee Clark was using his mop to swab the gory deck. He liked to run a tight ship.

3

"I wish you would have stopped him," said the man with the gray complexion. He was sitting behind a huge desk with an onyx top. Behind him, out the large picture window, was his seldom-admired view of Long Island Sound.

"Why?" Remo asked.

"We might have identified the body," Harold W. Smith said.

"Believe me, there wasn't anything left to identify. He blew up real good. You want to try a DNA test, go wring some samples from Lee Clark's mop."

"Use your manners!" said the little old man in the chair next to Remo.

"That's precisely what the Chileans did," said Smith, looking sour. But then, he always looked sour. And he always looked gray. Smith had been gray all his life, since childhood, but old age made him appear even less healthy.

"The poor guy was about to lose his marbles," Remo explained, "and it seemed like cleaning up the blood and guts was his way of working through it."

"It was a murder investigation," Smith insisted.

"Clark was one of the victims, Smitty, and he was the only victim not beyond help, so I helped him by not stopping him from helping himself. Under the circumstances it was the decent thing to do."

"It was not what you *should* have done," Smith insisted.

The old man in the next chair was regarding Remo with the distaste of a haughty parent who has just caught his prep-school son picking his nose. "He is always doing what he should not do, Emperor," said the old man in a high, lamenting voice. He was dressed in a long kimono of orange silk, decorated with a riot of hand-embroidered birds and animals in a rainbow of colors. The man was Korean, his features prominent despite his mask of wrinkles. He was Chiun, and he was very, very old.

Remo didn't respond to either Smith or Chiun.

"They were able to find several tissue samples on the boat," Mark Howard said. The younger man was sitting on the old couch, papers spread across his lap. "No match from the tests so far."

"See?" Remo said to Smith. "No problem."

"With more of the body we might have been able to make that identification," Smith said. "There might have been a finger capable of giving us a print."

"There wasn't. I was there, remember? Most of him

went into the ocean when he exploded anyway. Plus, I got you a whole, unexploded body. Where's my thanks for that?"

"More impertinence! I can only apologize for him," Chiun said.

Smith gave Remo Williams the sourest of looks, the expression of a man who had just bitten into a wedge of orange only to realize too late that it was a lemon. Remo had been on the receiving end of such glares more times than he could guess. He didn't even notice them anymore.

"Can we go home now?" Remo asked.

"On to other things," Smith announced.

"I didn't know there were other things," Remo said.

"Do you think I made the arduous journey from our faraway home for no reason?" Chiun asked scornfully.

"What? And carried your own trunks?" Remo queried. "You shouldn't exert yourself, Little Father. What if you broke a hip?"

"The other thing," Smith declared forcefully, "is quite serious."

"The pirates of the Drake Passage were not serious?" Remo said. "Not by your standards."

"Better than the pirates of the Caribbean," Chiun observed.

"I'm not going back to the Caribbean," Remo insisted. "I don't care if it's to save the President of the U.S. of A."

"This problem seems not to involve the Caribbean, but it could very well involve a threat to the President,"

Smith intoned. "May I be allowed to explain?"

Remo knew sarcasm when he heard it. "Go ahead."

Smith nodded to Mark Howard.

"This was the victim that brought the problem to our attention," Mark said, handing Remo a color eight-by-ten glossy photograph of a statue.

"It's a statue," Remo said. "Of a fat guy."

"Not a statue at all, but a genuine fat guy," Howard explained. Mark was Harold Smith's assistant, in both public and clandestine activities. The public affairs included the administration of Folcroft Sanitarium, a private hospital in Rye, New York, which served as a cover for CURE. CURE was the supersecret agency Harold Smith and Mark Howard administered. Remo Williams, with his mentor Chiun, served as its enforcement arm.

CURE wasn't an acronym, but was the actual name of the very small organization that had operated for years out of the same office in the private hospital on Long Island Sound. Smith had been its director from the start.

After a brilliant career in U.S. intelligence, Smith had been on the verge of retiring from the CIA when his reputation became known to the President of the United States, a young, idealistic and well-loved man who nevertheless had come to a harsh, realistic conclusion: the constitutional democracy of the United States of America wasn't working.

It wasn't working because the rights and freedoms spelled out in the Constitution were being used against the nation, in ways big and small. Crooks were tying up the courts claiming their rights had been violated. Killers went free on technical errors. Known felons were manipulating the legal system and escaping punishment for the most heinous of crimes.

The President, a man fated to die by violence, his assassination watched by the eyes of the world, had a bold plan. Harold W. Smith didn't want to agree that the plan was necessary or wise.

The plan called for the formation of an organization that would protect the people of the U.S.A. by flagrantly violating their constitutional rights. Strip their freedoms to protect them. Violate their privacy to find the criminals.

If this activity were carried out in absolute secrecy, under the control of a man with unquestioned loyalty to this country, then think of what good it could do.

Smith agreed to take the role of director of the new organization. There were two reasons he did so. First, he was a patriot to his core. Refusing a request from the President of the United States was unthinkable. The second reason was the privately held conviction that he could take on such a huge responsibility and not abuse the power that came with it—and he was quite convinced that anyone else the President might choose for the job would not show such fortitude. Smith knew something of human nature, and he knew himself and, with all humbleness, he knew he was quite simply one of the most trustworthy people ever to take employment with the U.S. government.

Despite CURE's outstanding record of funneling intelligence to law-enforcement offices across the country, it was unable to stem the tide of lawlessness in its first years of operation. Smith became a believer in CURE, and in what it did for America, but he thought long and hard before taking more drastic action. Finally, he came to believe that CURE needed an enforcement arm. Someone who could get in and take care of the problems that the police or the FBI could not, or would not, take care of. Someone with absolutely loyalty to the United States, and the skills required to serve as a hired assassin.

That was where Remo Williams came in. Smith had code-named Remo "Destroyer," and the name was a prophecy vast enough to escape Smith's understanding even to this day.

"His name was Frank Krauser, a Streets and Sanitation worker in Chicago," Smith added. "He was briefly infamous when he was the subject of an exposé by a local news channel a year ago. He was caught on tape spending most of his working day in a bakery."

Mark Howard next handed Remo a printout of a news video. The computer-generated Superman-style letters at the top of the screen said, "Slackers at Streets And San—The Exclusive Exposé!" The video itself showed what appeared to be the same fat man stretched out in a corner booth at a well-known doughnut franchise.

"I'm not sure if you can call Dunk-A-Donut a bakery, Smitty," Remo said.

"The exposé didn't get him in much trouble, apparently, because yesterday he spent the entire workday at a different bakery, a Krunchy Kreme. The surveillance tapes from the place show him arriving about nine. But this time he stayed past the end of his shift and called in to have one of his coworkers list him as taking a vacation day."

"He thought he was being videotaped again," Mark added. "The tape shows him watching a vehicle across the street. We didn't get a good look at the vehicle from the security tapes."

"He left about nine in the evening and wasn't seen again until the morning crew found a vandalized cement mixer at their work site," Smith said. "Someone had pried the extrusion end until it was big enough to admit insertion of a body. When they looked inside, they found Krauser."

Remo shrugged. "And?"

"He's dead," Smith said.

"So I gathered. But why do I care?"

"You may not care, Remo, but I do, because Frank Krauser is only the latest in a long string of murders that have been going on across the country, for weeks, maybe for months," Smith explained. "Even the CURE systems were slow to find a connection between them, and we're still not sure which murders are related and which are not. Mark?"

"The mayor of a small town called Old Crick, Iowa, was found dead in a hotel room with a Sioux City prostitute, strangled with electrical cords," Mark said, handing Remo a printout of the crime scene. "He's previously been accused of using municipal funds to pay for sex."

"They got in pretty quiet, it looks like," Remo said. "The mayor and the hooker were still doing the deed."

Chiun looked at the photo, then looked away. Death was of little consequence to him, but the wanton sexuality was another matter. "Filthy," he stated. "He got what he deserved."

Smith fired a disapproving look at Chiun, but the old Korean was facing out the window, cheeks slightly pink.

Remo took another photo. He saw the rear end of a man standing at a deep fryer in a restaurant, a clipboard still gripped in one hand. He was apparently leaning all the way forward into the fryer, which was steaming vigorously.

"Fried food will kill you," Remo said.

"It certainly will." Chiun examined this photo with more interest.

"Alabama state-licensed health inspector," Smith said. "He was targeted three months ago by a state anticorruption committee after the filing of a class-action lawsuit that names the state. He is accused of taking money in exchange for passing health inspection grades. Unfortunately, he passed a small restaurant and catering business in Muncie, Alabama. The next day it served tainted potato salad at a senior citizens' luncheon. Four deaths, fifteen serious hospitalizations. The restaurant was investigated and found to have multiple, serious health-code violations."

"I do not understand the problem," said Chiun. "This man was justly rewarded for his behavior."

"This man was murdered, Master Chiun," Smith said.

"He was guilty of the deaths of a bunch of seniors, stemming from his own corruption and greed," Remo said. "So somebody whacked him. What's the problem?"

"He was not guilty until proved so. The United States does not permit the killing of innocent people."

"Except by us," Remo added.

"Yes," Smith said. "Except by us."

"There are many other examples at the local and county levels," Mark said. "Lately we've seen an increase in killings of state workers, as well. We have state troopers who have been known to have racially biased ticket and arrest records. We have driver's-license clerks known to sell licenses to convicted drunk drivers."

"The pattern is obvious," Chiun said. "Someone is removing the rubbish."

"Exactly, and that might sound simple enough an explanation until you take in the scale of the murders," Smith said, removing the top sheet of paper from a small stack at his elbow and sliding it across the desk to Remo. It was a map of the forty-eight states, sprinkled with red dots.

"Don't tell me these are all killings," Remo said, disbelieving. "There's got to be a hundred of them."

"One hundred and forty-two." Chiun sounded bored.

"This is our best-case scenario," Smith said gravely. "In our worst-case scenario, we have this."

He slid over another printout of the contiguous forty-eight states.

"You're joking," Remo said.

"I don't often joke," Smith said.

"Yeah, I guess not." Remo peered at the printout, which was red with dots so thick they obscured whole states.

"There are so many that overlap I cannot count these," Chiun remarked.

"Seven hundred and eighty-six," Mark Howard said.

"Unfortunately, our belief is that the computer modeling for this result is likely to be more accurate than the first printout you saw. No matter how you look at it, the victims are in the hundreds," Smith intoned morosely. "The daring of the perpetrators is escalating, too. They are striking at bigger targets."

"Bigger as in the fat guy in the cement mixer?" Remo asked.

"No," Smith said sourly. "Bigger as in more important. State government officials, congressmen, members of the judiciary, election officials and so on. The list is long, and has started to include more federal officials, as well. A half-dozen in the past ten days, we believe."

"All the victims have a reputation for corruption in one way or another?" Remo asked.

"One hundred percent," Howard said.

"And the guys doing the killing aren't claiming responsibility, leaving any messages, leaving any clues, anything like that?" Remo asked.

"No." Smith was unusually somber. "A few of the murders have been tied together on the most superficial of evidence, but no one outside this room understands the full scope of the crimes. The fact is, the local and county types, like Mr. Krauser, are now only coming in close proximity to the bigger hits. That's why we want you to get to Chicago as soon as possible. There have been no murders of large-scale politicians in the area in the past few days, which means, following Mr. Krauser, the city is due."

Remo grimaced. "There's a lot of important state and federal officials around. There might be more than one unethical politician on the list. In fact, who isn't corrupt? I mean, it's Chicago."

Smith said, "If there is any commonality to the killings, it's their high-profile nature. All the victims have been publicly exposed as corrupt. Bearing that in mind, we think we know who the target is."

4

"You're awfully quiet, Little Father," Remo said. It wasn't that he didn't enjoy a little peace now and then, but it always worried him when he didn't know what Chiun was pondering so seriously.

Remo and Chiun had been companions for a long time, since the very earliest days of Remo's training with CURE. As a young beat cop in New Jersey, Remo was framed for a murder he didn't commit, railroaded through the judicial system with unprecedented speed and fried in the electric chair, only to wake up in a hospital bed in Folcroft Sanitarium.

Remo's only visitor in the hospital room was a one-armed man who was Smith's second in command at the time. The man gave Remo the choice of employment with CURE or death. Real death, this time. Permanent, in-the-grave, sorry-buddy-no-hard-feelings-blam! death.

Remo took the job.

Days later he began training with Chiun, along with training in firearms, interrogation, lock-picking, you name it. After a while he shucked all the other instruction and trained only with Chiun. There was nothing he needed to know that Chiun, the Master of Sinanju, couldn't teach.

They had been a team ever since, Master and student. Eventually Remo learned the skills of Sinanju to such a degree that he attained the rank of Master. Only recently Remo had become Reigning Master, making him the traditional Master of the North Korean village of Sinanju, birthplace of the ancient art, and owner of all the treasure that came with the position. However, Remo had honestly not expected the promotion to change his relationship with Chiun, and he was right.

"I have much on my mind," Chiun said vaguely. He was staring at the wing of the 777 that was carrying them into O'Hare International Airport. Chiun was looking for uncharacteristic wobbling or stress fractures that foretold of the wing spontaneously separating from the jet.

"Such as?" Remo asked.

"I do not understand this mission," Chiun said to the window. "I do not know why the addle-brained Dr. Smith would want this activity to cease, when this is exactly the type of busywork he has committed us to time and again."

Remo nodded. "Well, I like to think we go after bigger fish than the Streets And San slacker, but I see what you mean. I guess I don't get it, either. If they're all crooks, why not let them get offed?"

"Exactly," Chiun agreed. "It is possible that the doctor is losing his mental faculties."

Remo considered that. "He didn't act any different to me. Plus he had Junior agreeing with him every step of the way. They probably have some reason we don't understand. Wouldn't be the first time he sent us off on some fool's errand."

"You are a fool perhaps, but not I," Chiun snapped, turning to him. "I, at least, have come to understand Smith's rationale, even the most bizarre and incorrectly motivated. It is a cause for celebration when you understand enough to fetch the correct stick."

"Fine, you tell me what the hell we're doing this for?"

Chiun's eyes became vague, and briefly he stroked the white threads on his chin. "This time even my wisdom is dwarfed by Smith's inscrutability."

"I thought so," Remo replied, and opened the airline magazine. He hated airline magazines, especially the pap they printed up since the big budget crunch. "Smitty's probably just worried that whoever is doing all the killing is gonna give him some competition."

"Yes!" Chiun hissed. "That is the reason!"

"Naw. I was just pulling your leg."

"Do not touch my leg. You have bumbled into the correct answer, Remo Williams. The Emperor Smith is concerned that these upstarts will step into the spotlight and accept the glory for this work. And yet it is *we* who deserve the glory. Now Smith is regretting that he did not take my advice to proclaim the greatness of our achievements."

"I don't think so."

"Consider it. Time and again the glorious achievements of Chiun have gone unheralded, and thus the greatness of the Emperor Smith is unheralded."

"Oh, really? The glorious achievements of Chiun? Solo?"

"Chiun and his faithful houseboy, then," Chiun said, annoyed at the interruption. "Now this gang of upstarts will come in and do the work we do, but on a larger scale. Instead of assassinating a few ne'er-do-wells, they have come into assassinate hundreds of corrupt government workers."

"Yeah, like the guys who patch the potholes," Remo reminded him.

"This does not matter. It is not true value but the promotion of the value that matters to the dull-witted white," lectured Chiun. "If we say we assassinated twenty men and they claim they assassinated a hundred men, which number will the dull-witted, sofa-sitting American be most impressed by?"

"Are we talking about television commercials? I don't think Smitty'll go for that."

"And if we then try to explain that we have taken the high road and assassinated only the most dangerous and damaging criminals, what then shall happen?"

Remo waited.

"I asked you, what then shall happen?"

"I thought it was a hypothetical—"

"It was not! What then shall happen?"

"I don't know."

"Exactly. That same blank look. And then, of course,

click! They change the channel. Whites have such microscopic levels of intelligence that the simplest of explanations befuddles them completely and bores them utterly."

"You said it!" The tall, dark-skinned, clean-cut man in the next row was craning his neck over the seat, nodding. He looked like a vice President of accounting from a big, bland financial corporation. "The white folks I know can't think themselves out of a brown paper sack."

"Quiet!" Chiun barked. "You are as white as my buffoon of a son!"

"Sir," said Remo to Chiun, "I don't even know you."

"You calling me a white man? You are way whiter than me!"

"I am Korean," Chiun said stiffly.

"*You* are white!" the man proclaimed indignantly.

Remo tried to look uninvolved. "Oh boy."

"And where are you from?" Chiun demanded, his body rigid.

"Africa, originally. But I was born in Baltimore."

"Which makes you as white as snow."

"Oh yeah, yellow ass?"

Chiun's bony hand slithered over the seat, found the man's neck and slithered back. The vice president of accounting slept the rest of the way to Chicago.

"The point is this," Chiun continued doggedly, "these upstarts are intent on making publicity that should rightfully belong to me."

"Or us," Remo added. "But the other point is this—

Smitty doesn't want publicity. Publicity would shut us down. Publicity is going to shut these people down if they ever get any. Assassination is against the law."

"Laws are made by the rulers of the land," Chiun said.

"What's that supposed to mean?"

"It means nothing." Chiun looked out the window.

"It means something."

But Chiun was done with the discussion. He had a wobbling wing to watch.

AGAINST ALL ODDS, the aircraft remained in one piece and landed them safely at Chicago O'Hare, where a limousine awaited them. The driver was a tall blond woman who waved a white cardboard sign proclaiming "R. Middlesex".

"You Middle-sex?" She said it like two words and gave Remo a slow, salacious appraisal.

Remo checked his ID. "That's us."

"It is you. I shall ride along, however," Chiun sniffed.

"And we're late," Remo added. Somehow he just knew the driver wanted to engage in a little bit of hanky-panky talk, and he was not in the mood.

"Fine," she said, yanking the door open. "Clothes are on the hook."

Remo had forgotten about the clothes. It was a tuxedo, of all things. "Smitty doesn't really think I'm going to wear that, does he?"

"You going to the governor's big deal at the U of I, ain't you?" the driver asked. "It's formal."

"I'll wear the jacket," Remo said. "At least until I'm through the door." He dismantled the various components of apparel on the hanger and found the jacket, which he shrugged into.

"I like you, Middle-sex," the driver said.

"I dislike you both," Chiun snapped and jabbed at the button that raised the window between them and the driver. "I am glad Smith is too miserly to offer us this class of transportation on a regular basis. Limousine drivers are notoriously ill-tempered."

At that moment, for no obvious reason, the limo braked suddenly. Any other occupants would have been tossed to the floor. Chiun and Remo rode out the deceleration without discomfort.

"Do not say anything insulting, Remo," Chiun warned, "for I fear the harlot is invading our privacy."

There was a squeal of tires. As they started moving again, the driver got on the intercom. "Sorry. There were some skunks in the road."

"That explains the smell," Chiun replied.

They screeched to another hard stop. The driver was disconcerted that her passengers hadn't even been tossed out of their seats. Usually she could do some serious head knocking when she wanted to, maybe cause some concussions.

They disembarked at the entrance of the University of Illinois, Chicago auditorium, where the traffic cops waved them to the front entrance. The driver sneered her lip at Chiun, but he ignored her completely as he left.

Remo needed all his Sinanju-enhanced dexterity to dodge the sharp little pinch she targeted at the seat of his pants.

"OH, GREAT, more jokers."

Trooper Krucoff, commanding the governor's Antiterrorist Security Patrol, was also sick of the jokers, and sick of the jokes and sick of the just plain meanness that got leveled at him and his men. As if they chose the governor. As if doing their sworn duty somehow made them a part of the governor's agenda or alleged improprieties.

And marching right at him was another pair of ingrates, sure to give him shit. One was as old as Methuselah, if Methuselah was Japanese or Filipino or whatever this guy was, and he was wearing a shiny dress with dragons or something chasing themselves around the legs. The other guy was of indeterminate age. Maybe twenty-five, maybe forty-five, but sure as shit a goofball. He was wearing a black T-shirt and a tuxedo jacket.

Trooper Krucoff blocked the VIP entrance with his fists on his hips.

"Afternoon, Mr. Reeves." The younger man nodded. "Loved you in *Superman Versus the Mole People.*"

Krucoff did hear him, momentarily taken aback by the man's cruel dead eyes. If it weren't for the goofy getup the trooper would have been extremely wary of a man with eyes like that. He shook it off. "I can't let you in here."

"Sure, you can." The younger man reached inside of his jacket, which sent Krucoff and Trooper Azul into a quick draw for their own weapons, but they never even got the snaps off. The man with the dead eyes was un-believably fast on the draw; it was a good thing he only pulled out an ID wallet. "Special Agent Remo Middle-sex, FBI."

"Sure, you are," Trooper Krucoff said, taking the badge. He ran the badge through the electronic scanner and was surprised when the green light came on.

"Who's your sidekick?"

"Special Agent M.O.S.E. Chiun."

The Asian man was standing quietly with his hands in his sleeves, which had Trooper Azul a little on edge, and when the little man extracted something from his sleeves they both were startled into action again.

"Made you jump," the little special agent squeaked as he held out his badge, his face hard but his child-like eyes full of amusement.

Again the badge got a green light from the scanner, but Krucoff handed the badges to Azul.

"Call them in."

If they were insulted by the added precaution, Agents Middlesex and Chiun didn't show it. The little Asian man was at ease, hands once again in his sleeves, his eyes focusing on some wise thing that only elderly Asians could see. The goof in the tuxedo jacket and T-shirt was checking out the other VIPs, who got in without quite so much trouble.

"They're okay," Azul announced a moment later, handing the IDs to Krucoff, who unwillingly returned them to Agent Middlesex.

"Need a tie," Krucoff said.

"No, thanks."

"I'm not asking you, Agent, I'm telling you. This is a formal affair. I'm not allowed to let guests into the governor's skybox without a tie."

Something brushed against his neck and Krucoff realized the little Asian had vanished. He turned around quickly to find Chiun standing there, arms in his sleeves and apparently completely at his leisure, although he had not been there three seconds ago.

When Krucoff spun back at Agent Middlesex, the man was wearing a navy blue tie with his black tuxedo jacket, black T-shirt and brown shoes.

"Thanks," the agent said, and brisked inside the auditorium before Krucoff got a word out. Azul's face screwed up strangely. "Krucoff, where's your tie?"

THE TROOPER'S TIE joined the tuxedo jacket in the trash can as soon as they were in the VIP lounge. The glassed-in room stood above and to the side of the main floor, with a clear view of the quickly filling auditorium.

"All this for a politician who is about to leave office?" Chiun wondered.

"You have to give him credit for creating a truckload of favorable publicity. This guy should be the state's Richard Nixon. Instead he's actually going out on a high note."

"Yes," said Chiun thoughtfully.

The governor himself was prominently pictured in a silk-screened banner behind the stage, his face ten feet in height, serious yet smiling slightly. The likeness was flattering, even downplaying the man's famously bulbous nose and jowls.

"He still looks like Mr. Magoo," Remo noted.

"I know not this Magoo. Was he more competent a politician than Governor Bryant?"

"Definitely," Remo said. "Here come the convicts."

From the wall-to-wall picture window they had an unobstructed view. On the stage, a line of unsavory-looking characters in badly fitted suits was emerging from the wings and taking seats in the rows of chairs behind the podium. Some looked jubilant, some looked weary, and a few tried to adopt a street-tough swagger, but they were all extremely uncomfortable being where they were.

As the men filed into their seats, a row of students on the balcony across the auditorium rose to their feet and raised a banner that read No Amnesty For Murder. A loud chant began. "Killers, murderers, *crook!* Killers, murderers, *crook!*"

The processional of convicts on the stage reacted with laughter, a number of middle fingers and one outburst of temper. The protesters were ushered out of the auditorium by state troopers with great efficiency.

"Makes you sick," said the thin young woman with the fat highball glass full of something amber. "To think those kids want to incarcerate innocent men."

"Those men are innocent?" Chiun asked.

"They have not been proved guilty," said the woman, whose dress had not been tailored to match her recent weight loss. Remo guessed she was on one of those all-liquid diets that were all the rage. In fact, she was taking a big swallow of lunch.

Chiun looked at the stage and then at the woman. "How did these men become incarcerated if there was no trial?"

"Oh, there was a trial," the woman said. "A hollow sham of a trial, for every single one of them. They all ended up with life sentences, simply because each was labeled a recidivist. You really don't know about this?"

"We're from out east," Remo explained.

"Oh." She considered this as she sipped another two ounces of liquor. "Well, all these men were accused of doing horrible crimes. Rape and murder and, well, mostly rape and murder. They were brought to court and convicted on the evidence—without consideration of the fact that future technology might be able to clear them of their crimes."

Chiun stared at her blankly.

"It's like this," she said. "You know how there were all these guys who were convicted of murders and they got the death penalty, but then the along comes DNA testing that proves they did not commit the murder. So the governor said to himself, how do we know that some new technology might not come along next week, or next month, or maybe in ten years, that could prove one of these men was innocent of the crime that got him jailed."

"I suppose this is possible," Chiun agreed.

"So, obviously, you can't expect a man to rot in jail

just because the science hasn't reached the point where it can disprove the guilty verdicts."

"I see," Chiun said, nodding, then turned to Remo and said in Korean, "She is a drunkard and a lunatic."

"Probably, Little Father," Remo agreed, "but no more so than their governor."

"Do you mean to say her story is true? The governor of this province is taking this ridiculous stance? Why would he?"

"To draw attention away from the fact that he's facing federal corruption and conspiracy charges."

"Ah!" Chiun nodded sincerely and turned back to the woman, who had acquired a fresh drink from a passing waiter. She seemed befuddled but tolerant of the incomprehensible language, and beamed when Chiun addressed her in English. "The governor's constituency responds to his calls of clemency?"

"Oh, sure. Most do. There are some bad apples in the woodpile, you know, like those stupid kids."

"And this distracts the constituency from his looming indictments on federal corruption charges," Chiun added.

"My idea!" She toasted herself with the fresh drink, which was already down to dregs. "A PR challenge of the first magnitude! I'm his PR agent."

"I see!" Chiun said enthusiastically. "Ms.?"

"Johns. Sunny Johns." She reached out to shake his hand, but put it away as Chiun seemed not to notice it. "And you are?"

"Chiun." He shoved his fake FBI badge at her face.

"Moses Chiun," she said, squinting at it.

"Call me Chiun. May I have your card, Ms. Johns?"

Sunny Johns reached for her card with the hand holding the glass, sending the dregs trickling down her blazer lapels.

"So, really, any and all criminal convictions should be voided, pending the development of new technology that might clear the accused," Remo said.

"Yes, exactly." Sunny nodded as she thrust her card at Chiun, then stopped herself and put down the glass. She handed the card to Chiun with two hands, bowing over it.

"She thinks you're Japanese," Remo said in Korean.

"She is a drunkard and a lunatic, but talented," Chiun replied, taking the card in a whisk of motion that Sunny Johns did not follow. She looked on the floor for the card.

"But even ten years from now a convicted criminal would surely be able to claim that some other technology might be coming even further down the line," Remo insisted.

"I suppose so," Sunny said brightly.

"In other words, we should empty all the jails and never lock up another criminal because maybe, someday, he might be proved innocent."

Sunny beamed. "Exactly!"

"What a load of crap," Remo muttered.

Sunny loosed a peal of laughter. "Honey, don't I know it! But guess what, they're eating it up like hogs at the trough. Oh!" She clamped a hand over her mouth.

"I can't believe I said that. I never admitted that to any-body before."

"To have succeeded in this great deception indicates you are a woman of vast talent," Chiun said, giving her his best kindly-old-grandfather smile of approval.

Sunny removed the hand from her mouth and leaned in closer to Chiun, who halted his respiration to avoid her poisonous breath. "You haven't heard the best part."

"Yes?" Chiun asked.

"After the governor pulls this stunt he's gonna be worth millions. You know how many nutcase organizations will pay a hundred grand a pop to hear him give a speech?"

"Truly?" Chiun asked.

"And after today, the price doubles." Sunny's eyes were refusing to focus. "This is the peez-de-resistance! We got the networks. We got CNN. We got the BBC!"

She grasped the handrail in front of the picture win-dow as her legs lost their stiffness. "Truth is, Mr. Moses, I'm feeling a little bit awful about letting all those bad men out of the joint. They hurt a lot of people, you know."

There was no answer. Squinting through the blur, Sunny found that she was getting nasty looks from the governor's staff, but the nice little man who was her con-fidant had gone away.

"Aw, hell," she blubbered.

"SHE IS JUST what we need, Remo!"

"I wasn't impressed, tell you the truth," Remo said. "You said yourself she's a drunk."

"Many artists are."

"Artist?"

"She performed a great work of promotional creativity. Even I would not have deemed the whites of this nation gullible enough to swallow this ridiculous philosophy!" Chiun stopped and looked at Remo worriedly. "The people of this state, are they considered exceptionally stupid, even by American standards?"

"Depends who you ask," Remo said. "I think they're about as smart as the next state."

Chiun clapped his hands. "Wonderful, then Sunny Johns can work her magic for us on a national scale."

"And what exactly is she supposed to do for us, Little Father?"

"Publicize us!"

"Who's us?"

"Myself, of course. And Emperor Smith, and his heir apparent, the Prince Howard. Even you. We will let the nation know of our grand efforts to protect them from the evil that walks in their midst. With the right advertising and promotion, we will shine out like stars of justice and righteousness, while this band of upstarts will be just another band of playground bullies."

"You going to get the okay from Smitty before you book the commercial time?" Remo was only half listening as they emerged into the auditorium seating areas close to the stage. He was scanning the crowds, looking for signs of a possible attack.

"He would likely wish me to consult with him first," Chiun admitted.

"Probably."

"But he might attempt to interfere."

"He just might."

They helped themselves to empty seats in the front row of the side section as the house lights dimmed. Even Remo's sharp eyes had trouble negotiating the swarms of human beings among the erratic and polarizing stage lights. "You see anything, Little Father?"

"Yes, there she is," Chiun answered, standing on his seat and gesturing back to the great glass picture window of the private box. Sunny Johns waved back and wiped away tears as she leaned against the glass.

"Down in front!" shouted a man a few rows back. A soda can flew in Chiun's direction, and just as it was about to bounce off his pale, wrinkled skull it seemed to reverse course at a tremendous speed, colliding into its thrower with force enough to rob him of consciousness.

"Not her, Chiun. We're here to watch for the bad guys, remember? Gonna assassinate the corrupt governor and we're supposed to stop it? Ring a bell?"

"Why, again, are we doing this?" Chiun asked, taking his seat and scanning the crowds.

"I forget, exactly."

The music blasting out of the sound system was the same 1970s techno-pop used by the city's pro basketball team, whose five consecutive world championships had led to the firing of the entire coaching staff and the departure of all the talented players. The basketball franchise had now settled comfortably into the traditional role of a Chicago sports team, which meant losing with dogged consistency. The song, dating from the team's glory years, still got the crowd revved up for the arrival of the soon-to-be-ex-Governor Jerome Bryant. To deafening applause, Governor Bryant waddled out of the wings, waving a hand to the crowd.

"Cripes, I expected a leather boy on a Harley to come roaring out after that build-up," Remo said.

"Instead you get a trained walrus," Chiun observed, but his interest in the spectacle was obvious.

Governor Bryant waved and lifted the sides of his mouth in an attempt at a smile until the weight of his sagging jowls made the effort too great to sustain. The applause died down after a long minute; only then were the five groups of chanting protesters heard. The crowd resumed its wild applause to drown them out while the state troopers extracted the protesters.

Bryant began delivering his speech, as dry as stale bread. He decried the state's flawed judicial system. He counted as heroes the criminal investigation students of the university who had uncovered new DNA evidence that overturned the convictions of a convicted murderer who had been sitting on death row for years, all the while protesting his innocence.

Remo could appreciate that. After all, he once sat on death row for a crime he didn't commit. If he had been able to use DNA evidence at the time, maybe he would never have gone to the electric chair. He wondered idly where he would be today.

Right where he was, he realized. The frame-up had been engineered by none other than Dr. Harold W. Smith himself, and if there had been a chance DNA evidence would be used in the trial of Remo Williams, then damning DNA evidence would have been planted at the scene of the crime he was accused of.

Then the governor began talking about the further efforts of the university students—actually, it was the next group to come through the same criminal investigations program at the university. They apparently couldn't locate other cases of wrongful conviction that could be proved with a fresh look at the evidence, but they did find many convictions that might be proved false, if and when new technology was developed to cast doubt on the physical evidence used to gain the convictions.

"That trained walrus you talked about would have been more entertaining," Remo said. "Only this guy could make a wild story like this sound like an accounting lecture."

Remo had to admit this guy seemed like a likely target for anybody out to clean up government. He felt like popping the creep himself. Nevertheless he diligently searched the vast crowds and the stage seeking any sign of an imminent attack. The speech ended, and the governor began calling up the convicted murders and rapists by name. Some had nodded off and had to be nudged awake by the governor's aids. One of the sleepers came awake with fists flying and the aide went down for the count, but the ceremony was otherwise uneventful for the first half hour.

Then the pace picked up considerably.

Remo stood, eyes locked on another skybox across the main floor and almost at the rear of the auditorium. The glass of the picture window reflected the stage lights, and inside the skybox were only the tiniest visible glimmers of an exit light.

"Remo?" Chiun asked, standing up beside him.

"Maybe nothing, but check out that skybox."

Chiun's wispy white eyebrows came together as he concentrated on the glass front. Vision was just one of the highly enhanced senses of the trained Sinanju assassins, and the skybox was not far from where they stood, but the auditorium environment made the glass into a mirror that even Chiun couldn't penetrate easily.

Remo had been scanning the back corner of the vast theater when he thought he saw the silhouette of a man beyond the glass with a rifle. When one of the spotlights changed its angle, the reflection decreased for a moment and the two Masters of Sinanju saw into the shadows.

"Sniper," Remo blurted. "I'll go."

That was the moment that the usher came alongside the front row of their balcony. "You want to take your seats, please?" he complained.

Then one of the two men he had been complaining to was gone, and the usher saw him a second later sprinting across the auditorium. Running on heads.

5

Remo hardly allowed his feet to brush one head before he was on to the next. A small ripple formed in the audience as the diagonal line of people looked up to see what had swept over them.

Remo moved fast, like a harsh wind, and he knew it wasn't fast enough when he saw the silhouette in the skybox crystallize into a man aiming a heavy rifle. As he bounded off the main floor and maneuvered up the balcony over the backs of chairs, over shoulders, over heads, he saw the muzzle-flash and heard the heavy thump of the weapon being fired. The picture window now had a jagged round opening about the size of a rice bowl. An inch of the gun barrel jutted through the hole and fired again, but that was when the sniper spotted Remo coming at him over the heads of the balcony audience. It spoiled his aim.

Remo was moving fast when he spun and slammed his back into the shatter-proof glass. The window was designed to withstand beer cans and Frisbees and all kinds of objects thrown in the auditorium during ball games and rock concerts, but not this. Remo transformed the solid sheet of glass into hundreds of thousands of tiny shards of crystal that flew inward in a deadly hail.

The sniper briefly understood that he was seeing death come at him, too fast to even squeeze his eyes shut.

Remo grabbed the sniper in an unaffectionate embrace and propelled them both toward the rear of the skybox, feeling the crystal shrapnel chasing him. He and the sniper went into the door with all the grace of a wrecking ball going into a Vegas hotel, then Remo twisted hard, spinning himself and the sniper out the open door frame. The hailstorm of glass came too fast to avoid completely, but Remo moved so fast that the glass skidded across the flesh of his forearm like the grit of a sandstorm and failed to penetrate. Then he and his burden were clear of it, and the sound was like rushing water for a moment until the glass splinters sprinkled to the floor.

"Ah, crap," Remo muttered as he saw the condition of the sniper. The man's body was broken up by the brutal manipulations and he slumped to the floor, his eyeballs rolling up. The man was wearing a white balaclava, and around his mouth it was now soaked with blood. Remo ripped off the hood. "Hey, gun boy, you still with me?"

The sniper forced his eyes to focus, and when he tried to speak he leaked a lot of red stuff. His head rolled to the side.

"Help him," Remo ordered to the skybox waitress

who had just arrived with a tray of bottled beer and water. She just stared.

Remo left her to figure it out on her own. Not that it made a difference to the sniper, who was dying too fast even to answer questions.

Remo went back through the skybox, bare except for its fresh carpet of crystal. The sparkling glass was like snowfall, and Remo went over it without even making it crunch beneath his feet. He slithered into the crowd, which was still trying to figure out exactly what was happening up on stage.

Governor Bryant had pulled some wild stunts in his abbreviated, controversial stint as governor, but this one was the most dramatic and attention-getting. Unfortunately for him, it involved most of his head flying around the stage in little chunks.

CHIUN WATCHED Remo speed away and his vision turned back to the stage, only to momentarily polarize under the glare of the usher's flashlight. He slapped the usher's hand. The crushed flashlight was airborne for thirty feet before it hit a concrete support column. The usher took a moment to realize his hands were in the same condition as the flashlight, then came the pain of many broken hand bones. As he was inhaling to yowl, he couldn't help but notice that the little old man had vanished.

Chiun seemed to flutter over the heads of the crowds like a butterfly and he zeroed in on the idiot governor, only to see the flash of red flying from the governor's shoulders. With that priority nullified, he leaped onto the stage and snaked around the corner of the fifty-foot-tall stage curtains, emerging and vanishing from the view of the audience so swiftly that no one could swear they even saw him—and most were paying attention to the spectacle of the collapsing, half-decapitated governor.

Chiun ignored the rising tide of collective horror coming from the crowd and trained his senses into the stage wings, where he hugged the shadows. First a knot of law-enforcement officials tromped onto the stage from the opposite end of the stage, their guns drawn. Chiun could see in their faces that their adrenaline was peaking so swiftly they might start directing their boom devices at the crowds.

Others came into the wings behind the law-enforcement officers and on Chiun's end of the stage, with more controlled purpose. They materialized into knots of ridiculous-looking soldiers in black, skintight suits. Blacksuits were worn by the not-very-special forces of the world, Chiun was well aware, and this was a technique borrowed from the Japanese ninja, who had stolen every useful gimmick they knew from the sun source of all the world's martial arts, Sinanju.

But this particular group had augmented the traditional blacksuit in ways both foolish to look at and foolish strategically. They wore masks of white, and gloves of white! The white gloves made their weapons especially vivid to Chiun's eyes, and he floated through the darkness to intercept the nearest foursome as they aimed their stocky machine guns across the stage.

Before the first finger tightened on a trigger, there was a blur of vivid color and the point man felt his arm grow lighter. He stared at the fountains of blood where his hands had once been firmly attached.

His neighbor saw the gaudy swirl and tried to line up his weapon on the whirlwind of color, then felt a jolt as the stock of his weapon rammed into his abdomen and crushed his organs, killing him before he thumped to the stage.

The other two gunners were turning their weapons on Chiun, and he regretfully pulled the blows he delivered to each of their heads. Their skulls collided loudly, although with none of the bone-shattering quality that would have been satisfying to the old Master. He knew Smith would want survivors for interrogation, and that bumbler Remo was likely to kill any antagonist who didn't sit on the floor calmly with his hands folded in surrender.

Chiun felt the pressure waves that rippled through the air ahead of a stream of bullets and he moved himself out of their way. As the gunfire flew across the stage from the wings on the opposite side, Chiun advanced on the gunners like a phantom.

THE MAN with the binoculars almost whooped for joy when he saw the splash of color that marked the end of the worst governor in the United States. Perfectly dead. Wonderful!

Then he heard the crash and his binoculars traveled to the enclosed booth where his sniper had been stationed. The window was gone. The skybox was empty. The safety glass was supposed to remain intact even when a shot penetrated it, but the window had clearly disintegrated from the gunfire. His gunman had to have run out to avoid falling glass.

Then his binoculars picked up a dark, fleeting figure that floated from the skybox and disappeared into the crowd. He lowered the glasses and peered at the crowd, trying to find the ghost that he knew was not his sniper.

The man was traveling over the sea of people faster than most men could run on open ground. Gunfire started on stage, but the man with the binoculars knew something was missing. He should be hearing eight mini-Uzis. Was half the team tardy?

The figure traveling over the crowds never hesitated, as if he couldn't even hear the gunfire and couldn't see the contortions of murder occurring on the stage. There was something else, too, another fluttering ghostly figure, this one a blur of color that danced among the flying machine-gun fire and never slowed before vanishing into the wings. Then the figure from the crowds gained the stage with a single leap and was gone.

The gunfire halted.

The man allowed the binoculars to dangle on their strap, feeling his shock turn to dread, and he thumbed his radio. "Come in, Team Justice. Justice Leader, do you copy?"

Something flew out of the wings and plopped onto

the stage. One of the mini-Uzis. A pair of hands with bloody stumps still gripped it.

"Team Virtue, come in," the man radioed, already aware it was a lost cause. Still, he tried, opening the channel. "All White Hands, report in!"

Nothing.

"Report in, all White Hands!"

"White Hen reporting in," the radio crackled. "You must be the top chicken."

The man stared at the stage, then snarled into the radio. "Who the hell are you?"

"Just one of your little White Hens."

"That's White Hand, idiot!"

"Not very white hands if you ask me," the radio said. "Kind of red and messy hands."

"You're going to pay, whoever you are," the man seethed into the radio. "You will not obstruct our righteous work!"

"Wrong again, Mr. White Hen," the radio said. "Can't say I can find a lot of fault in your work so far, you understand. The guy in the cement mixer this morning, who's to say he didn't deserve it? Not me, that's for sure."

The man was ready to interrupt the babble on the radio when he saw the blur of motion across the chaos of the crowds. It was the same color as the figure that had crossed the stage. Damn it! He stood there letting the fool on the radio distract him while his partner came to get him. And he had almost allowed it to happen.

Almost. Now it was time to start acting smart again.

He swiftly thumbed open the plastic control panel in the base of his radio, flipped on the arming switch and jabbed the red fire button the instant it illuminated. He was pleased to hear the distant blasts of small charges coming in quick succession.

Then he inserted himself into the terrified crowds.

REMO WILLIAMS DROPPED the radio and moved away from the fallen gunners in a single leap. In quick succession the radios belonging to the four gunners on his side of the stage erupted. Two of those gunners had still been alive, but they most definitely were not now.

A moment later Chiun returned, shaking his head. Whoever it had been, he had blended with the thousands of panicking people before allowing himself to be spotted.

"So much for our intelligence coup," Remo bemoaned.

"What are they doing?" Chiun asked, nodding at the stage, where the surviving convicts were brawling amid the bodies of dead police and the dead governor.

Remo smirked. "Trying to collect their commutations. It's the governor's signature that frees them."

Chiun looked at Remo without saying a word, but even the look was unnecessary. Remo was already marching onto the stage, where he began snatching rolls of paper in blue ribbons out of the hands of killers and rapists.

"Sorry, this ceremony is canceled," he announced.

A hugely obese figure with a mop of sandy brown straw hair stared at his empty hands in dismay, then his face inflated with indignation. "That is my document, and you got no legal right to remove it from my person."

"Sue me," Remo said, his hand snatching paper rolls at lightning speed and adding them to the crushed wad in his other hand. He found a small wastebasket under the podium and used that for convenience' sake.

The fat man stepped gingerly through the mess of gubernatorial gray matter and waddled at Remo defiantly. Remo ignored him as he sped in pursuit of a pair of identical twin slimeballs who were making a run for it. They didn't get more than five paces before the commutation decrees were slipped from their fists.

"Stop there, little boy! I got matters to discuss with you!" The fat man was breathless from his five-yard dash.

Remo ignored him as he counted the rolls in his wastebasket, then counted the angry mob of convicts moving into position around him. Finally he stood on his toes to count the convicts who had been gunned down in the melee.

"What's thirty-three plus eighteen?" Remo asked the fat man.

"Them's our tickets to freedom. Hand 'em over, little boy," the fat man said, his tone reasonable but determined.

"First answer the question, scumbag," Remo insisted. "Thirty-three living scumbags plus eighteen dead scumbags is how many total scumbags?"

"Little boy, don't play games with me! That's my life you got there in that can!"

Chiun appeared at Remo's side. "Perhaps you should carry a calculator."

"The sisters always said I might need to use math some day, and I never believed them. And they were right, what do you know?"

Chiun sighed. "The answer is fifty-one scumbags."

Remo smiled and waved his wastebasket at the convicts. "Good, then I got all of them!"

"And you best be returning them to us directly, little boy," the fat man said threateningly.

"Certainly, thief, return them at once!" Chiun squeaked, and yanked the wastebasket from Remo. Chiun shoved one hand into the wastebasket, whirling his hand inside like some sort of industrial food-preparation machinery. His fingernails were as sharp as razors and strong enough to cut steel pipe. They worked well on paper, too.

"Here you are," Chiun announced, and flung the contents of the wastebasket at the convicts as if he were dumping a bucket of water on a barn fire.

The fat man was engulfed in a cloud of paper particles too small to be called confetti. He roared in fury, but made the mistake of inhaling afterward, coating his lungs with particles.

"You're breathing my commutation!" accused a tiny Puerto Rican with an Elvis bouffant, who placed a hard right into the obese man's stomach. The blow didn't penetrate the fat layer, and the little man next rammed the fat man with his head, hard, disappearing to his shoulders in the spongy blubber. The hacking fat man gagged up bile and collapsed with the Puerto Rican underneath him. The Puerto Rican cracked and went limp, and the fall raised a fresh billow of paper particles that the other convicts scrambled after, trying to scoop them out of the air in their cupped hands.

Remo and Chiun were long gone, but the clouds were still hanging in the air when the city SWAT teams stormed the auditorium and cuffed every single person on stage, alive or dead, including the deceased governor.

Nobody on the SWAT teams had really liked that governor.

6

Dr. Harold W. Smith stared at the computer monitor under the surface of his desk. It was a brand-new flat screen, recommended by his assistant, Mark Howard. Mark helped him remove the old, heavy unit. The new screen that was bolted in its place looked like a toy to Smith. It was only an inch thick and weighed just a few pounds. Still, Smith never allowed himself to become outdated in his computer technology. The success of CURE depended in part on state-of-the-art technology.

Sure enough, the nineteen-inch flat panel provided a brilliant image with high resolution. When they had turned it on that morning for the first time, Smith had gazed into it and experienced a strange lack of tension in his eyes. He realized that he had been squinting into his old monitor for so long it had become an unnoticed habit.

"This enables digital video feeds," Mark explained as his fingers rattled on Smith's keyboard and brought up four windows, each showing a digital television channel, now a part of the standard media feed being channeled into the CURE computer systems.

"And this allows you to adjust the screen resolution at a touch," Mark added, maneuvering the mouse to an on-screen button and clicking it once. The screen images magnified. They looked huge, but the width of the display meant Smith was seeing as much information now as he had seen on his old, smaller monitor.

"I use this all the time when my eyes get tired," Mark explained, vacating the seat so Smith could test out the new display.

Smith appreciated the comment, but he knew why Mark was showing him this feature first of all. His eyes were tiring more easily as he got older. Smith was not a young man.

"So?" Mark asked. "How do you like it?"

"Like what?" Smith asked without tearing his eyes away. "Oh. Yes, fine, but we've got trouble, Mark."

Mark looked over Dr. Smith's shoulder. One of the news network's digital satellite feeds was displayed in the top right window. The network was interrupting its regular program for a breaking news story. Dr. Smith brought the volume up so they could hear the anchor inform them of "Reports of gunfire in Chicago at the auditorium where Governor Bryant..."

"I'm on it," Mark Howard announced, leaving for his own office. After working together for a short time, Howard and Dr. Smith had developed an efficient two-pronged approach that allowed them to scour the global networks and their own information sources for valuable intelligence at the first sign of a crisis.

This crisis was still evolving. Between the two of them they learned just one meaningful bit of data, soon verified by the media: the controversial governor was dead.

Minutes later all the networks were showing video footage of the gunshot in almost constant rotation and sometimes in slow motion, and the brain bits were clearly visible flying into the rows of seated convicts.

THE TWO PHONES RANG at almost exactly the same instant. Harold W. Smith grabbed them both and said into the red one, "Hold please, Mr. President."

Before the leader of the free world could respond with "Hell, no," Smith had lowered the red receiver to the desk and spoke into the blue one. "Remo, what went wrong there?"

"Well," Remo said, "first they elected this really bad man to be their governor, then a few years later somebody shot him."

"Remo, I have the President on the other line and I would appreciate a straight answer," Smith said icily.

"What could be straighter, Smitty?" Remo demanded. "You want the important facts, you just got them."

"Did you question them?" Smith demanded.

"They're all dead."

"You killed them? All of them?" Smith's voice rose slightly.

"Whoa, there, Smitty, I didn't kill them all."

"Did Chiun?"

"I most certainly did not!" squeaked a distant voice through the phone. "I spared several of the worthless cretins so that we might interrogate them fully, just as you requested, Emperor," Chiun insisted, getting closer to the phone.

"Give that back!" Smith heard Remo say.

"It was Remo who allowed the unslain men to boom themselves," Chiun accused loudly into the receiver.

"Give me that."

"Ingrate!"

Smith's hand gripped the receiver so hard it turned from gray to white. "Would you both stop bickering like children and give me a report, please."

There was silence, as cold as the deep freeze of a miserable winter. Finally Remo came on the line saying, "Now you've done it."

"Did you learn *anything*, Remo?" Smith asked.

"N-O spells no, how many times do I—"

Smith put the blue phone down and spoke into the red one. "I'm sorry, Mr. President, I was just getting a report from Chicago."

"Dammit, Smith, what went wrong?"

"I do not know yet, sir."

"All they had to do was protect one man. I thought your guys were supposed to have wonderful, strange abilities, but they can't protect one public official?"

"Mr. President," Smith said deliberately, "if my men had been instructed to protect the life of the governor instead of watch from the sidelines, then the governor would be alive right now. As I told you this morning, this event was foolhardy and by its very nature impossible to secure."

"I tried to talk him out of it," the President said. "That fool wouldn't hear of it."

"We also discussed increasing the security level at the auditorium," Smith reminded him.

"Bryant wouldn't go for that, either," the President said. "My boys said it would have taken days to set up and you know his term was ending Monday. That old bastard wouldn't let anything get in the way of his farewell extravaganza." The President sighed. "Guess he went out with a bang like he wanted."

"Yes, sir," Smith said. "I'll update you when I learn more." He disconnected the line.

"Remo, you still there?" Smith asked into the blue phone, but he heard only the distant sounds of a public place somewhere in Chicago. An intercom in the background said something about a cheeseburger with ketchup and extra-extra pickles.

Smith hung up and stared at the crystal-clear, ultra-slow-motion video replay of the governor's exploding head.

7

Dr. Donald Lamble watched the replacement governor mumble his way through a press conference, his head hanging sorrowfully.

"He is talking to his shoes, not the reporters," Lamble observed.

"A shameful performance," agreed Dr. Lamble's campaign manager as she used a drapery steamer on his lapel. One corner wanted to curl. "Nobody is going to believe he's sorry about it," she added. "Best thing that could have happened to him."

"Yes. Exactly," Lamble said. The lieutenant governor had profited greatly from the screw-ups of his predecessor, including landing in the governor's seat when the scandal-plagued Bryant announced he would resign months before his term was scheduled to end. Bryant's death meant the lieutenant governor's chances of being indicted as party to the corruption scandal were greatly reduced, plus it gave his own administration credibility he would have otherwise lacked—and that added legitimacy to his campaign to be elected to a full term.

"The idiot thinks he has to look mournful," Lamble observed. "What he really should do is come out swinging. Tell the state they are better off without that man Bryant. Ouch!"

His campaign manager mercilessly triggered hot steam into the stubborn lapel, scalding his chest in the process. Lamble stood as straight as an arrow and grimaced through the pain. She wouldn't have stopped if he asked her to, and he wouldn't have asked her to. After all, he had to look sharp. He had to be perfect. Nobody could be cleaner cut than Dr. Donald Lamble. If he had to endure a minor burn to get his lapels to fall into place, then he would endure it.

His campaign manager, third cousin and occasional lover, nodded in satisfaction and stepped back, appraising Lamble critically. "Looking good."

"You're the best, Madge."

She flicked his nose sharply with one finger. "Contractions are for junkyard rabble!"

Lamble flinched. "Sorry. You are the best, Madge."

"Thank you. I know. Now go show them how it is done."

DR. DONALD LAMBLE was the picture of confidence when he stepped out into the crowded little room in his campaign headquarters. His campaign staff and volunteers applauded politely, but there was no mistaking the excitement in their eyes. They were Lamble's people.

They believed in him and his message. That faith was his fuel.

He greeted them with smiles, his backbone ramrod straight. He didn't need to be a humble man. He was a man with a message he knew was right, and there was no need to be humble about taking the ethical high road.

Only a few reporters were on hand, and Lamble knew that others had been turned away at the door. That was one of the techniques from the *White Hand Book*. It seemed like bad public relations until you thought it through.

Reporters were just nosy troublemakers who liked nothing more than getting what they couldn't have. The practice of letting in just a few journalists for important press conferences made Lamble's events all that much more newsworthy. The local media had begun getting competitive about who could and who should get in to his media events.

The other purpose was more subtle. No reporter, however jaded, however politically disenfranchised, could remain unenthusiastic when he was surrounded by a crowd of supporters. Today the handpicked media were all those who had begun to lean in Lamble's direction. He needed sympathetic ears for what he was about to say. But the *White Hand Book* said this was the time for it. Lamble believed in the *White Hand Book*—he had faith in it. You had to have faith in the book to have faith in the party, because without faith there was only failure.

Lamble smiled, the picture of self-assurance, tolerating not even a glimmer of doubt to flutter through his head as he thanked his campaign staff and the reporters and launched into his comments on the assassination of governor Bryant.

"The violence visited upon the governor of our neighbor state today was a horror," he said. "But what we have witnessed today is a perfect example of how bad government is ruining this great nation. Ironically, Governor Bryant was a victim of the very violence that his corrupt administration allowed to flourish unchecked."

There was a murmur among the people. The reporters who had shown signs of being Lamble converts were now showing suspicion and surprise. Saying bad things about the recently deceased was a big political no-no.

No need to worry. The idea was on the table. Time to convince the people, including the reporters, to see the message in the same light as Lamble.

"Governor Bryant was a man who furthered his career through the corruption of his elected office. There are more than sixty corruption counts in the charges brought against his former staff, and yet Governor Bryant claimed he knew nothing of it."

Lamble knew what every person in the room was thinking—Bryant was never charged with any crime...

"My Washington sources tell me, in fact, that an indictment against Governor Bryant was delivered two days ago and ordered sealed by the courts—a legal stipulation that becomes null when the defendant dies. Therefore I can reveal now that this man was charged by the government of the United States with twenty-seven counts of corruption, racketeering, and misuse of public funds. These charges extend beyond the campaign scandal of his secretary of state term and include accepting bribes in exchange for state contracts, for state jobs, and for the commutation of harsh prison sentences against convicted murders."

There was a buzz in the room. There had been speculation of such things throughout the brief stint of Bryant's term as governor, and now there was confirmation. If Lamble said it, then it had to be true. If it was true, then Bryant was indeed a bad, bad man.

"Governor Bryant brought corruption into the highest office in his state. He made his own self-interests more important than the welfare of his people. He put murderers on the streets to make himself rich. He put his friends into jobs for which they were not qualified, then took kickbacks. These are not rumors or speculation, but the very words of federal prosecutors as written in charges against the governor."

The reporters were practically drooling and the campaign workers' eyes were shimmering with excitement.

"Governor Bryant allowed corruption to fester in his state, creating an environment for violence to thrive, and that violence killed him," Dr. Lamble intoned. "Is it any surprise?"

"No," answered some in the crowd.

"And this violence was visited upon him in the minutes before he could commit the most egregious and self-aggrandizing act of his administration—putting even more violent criminals on the streets," Lamble said. "I call it just deserts."

The applause was more than polite. They were actually buying it. "The message is this," Lamble said. "Those who live by corruption will die by corruption."

"Excuse me, Dr. Lamble," interjected one of the reporters.

Lamble made a show of stopping with his mouth open, smiling, clearly not taking offense at the interruption. His people would take offense for him. "Yes, Mr. Rode?"

"Are you saying you condone this violence?"

"Not at all."

"Are you saying that vigilantism is an unacceptable method of removing politicians from office if they are perceived as being corrupt?"

"No, Mr. Rode. When a Mafia boss is gunned down by a rival crime Family, that is poetic justice. When a gangbanger has one of his own cheap guns blow up in his face, that is poetic justice. And when Governor Bryant is assassinated along with a bunch of convicted murderers and rapists, it is poetic justice."

As smooth as silk, Lamble thought, as the applause filled the room. People were whistling. People were shouting. Their faces shone with their adoration. Even the rude reporter was nodding as he jotted down his messages and checked his audio recorder. It was a bold message and Lamble had delivered it perfectly.

Man, did he know how to push the good people's buttons or what?

8

Orville Flicker watched the news feed from the Midwest, where candidate Dr. Donald Lamble was pretending not to be overjoyed by the hoots and cheers.

The network cut back to the anchor. "Strong words from Senate candidate Donald Lamble. Not the sort of aggressive stance I would have expected from an independent running at least four points behind the two major-party candidates vying for the same seat. Sam?"

"That's right, Sam," said the hastily arranged expert, a commentator from the nightly news show who was added to the normally second-rate afternoon line-up just to give it a shot of credibility. The camera pulled back to take in the elderly man who had been a network news fixture for decades.

Two Sams, Flicker chuckled. Some producer was probably being fired that very minute.

"It is just the kind of remark the public will take as coldhearted," Commentator Sam opined.

"Although his constituency seems to agree with him," the anchor said.

The old commentator gave the younger man a patronizing, gin-soaked smile. "Important to note that those are not his constituency, Sam, but his campaign staff. I think we'll see quite a different reaction from the voters Dr. Lamble hopes to represent."

"Perhaps, Sam," said the younger anchor doubtfully.

"Count on it, Sam," snapped the commentator.

"I wouldn't count on it at all, Sam, you old sot," Flicker told the television.

"What's that, Mr. Flicker?" Noah Kohd thumbed off a mobile phone and looked at the television, just one of three that folded down from the roof of the limousine. The other two were silently showing broadcasts from other networks.

"I know that old drunkard better than my own Dad," Flicker complained, waving his remote at the screen. "He dropped out of high school, for Christ's sake. He never would have made it to the networks if he hadn't been in the trenches in Korea, and he only made it there because he was too sauced to know any better. Then he spends the next fifty years on the air acting like he knows what he's talking about. He's a moron. You should have heard some of the questions he used to come up with for the President."

"Yes, sir," Kohd said as his phone tweeted and he placed it to his ear. Kohd listed to the phone with one ear and to his boss with the other, although he knew perfectly well that Flicker was about to tell him about the time the commentator fell asleep during a White House news conference.

"One time he fell dead asleep during a White House news conference and started snoring. I wanted to have the old booze hound blacklisted after that." Flicker bit the inside of his cheek out of habit. "Of course *that* didn't happen," he concluded for his own benefit.

Orville Flicker sat up straighter. Got to look good. No slouching. He knew he was not a terribly appealing man physically, and only persistent attention to posture and behavior could overcome his physical failings. Small of stature, gaunt without looking fit, he was in his midforties and already his murky brown hair was showing signs of gray. His skin was pasty and his lips thin.

What he needed was an image consultant. Not one of those Hollywood sleaze merchants, but a real man who knew what a real man should look like. Someone who could train him to smile like he meant it. Someone who could make Flicker look like he had stature. Presidential stature.

Kohd nodded into his phone. "Okay," he said, and thumbed it off. "Check BCN, sir."

Flicker expertly muted one screen and brought up the sound on another just in time for the BCN Instant Opinion Poll.

"Well, it looks like the people have spoken!" cheered the anchor. Frank Appee was the new afternoon man at the BCN news desk. "Senate candidate Donald Lamble has got a few folks jumping-up-and-down mad in his home state, no doubt about it."

Flicker froze, eyes locked on the screen.

"But the angry types are in the minority! Just look at how the chips are falling in America's heartland, folks! Our results show eighty-one percent agreeing with Doc Lamble. You heard me. That's eight out of ten think Lamble's on-target when he says that Governor Bryant was a crook and he died like a crook. Ten percent are undecided and another nine percent think it's Lamble who ought to be shot for saying bad things about the recently deceased."

Flicker smiled. Kohd saw his boss relax with relief. Flicker had worried that public reaction would not be sympathetic to the party line. Kohd had never worried for a second. After all, they had been following the *White Hand Book*. The book was always right.

Kohd put the phone to his ear as it rang again. "Right," he said, then nodded at the first screen. "Sir."

Flicker snapped BCN into silence and brought up the sound on the first screen, where the two Sams were staring offscreen. "—think you can fire me? You can't fire me! I quit! You can take your old drunkard—"

The offscreen tirade vanished and was replaced with a commercial featuring a floppy-eared Irish setter bounding overhead. Flicker snapped it into silence, thinking that he might recognize the voice of the producer who had just ruined all his future possibility of getting employment in the network news business. On the third screen another poll was coming up, and he brought the sound. The anchors were talking in sonorous baritones.

"This is quite unprecedented but it is just as I expected, Karl," said the man with the vast toupee and the heavy eyebrows. "The people are fed up with the corruption."

"How so, Kent?" asked his partner. "We have had corrupt politicians before."

"That's an understatement, Karl."

Both men laughed politely, although the expressions on their faces were cast in stone.

"Yes, we've certainly had our share of unethical elected officials, Kent, but historically there has always been a sort of break in the public's awareness of unethical behavior. During this lull, the people tend to forget or downplay the scandals of the past."

Kent nodded somberly.

"This PLOC, or Perceived Level of Corruption, rises and falls with the media attention paid to political scandals," Karl continued, "but in the recent years these scandals have been unceasing. Therefore the PLOC level has remained high."

"In other words, there has been no PLOC lull," Kent said in an undertaker's voice.

"Exactly," Karl agreed expertly. "And without a significant PLOC lull, the public becomes overly sensitive to unethical behavior and more harsh in its judgment."

Kent and Karl, as wise and incisive as economics professors, considered the dire and meaningful implications of this. "This raises some interesting questions," Kent said leadingly.

"It certainly does," Karl responded. "If we had experienced a PLOC lull instead of a consistently high PLOC, would the people have been more forgiving of Governor Bryant's alleged corruption?"

"Absolutely not," Flicker responded to the screen. Kohd, on the phone with another call, nodded in agreement.

"If there had been any kind of a meaningful PLOC lull at any time in the recent past, would we see such broad-based support for the comments of the Senate candidate? After all, one of the unwritten laws for U.S. politicians has always been to never speak badly of dead opponents. It is seen as disrespectful."

"Not if their opponents are criminals," Flicker growled.

"What candidate Lamble has achieved," Karl concluded, "is change the perceptions of the public. The people won't mourn a dead criminal. Lamble has convinced the people—at least some of the people—that Governor Bryant was a criminal and he should not be mourned."

Flicker's face tightening into a smug grin. "Damn straight," he said.

Kohd gasped and disconnected his call without saying goodbye, then sat and looked at his boss with amazement. Flicker's confidence was in high gear. "Excuse my language, Mr. Kohd."

"I should say so, Mr. Flicker," Kohd responded.

Flicker tried not to roll his eyes. He wanted to tell his assistant to get the hell off his fucking high horse, but if he heard more than a single four-letter word in an hour Kohd would probably cover his ears and run screaming into the hills. The man was just so damn *straight*. Flicker considered himself straight, in every sense of the word, but nothing and nobody was more clean-cut, more spit-and-polish, more sinless than Noah Kohd.

Which, believe it or not, could get on a guy's nerves after a while.

9

The *White Hand Book* had something to say about a grassroots political campaign: it had to look like it was grassroots. If it looked planned or organized or prefabricated, it would have no credibility.

If the *White Hand Book* had one golden rule it was this: perception is everything.

Orville Flicker understood that rule. He had been born understanding it. He had meditated on its meaning for more hours than a philosopher considered the meaning of existence.

After all, existence was less important than perception. Without perception, existence was meaningless. On the other hand, perceiving something existed was the same as that thing actually existing for as long as the perception continued.

Flicker understood this when he was a little boy and he believed all the lies told to him by grown-ups, which meant his mother. He was allowed contact with no other grown-ups, or children. He invented his friends, a dragon named Hobbs and a cow named Whom, and spent hours playing with them.

When Flicker started school it was a small, home-based private class with only five other children. Five other children were more than enough to permanently scar his psyche, and it happened the very first day. Not long after he enthusiastically introduced the children to Hobbs the dragon and Whom the cow, he was ridiculed until he cried. He cried until his mother came and took him away from those awful children.

That night, Hobbs the dragon unceremoniously tore the meat off Whom the cow and ate her alive, only to get worms from the uncooked meat. Hobbs was dead by morning.

In his mind, for months, Flicker still saw the rotting dragon carcass and the scattered, moldering bones of the cow, which amazed him, because he was smart enough to know now that he was seeing an illusion created by his own mind.

He began to wonder how he could make other people believe in what he wanted them to believe, whether it was true or not. This sort of thinking led inevitably to a career in politics.

Perception was the *only* thing in politics and advertising. Nothing else mattered. Flicker knew it. Every smart politician knew it. Flicker's uncanny understanding of what perception was, why it was important and how to create it got him far.

But all it took was one serious lapse in his good judgment to ruin his career in an instant.

That was in the past and best forgotten. If people didn't forget, then you made them forget. You washed the past out of their minds with illusions of the present and dreams of the future.

Lucky for him, some memories were too entrenched to be forgotten, such as the reputations of the reigning political parties. In the United States of America there were two choices: bad and worse. The political parties that monopolized elections had been around so long that nobody truly believed there was an alternative. Orville Flicker was about to conjure an alternative out of thin air.

But it couldn't look conjured. It couldn't look like the product of planning or strategy. It had to be perceived as spontaneous. The people had to believe this new party was their creation, like a mythical bull springing into existence full-grown from the brow of a deity. The new party would appear to come into being in just that way, and all the people who joined it would never know how carefully Orville Flicker had been planning to use them to take over the U.S. government.

10

The Master of Sinanju Emeritus sniffed as he approached the automatic doors. When they parted, the air from outside wafted in at full strength and he stopped.

"Keep moving through the automatic doors," said the young woman on the stool. She had a uniform, a security badge and even a billy club in her belt, but she wasn't really charged with handling airport security. Her responsibilities began and ended with keeping people from stopping between the automatic doors.

"Come on, Chiun, what're we waiting for?" Remo was balancing a lacquered chest on each shoulder. Each was a unique work of art, the wood hand-hewn, the exquisite designs startling in their beauty. Remo had no idea what was in the chests, but Chiun never went out of town without several of them.

"Remo, there has been a terrible mistake," Chiun declared. "The pilot of the wobbly winged aircraft has landed us in Mexico."

"Naw. It's just Denver."

"Sir, please move out of the way of the automatic doors. They may close unexpectedly," the young woman explained.

"Smell it if you dare," Chiun said. "It is the oppressive stench of Mexico City."

"It's just Denver," Remo insisted. "Sometimes the smog gets trapped by the mountains."

"Sir, the doors might close and cause injury!" said the door-minder urgently.

"It is the door that will receive injury if it dares to close on me," Chiun snapped. "Tell me, what town this is?"

Fearfully watching the doors, which quivered in the open position expectantly, she only half heard the question. "It's Denver, of course, what do you think?"

"Not Mexico?" Chiun demanded.

"Sir, the doors might close!"

"What's with the nutty Chink Munchkin?" demanded a business traveler in the gathering line of people waiting to exit.

"Hoo boy," Remo muttered.

"Remo! I demand to know the meaning of the word Munchkin!"

"Well, he's nutty but he's got good hearing," the businessman muttered.

"That's not all he's got good," Remo replied conversationally.

"Oh yeah? He a tough guy? What's he gonna do, gum my leg?"

"Sir," the young door-minder pleaded, "the door could close!"

Everything happened all at once. The door started to close. The door-minder shrieked, knowing she was about to see the little Asian man crushed. The businessman's chuckling became a gag. Remo became intensely interested in a Pomeranian in a nearby pet carrier.

"Hi, doggy."

The Pomeranian's snarl died as it witnessed a surprising flicker of motion.

"You are correct," Chiun announced. "It is not Mexico City. The stink is slightly cleaner."

Remo chose not to see the businessman who was now paralyzed, stiff as a plank and jammed in the doors to keep them from closing, although the servomotors were trying their darnedest.

The door-minder turned to Remo. "The little man! He, he..."

"I see nothing." Remo stepped over the businessman.

"We have been to this place before, and it was never so oppressive in its atmosphere," Chiun said.

"Blame El Niño," Remo said, nodding at a cab, eager to get out before airport security or the sky marshals charged to the scene.

The driver of the first cab in the queue was staring at them. He'd seen the whole business and he knew trouble when it was about to get into his taxi. He floored it.

"Hold these for me, would you, Chiun?" Remo

asked, tossing him the trunks. There was a shriek from the tiny Korean and a chirp from the cab as Remo used his free hand to grab and lift it by the front end. The clonk and the honk were the driver's head slamming into the steering wheel and hitting the horn.

"Remo! You cast aside my precious trunks?"

"I did nothing of the kind. I handed them off to you," Remo growled.

"You," he said to the driver, who opened his door to flee but had it slammed in his face again. "Stay where you are. I need a ride and you're elected."

"Off duty!"

"You did not hand them off! You cast them away like worthless trinkets! They might have been scratched or—or worse! Just imagine if they had crashed to the ground!"

"You caught them just like I knew you would." Remo busily stowed the blemish-free trunks into the rear of the cab, then he got in back alongside the red-faced Chiun.

"You are an ungrateful ingrate!"

"Isn't that redundant?"

"No!"

"Look, Chiun, the only way your precious trunks would have gotten dinged is if you fumbled them."

"I, Chiun, never fumble."

"So the trunks were never in the slightest danger."

"Cannot drive! Off duty!" The driver gestured with shaking hands at the Off Duty sign on the fare meter.

The tiny Korean man weighed half as much as the

cabdriver, but the dark-skinned man at the wheel could never in a million years have turned his face the same shade of boiled-lobster red. Other things the cabdriver could never have done included smashing the bullet-resistant Plexiglas safety panel with one bare hand and twist the fare meter out of the dashboard like an old village woman wringing a chicken's neck.

The fare meter went through the windshield of the cab, raining glass twenty feet in all directions.

Not only was the fare meter gone, but the radio, the glove box and most of the right half of the dashboard now littered the pavement in the Denver International Airport cab queue.

"On duty," Remo pointed out. "Can drive."

The cabbie used his fingertips to leverage the metal shard that had once been the gearshift, pulling into traffic with a longing look at the troops of sky marshals he glimpsed marching through arrivals to the scene of the suspected terrorist activity.

"Smitty is going to shit a brick," Remo commented. "You know, shutting down airports does not have to be standard operating procedure."

"I shut down no airport."

"That's funny, because you just left the airport and ten bucks says they'll shut it down to find the suspected door terrorist."

"It is you who carries chaos around with you wherever you go."

"Yeah."

"It is a potent cloud, it hovers around you, you cannot shake it loose but it still affects everything you come in contact with. It is like, like—"

"Like cabdriver BO," Remo said helpfully.

The cabdriver glanced into the rearview mirror, but it was dangling by a single screw and showed him his own flannel shirtfront.

"News flash, for you, Little Father," Remo said. "You started all the excitement. All I did was talk to an ugly rat-dog in a box."

"Already your memory of the sequence of events is degrading," Chiun said. "I was angry with you, my son, but now I am only sorry for you."

"I appreciate your sympathy, Little Father."

Chiun nodded, his yellowing chin whiskers dancing in the blast of air coming through the windshield. The cabbie managed to bend the rearview mirror back into place and he glared at Remo in the mirror.

"You I don't need," Remo warned.

"Kill me if you must, but do not insult my hygiene," the man said in a thick accent.

Remo snorted. "I have news for you. You got all this circulation and it still smells like an untreated septic tank in here."

Chiun was shaking his head.

"What?" Remo demanded. "What?"

The driver looked crestfallen. "You smell the city, not me."

Remo considered that.

He was still considering it as the cabbie dropped them off at a bank in a hotel district. Remo went inside for a minute and came out with an envelope.

"Listen, I'm sorry I insulted you," he told the cabbie as he extracted Chiun's trunks from the back of the cab. Chiun wandered down the street with his nose held a quarter-inch higher than necessary. "My dad gets me cheesed sometimes."

"One never grows accustomed to the insults. You are like many Americans who ride my cab," the cabdriver said with an odd mixture of sorrow and fear. Then he glanced at his missing dashboard and added quickly, "In your attitudes about foreigners, I mean."

"Yeah, you're right," Remo said. "Sorry."

The cabdriver was sure the tall man with the vicious eyes was being ironic as a prelude to throttling him. But the throttle never came, and the cruel-eyed man handed him the envelope. It was bulging with hundreds. He looked at the bank, sure the cruel-eyed man had just robbed it, but business was going on inside without sign of alarm.

When he looked again, the cruel-eyed man was jogging down the street with the beautiful chests balanced on his shoulders.

The cabbie had led a hard life. Tortured by the Baath regime that killed his family, he had escaped Iraq's despot during the opening mayhem of the Shock and Awe bombing campaign. He had never really believed in the American Dream, but in the past half hour his luck finally turned around.

He marched directly into the bank and opened a checking account, and the first check he wrote bought him a whole new cab.

11

"Holy Toledo, Remo, was that really necessary?"

"Yeah, Junior." Remo sighed. "Give me Smitty."

"He's out. You know how much you gave that guy?" Mark Howard demanded on the hotel phone.

"Of course I do," Remo said, trying to remember how much he gave the cabbie. "Can you stop asking amazed questions, please?"

"I'm not amazed. I'm aghast."

"I'm going," Remo said.

"You know, even I don't make that much in a year."

Remo sniffed. "Come on, Junior."

"It's true."

"Okay, you got me. How much did I give that guy?"

Mark Howard read off a long number with the words "dollars" at the end.

"Well," Remo said, thinking fast, "the guy needed a new cab. Chiun destroyed his old one."

"But it was Remo who destroyed his self-esteem," Chiun called. He was on the floor in front of the thirty-inch television watching a trio of weeping Hispanic women accuse one another of horrific betrayals.

"What's he mean by that?" Mark Howard asked.

Remo steered the conversation in a new direction. "Junior, you have to be kidding me. Your salary is less than that?"

"Yeah. So what?"

"Annually?"

"Yeah. But it wasn't exactly a small chunk of change, Remo," Mark Howard said, and now it was his turn to be on the defensive.

"It was a hell of a tip, yeah, but it's lousy take-home pay for a guy who does everything that you do," Remo insisted.

"Compared to you, maybe—"

"I don't care who you compare it to, you're underpaid. No wonder you live in that dive in Rye."

Mark Howard tried to make sense of the rapid-fire insults and compliments.

"Don't worry about it, Junior. I'll take care of it."

"Remo, I do not want you interfering in my relationship with Dr. Smith."

"Working with Weird Harold's the very reason you ought to be making a hell of a lot more than you do," Remo said.

"Can we discuss the mission, please?"

Remo was pleasantly surprised that, for once, it wasn't him being bogged down in idiotic minutiae. This time, he was the bogger instead of the boggee.

"Okay, shoot, what's on the agenda?" He couldn't help but grin.

Mark Howard made a sound like he was trying to massage the stress out of his forehead. "Federal Circuit Court at 1:00 p.m. A bunch of state employees hired by the last governor—get this, a bunch of wealthy campaign contributors found a loophole that makes it legal for them to give a personal cash gift to the governor and get employment for their wives or kids or friends in return, and the new job pays more than the cash gift. But the employees were fired by the incoming governor, which he technically did not have the right to do. They're suing to get their jobs back."

"Yawn," Remo said. "Can't we go after some of the real lowlifes? There's crossing guards out there selling crack to grammar-school kids. Aren't they getting offed by the same bunch of do-gooders?"

"This is the most high-profile case in the country involving blatant corruption," Mark said. "We tracked a Colorado killing this morning that was probably a White Hand murder. We think it's a prelude to something big and this is it."

"I hope you're right," Remo said. "This is turning out to be an expensive business trip for the company."

12

Boris Bernwick was experiencing a high level of career satisfaction. How many people who liked to murder—professionally, or just as a hobby—got so many opportunities to commit murder? Talk about your dream job.

And to think how far he'd come.

Bernwick had started out as a soldier with the good old U.S. of A. and had excelled. Basic training was like a playground romp. The other recruits hated him because he tended to bawl them out after their sarge had already bawled them out. But they deserved it. They were pussies, and they needed to know they were pussies. Bernwick, as the one and only nonpussy, had the responsibility and the obligation to inform said pussies of their pussy status. Eventually, a gang of the other recruits tried to give Bernwick a lesson in teamwork. It happened in his bunk in the middle of the night. They whacked him with a few lengths of pipe that were then hastily reattached to the urinals. The sarge, an understanding sort, allowed Bernwick to individually box his five attackers, bare-knuckle. He knocked them out, every last one of them, sent them to the infirmary, and they all had to repeat basic. Losers.

Bernwick was quick to rise through the ranks, and if he had one complaint about being in the Army it was that the Army was so damn peaceful. He saw precious little action—until Iraq.

Bernwick had heard the stories about the first campaign in Iraq, when some soldiers unofficially committed a few atrocities against the Iraqi soldiers. Bernwick never did quite see the problem with killing the enemy. That was the whole idea of Desert Storm, wasn't it? So what if the enemy was unarmed and surrendering at the moment they were killed?

He never heard of any U.S. soldiers being disciplined for such actions in Desert Storm, and sure as shit no solider was going to get disciplined for it in 2003.

Fucking embedded journalists.

See, those fucks were supposed to be on video blackout during the fighting. How was Bernwick supposed to know the blackout was lifted during certain lulls in the hostilities? The idea was to send front-line video back home showing the U.S. military offering humanitarian aid and succor to the surrendering soldiers of Iraq.

Humanitarian aid to the enemy? No way, Bernwick thought. Succor? He had something the Republican Guard could succor.

Bernwick shot a few of them, four or five, so what? And so what if they were processed and shackled and scarfing down MREs because they hadn't been fed in days and they weren't armed with any weapon more lethal than a plastic spoon? So what? They were Saddam's solders. They were the enemy.

But you should have heard the bleeding hearts go yap yap yap, just because Bernwick got caught on video hosing down the POW picnic and just because the video happened to be on the air, globally, within twenty minutes of the last towel-head flopping over dead with a mouth full of half-chewed ham steak.

It seemed even less than twenty minutes before Bernwick was facing a full-sized court-martial. His military lawyer told him that his "They were Iraqis! They were the enemy!" defense was simply not going to work.

"Because of the damn media, right," Bernwick demanded. "Nobody would have cared if I wasted a bunch of camel jockeys if that fuck from the network wasn't there filming it all. Am I right? Well, am I?"

"I'm sorry to say you are not right, Captain," his lawyer answered regretfully. "You would face court-martial regardless. The fact that you created a huge amount of negative public relations during a time we can't afford it—that does make this a high-profile case."

Bernwick shook his head, laughing bitterly in his jail cell on the Kuwaiti base. "You may be educated, pal, but you ain't got a clue, know what I mean? The only reason I'm knee-deep in the shit is cause of that fucking cameraman. If it weren't for that, it would have been no big deal. Just another truckload of dead Ay-rabs and they're a dime a fucking dozen."

Bernwick found out later that his Army-appointed defense lawyer, whom everybody call Al, was really Army Colonel Akhmed Al-Duri Bey.

Bernwick left that whole mess behind and good riddance. It was his old sarge from basic training who saved the day. The old sarge had been treated bad, same as Bernwick, and got knocked back down to sarge and now he was managing a bunch of mechanics who worked on Hummers and Bradleys.

"I'm outta here," said the sarge. "I had enough of this-here puss-army. And I got some prospects, son, and maybe I got you a way out."

Bernwick was all ears. He liked what the old sarge had to say and he mostly liked the idea of not having to sit through the court-martial hearings.

"Count me in, Sarge."

"I ain't through tellin' you yet, son."

"I heard enough," Bernwick said.

The old sarge nodded, and his eyes became moist. "You're a good man. You got real guts. I'd trade my own good-for-nothin' boy to have a son like you what I could be proud of."

Bernwick was deeply touched. The sarge's son was with the Pentagon, technology research, developing nonlethal weaponry.

Nonlethal weaponry! The pussies who wanted nonlethal weaponry were the same pussies who got irate when a bunch of Iraqi enemies were shot dead while shackled together eating U.S. Army Meals Ready to Eat.

"I don't even care what else you have to say, Sarge," Bernwick had insisted, fighting back his own emotions. "I trust your judgment. Count me in."

Sarge smiled, revealing several gaps in his teeth, and held up a security card. "First, though, I get you out."

Sarge and Bernwick walked out of the lockup, but they didn't get far. The alarm sounded. The base was full of MPs. The place was practically deserted, what with most of the forces on a camping trip in Iraq, and losing themselves was impossible. Sarge and Bernwick took out a couple of MPs really quiet, bashing their heads in and stealing their vehicle. More MPs came after them. Sarge drove and Bernwick emptied the stolen rifles. Scored at least two more Military Pigs.

It never even crossed his mind that he was killing the same soldiers he had fought beside for six years. Later he thought about it, but his conscience was clean. After all, it was *them* who fucked *him*.

Anyway, Sarge took a hit. He slumped over with blood coming from his shoulder and Bernwick grabbed the wheel, yanked the sarge into the back and drove like a bat out of hell with automatic rifle fire burning the air around him.

Four MP vehicles waited at the base entrance and the rolls of barbed wire were being put into place over the entrance.

He wasn't going to make it.

That was when Saddam Hussein stepped in and gave Bernwick a little bit of friendly help.

The air-raid sirens went off and the MPs at the gate began to don their chem-bio suits. It was the whoop of the top-level siren. That meant full body protection was needed.

Morons, Bernwick laughed. None of the SCUD attacks had yet included biological or chemical agents, not to mention the fact that those pieces of missile shit flew off course like an old lady driving at night without her spectacles. And half the time they were blown up in the air by a U.S. Patriot missile anyway.

So, while the morons were suiting up, Bernwick took a deep breath of the clean desert air and plowed into them full speed.

To this day he got a chuckle out of remembering how those MPs went flying in all directions, one guy still holding his headgear. The barbed-wire barrier was taken out by a pair of bodies that sailed into it and yanked it off the gate before flopping across the sands in a thick tangle of wire and bleeding bodies.

His vehicle was still in working order, so Bernwick drove away.

Half an hour later, he bashed in the sarge's head with the crowbar from the jeep.

Sarge showed his yellow belly right there at the end.

"Son, I ain't dyin'! It's a shoulder wound, for God's sakes!"

"You'll slow me down, Sarge," Bernwick explained, disappointed in the old soldier.

"Then just leave me for the Army, son!"

"You think they won't get the truth out? About where you and me were headed?"

"My lips are sealed, swear to God, son!"

"You know what they'll do, Sarge," Bernwick said in an even, emotionless voice. "You were the one who told me what they do to a man who won't talk."

Sarge's wet eyes focused on the sky.

"They say that they shame a man into tellin'," Sarge said resignedly, then he looked purposefully at Bernwick. "I don't want to be shamed, son."

"I know you don't, Sarge," Bernwick said. Then, after the sarge's skull was cracked open, he said again, "I know you don't."

Sarge had some stolen military ID for Bernwick, and that got him home, months later, through Turkey. Once he was back in the good old U.S. he arranged to meet a man at a restaurant in Alexandria, Virginia.

The man was young, scrawny, pale, but he had a way about him. You listened to him talk and you *believed* in him. You listened to his opinions and you *agreed* with him. You experienced his sermons and you had *faith* in his vision.

"This war will be fought on two fronts, Mr. Bernwick," the man said with grave enthusiasm. To everyone he was simply the White Hand's head of armed forces. "Call me Haf." Haf always wore a high-quality fake beard and a wig.

"There will be the public face of our organization, people being groomed to take on the role of spokesmen and legislators. But they will never stand a chance without the backing of true soldiers. I need warriors who are not afraid of dirty work, not afraid to fight for our cause, to open the doors to the future. Without those soldiers, there really is no future for us."

Bernwick wanted to jump up and down like a little kid on Christmas morning. "I'm in."

Haf closed his eyes for a moment, as if saying a silent prayer of thanks. Bernwick never felt so valuable in all his life, and he walked out of the restaurant in Alexandria, Virginia, with his self-esteem up in the stratosphere.

Nowadays he was General Boris Bernwick, and his self-esteem was still floating around up there, right under the feet of the angels. He loved his job, he was good at his job, and he was helping to make his country a better place. Hell, he was helping to carve out the future.

TODAY THEY WERE doing some good. They were making things better for all of America. All it took was a little janitorial work. You go in with your room-broom automatic rifle, sweep up some of the filth and go away.

Haf put his hand on Bernwick's shoulder and smiled at the description. "Janitor? Boris, don't sell yourself short. In my mind, you're more like a doctor. One of the specialists at the cancer hospitals who go in and cut out the tumors that no other doctor could cut out."

Yeah, a doctor was way better than a janitor.

"You're the surgical specialist, Boris," Haf said. "You go in and cut out the rotten growths. Then the front-end people are the healers, the ones who transplant in the good parts to replace the discarded ones."

Bernwick liked that a lot.

"There have been political parties in the past who have tried to do what we do," Haf explained. "They have good ideas and a strong ethical backbone. They take out some of the cancerous organs and replace them with healthy organs. But you know, it's never enough, is it?"

"No," Bernwick said as if he understood, but he wasn't sure he did.

"Think about it, Boris," Haf said. "If I have cancer of the lungs, stomach, spleen and colon, the doctors don't go in and just take out the lung cancer."

Now Bernwick understood. "'Course not. Your patient is still sick."

"Exactly," Haf said. "And getting sicker all the time, even if his lungs are better. The patient is still dying."

Bernwick nodded. "You got to cut out all the cancer and stick in all healthy new organs. Even one piece of cancer could still kill the guy."

"Or the nation," Haf said, his eyes ablaze with passion. Bernwick felt it, too, the drive to do what was right.

"Boss," Bernwick said seriously, "you point me at the bad organs and out they'll come, even if I got to cut them out personally." He gestured with his hand as if digging around inside a human body with a small surgical tool.

"Dr. Bernwick," Haf said with admiration, "I know it. I see the fire in your eyes. And when the bad ones are out, I'll have plenty of healthy organs to replace them. We'll save the patient yet, you'll see."

Bernwick smiled to himself as he stood in the darkness. The whole damn nation was going to see. It was going to be better than a recovery. This time the patient was going to come out stronger than when he went in— stronger than ever before.

Bernwick touched his watch and the glow showed him it was 9:04 a.m. Court was now in session.

"General, our spotter says the courtroom is full up," reported one of his Special Forces recruits who pressed an earpiece to his head. "Right on schedule."

"Good," Bernwick said in a low voice. "I know it's not too dignified spending the night in a storage closet, but you're all real soldiers and you've shown your professionalism today. Now it's payoff time. We'll move at 0920, as planned."

There was a murmur of relief from the commandos. They had all known active duty with Special Forces, but this overnight wait had been tense. They could not ignore the nagging uncertainty stemming from yesterday's mission by their brethren in Chicago—a mission that cost the life of every member of the Midwestern cell of the White Hand.

Bernwick had tried to hammer it into their heads that the Chicago mission had not failed. The target was achieved. But even he didn't buy that load of bullshit.

A lot of their comrades died yesterday. No matter how dedicated you were to the cause, it was tough to look at the job as well done when you got killed doing it.

He had been able to keep his cell isolated from the news pretty well, but then, last night, they had slipped through the security in the courthouse and taken up their station, and then they sat there with nothing to do for six long hours except think about Chicago.

Time to address it again, head-on, no more bullshit, Bernwick decided. "This is not going to be a repeat of yesterday. Is that understood? We have a smaller space, fewer participants. Our job is easier because the environment will be under our control. I guarantee you this—we go in aggressive and alert, we're going to be invincible. Nobody, but nobody, is going to stand in the way of a professional soldier. Is that understood?"

"Yes, sir," said a chorus of voices.

"Good," General Bernwick said, his own confidence ratcheting up a notch. "Now let's go shoot some civilians."

13

"It is no wonder that your courts are not trusted," Chiun stated imperiously. "This trial is a farce."

"Can't argue with you there," Remo said. They had VIP seating, in the third row behind the families of the fired state workers. Remo knew little and cared little about style and fashion, but he knew expensive clothing when he saw it. Lots of custom tailoring, designer labels and dead animal pelts. This bunch was not hurting for cash. But to hear the opening arguments, every one of the families of the fired workers was on the verge of poverty.

"It is a sad story the attorney tells," Chiun said, leaning slightly over to whisper to a hippopotamus-sized woman in her early fifties. Her face paint revealed her suspicion, but she saw sympathy in the childlike eyes of the ancient man.

"It has been horrible to lose my job," she whispered in return. "It makes you feel helpless."

"It is a despicable breach of trust when a king promises to support his people, then does not."

The woman considered that, then nodded sincerely and rotated her girth to face Chiun more fully.

"You are a very incisive gentleman," she said.

Chiun smiled and closed his eyes in gracious acceptance of the compliment. Remo scooted to the left, opening the gap between himself and the conniving old Korean. He concentrated on listening for unusual noises, but he couldn't help overhear the conversation next to him.

"I come from an ancient lineage," Chiun said. "My ancestors left their village in Korea to work for rulers around the world and there were many times that we were cheated by rulers who promised us payment."

"Ix-nay," Remo muttered. Chiun knew good and well that he was not supposed to talk openly about Sinanju.

"My goodness, how awful! I know just how it was for you to suddenly lose the income you have been promised. It was terribly anxiety-producing to my family."

Chiun nodded. "You have many mouths to feed, and now nothing to feed them."

The woman looked uncomfortable. "Well, there's actually just Raymond and myself. The twins are at Notre Dame and my daughter is a state representative. But we do have the schnauzers, Jack and Jill."

Chiun nodded, his expression without judgment. "In my village," he said, "there were many families, and no fishing or work. All the village relied on the income that came from foreign rulers. When the money did not come—" he shrugged simply "—then there was no food."

"Oh, my."

"It is a sad thing to see a child die slowly from starvation," Chiun said. The blood drained from the face of the big woman. "It is sadder still to see the mother or the father grow gaunt because they sacrifice their share of what little food there is to their children."

The big woman's lower lip trembled.

"And it is not a mercy to prolong the life of a starving child," Chiun intoned in a low, matter-of-fact voice. "If there is no hope of food, then why allow the little one to suffer more than is necessary?"

"I don't..." She couldn't say anything more.

The lawyers for the state were now giving their opening arguments. "...we will show federal tax returns as evidence that, far from being destitute, the fired state employees have annual family incomes ranging from five hundred thousand to three million dollars, and that does not include the salaries they would have received had they continued working for the state."

The big woman wasn't listening to the lawyers, her attention riveted on the mild little Korean man who spoke almost in a whisper.

"In fact, it is an act of mercy to end the suffering of the babies, for their sake and for the sake of the village."

The woman's heavily painted eyes brimmed with tears.

"We live on a bay, you see, and we call this act of mercy sending the babies home to the sea."

Then Chiun did something amazing. Astounding. He produced a tear. It rolled down the ripples in his ancient face, and he allowed his mouth to tremble.

The hippopotamus woman gasped and sobbed loudly. She thrust her great rear end off the seat and grabbed her millionaire husband, Raymond. She towed him out of the courtroom, blubbering and sobbing all the way. The trial proceedings had halted and only slowly did people begin to react to the display.

Chiun sat back in his seat and couldn't hide the slight upturn of his mouth.

Remo couldn't stop being amazed. "Little Father," he whispered finally, "that's one of the coolest things I've ever seen you do."

"Heh-heh-heh."

"How long has it been since Sinanju actually sent any babies home to the sea? Like three thousand years?"

"Heh-heh-heh."

THE TRIAL BEGAN in earnest, Remo fought the inevitable boredom that came whenever he was in court—not that he was in court often in the past, well, couple of decades. When he was a cop in New Jersey, there had been regular court appearances. Then, of course, there was his own trial for murder. He had been framed and the trial was rigged and Remo Williams was found guilty. Next thing he knew, wham, bam, sizzle, he was in the electric chair.

The entire trial and execution were orchestrated by CURE, which then consisted of Harold Smith and Conn MacCleary, who had once been an agent alongside Smith in the Central Intelligence Agency.

Which got Remo wondering again about his current

endeavor and why he was doing it. Everywhere you looked, there was corruption. Somebody was removing the perpetrators of the corruption. Was that really a bad thing to do?

And what was the difference *really* between these guys and CURE?

Maybe stopping the corruption vigilantes was actually the wrong thing to do.

Chiun had moved down and was speaking to a well-proportioned but meaty middle-aged woman whose husband keep shushing her. The former governor had given the man an accounting supervisory position that took him away one afternoon a week from his nine-to-five job as comptroller for a three-billion-dollar airline.

"My people have long faced starvation," Chiun intoned sadly.

"We're not exactly starving," said the wife, who giggled in a desperate attempt to move the conversation away from all this negativity.

"You are an extremely fit woman," Chiun said approvingly.

This was more like what she wanted to hear. Older than dirt or not, she had a hankering for the vivid little Asian man. "Why, thank you."

But Chiun shook his head morosely. "Your fat stores are insufficient to support you during starvation."

She frowned, unable to decide if this was complimentary or not.

"And, of course, there is very little stored fat in your

plasticized udders," Chiun added with such seriousness the woman took a few seconds to believe she had heard what she thought she heard. "They will fail to sustain you as you begin to starve. Soon your flesh will become paper thin and cling to your bones, and then your fleshy protuberances will be a mockery to your agonized wasting."

The woman struggled to decide how to react. Remo enjoyed watching her, but he heard something that made him forget her entirely.

Chiun heard it, too.

"Front and back. I'll go front," Remo said.

Chiun nodded and then the two of them were bounding over the rows of wooden benches while the court erupted into pandemonium.

14

Remo cursed himself and cursed Chiun. If he had been listening more closely to what was going on around them, instead of eavesdropping on Chiun's game-playing with the rich idiots with the lawsuits, maybe he would have heard the guns earlier.

No. That wasn't fair to either of them. There were people all over this place. Cops and media and interested public and lawyers and court personnel. The gunners had taken their positions outside the rear entrance to the courtroom and in the judge's chambers, and only then did they extract their weapons and create the distinctive noise of firearms.

The gunners weren't wasting time and they weren't taking chances. The crew in the judge's chambers started shooting without even opening the door, and the torrent of bullets mangled the bolt and shoved it open.

There were two gunners, one crouched and one standing, and when they saw the flash of movement coming straight at them they concentrated their gunfire on it.

Remo dodged and spun and slithered around the bursts of autofire, moving as fast as he dared without intercepting one of the rounds himself. It took just an instant to reach the gunners, but how much gunfire had he allowed to spray into the crowded courtroom?

The two gunners were too slow to think about the bullet-dodger before he struck them dead. One expensive Italian shoe shattered the skull of the crouching man while the standing gunner got the finger. The finger penetrated the bridge of his nose and opened a channel into the brain itself. Remo's finger found the brain switch and turned it from on to off.

There was another gunner just behind them, where he had failed to see all that Remo did. The bodies of his companions had only started collapsing before he found his submachine gun removed from his hands and twisted with a groan of metal.

The gunner faced not a man but a dervish. A whirlwind. A creature too fast to be human tossed the gun into the wall, where it embedded itself, then grabbed the commando by the hair and began slashing him with a knife, but the knife moved too fast to see.

The commando's battle harness, his handgun holster, his blacksuit and white gloves and mask—all were shredded and seemed to disintegrate from his body like water flowing off him.

The commando found himself standing stark naked in the judge's chambers.

Remo snatched up the items that resulted from his

quick disrobing of the gunner. He came up with a hand-gun, a knife, a magazine for the rifle and a walkie-talkie. He twisted the gun, dismantled the radio and snapped the knife. No explosives. Hidden in the bullets? Seemed unlikely.

"Where's the suicide charges?" he demanded.

"The what?" the naked man asked.

"They've got you rigged to blow up if you blow the job, Dinky," Remo said. "Didn't you hear about yesterday's screwup?"

The naked commando looked blankly at Remo. "Huh?"

"Very helpful." Remo didn't have time to deal with it. Maybe this guy didn't have a self-destruct mechanism, but that didn't mean the two corpses weren't booby-trapped.

"Come on, Dinky." Remo lifted the commando by his hair and propelled him into the courtroom. Chiun was nowhere to be seen, and crowds crammed to get out the back entrance of the courtroom. Almost nobody noticed Remo until the bailiff swung in his direction, his revolver in a two-handed grip that meant serious business. The judge cowered behind him.

"Who the hell are you?" the bailiff queried.

"Justice Department," Remo blurted, since he couldn't remember what kind of ID he was carrying today. "Get the judge away from here—those bodies are rigged to blow."

"What the hell are you doing with that guy?" the bailiff cried at the sight of the naked guy.

"Dammit, get to the back!"

"I don't trust you for shit!" the bailiff shot back.

"Fine, I'll handle it. God forbid anybody lift a finger but me!" Remo slipped into the bailiff's personal space in an eye blink, batted the revolver skyward and snatched the officer of the court by the collar and belt.

The bailiff grunted, then heard, "Bailiff coming!"

Remo tossed the man with a quick flick of the wrists and sent him careening down the center aisle of the court. Budget cuts had made floor waxing and polishing a less-than-monthly event, and the bailiff screeched as the friction heated his flesh through his shirt and trousers and instantly burned his forearms.

"Judge coming next," Remo warned even as the bailiff bowled into the legs of the crowd and brought down eight gawking bystanders. Remo knew a seven-ten split when he saw one and he whipped the judge right down the middle of the aisle, giving the throw just enough English to send the judge into a last-second swerve that brought him lengthwise, taking out more of the panicking rabble. The judge's robes at least protected him better from friction burns.

"Sorry, Dinky," Remo announced to the shell-shocked, clothing-optional commando.

The man was a soldier, veteran of Gulf War Version 1.0, Bosnia and Afghanistan, and he had laughed at death, but now, finally he knew utter terror. He saw the burned arms of the bailiff and knew his own immediate future.

He tried to run, but the madman that was Remo Williams snatched him off his feet and got him the hell out of the blast range as fast as he knew how to do.

The commando was screaming even before he hit the floor at roller-coaster speed. He didn't slide on the unpolished floor so much as scorch across it, every inch an agony of fire as the great speed and the inordinate amount of exposed human flesh resulted in skin-peeling heat and friction of a massive degree.

Remo would have liked to watch, but he didn't have time. In all the chaos and screaming and movement, Remo had sensed something that didn't belong.

It took him two precious seconds to realize what it was. Air shifting, not ventilation, something strange and out of place, something from above.

A commando was looking down from the roof, where an opaque plastic skylight bubble had been removed. The commando was taking action—he had a remote control.

"Grenade!" Remo shouted, because he couldn't think of anything to better mobilize this herd of morons.

As he shouted, he leaped away from the rear of the courtroom where the two commando corpses were sprawled in the door to the judge's chambers. He saw the flash of light come from that direction a microsecond before the shock wave rolled into him and he plummeted into the third row of the court benches. As the crunching impact of the blast traveled across the courtroom, Remo wondered if maybe, just maybe, the com-

mandos were booby-trapped with explosive supposi-
tories.

Far-fetched, yes, but dammit if that wasn't the way
his luck had been running of late.

He filed away the thought, unpleasant for more reasons than he could count, and his hands came away from
the bench back in front of him holding a foot-long splinter of shattered wood. It was two inches thick at the base.

Remo leaped to his feet, spotted the commando on
the roof aiming his weapon at the crowd at the rear of
the courtroom and let the splinter fly. It seared the air,
moving at bullet speeds, but Remo's luck had wandered
away a heartbeat earlier in search of somebody more de-
serving. The man at the skylight pulled away fast, never
seeing the missile until it missed his sternum and penetrated clean through his pectoral muscle.

Remo heard the scream and followed it.

15

The bloody puddle had collected at the base of a maintenance ladder, and the drops vanished at the curb next to a No Parking sign.

Remo consoled himself with the knowledge that he still had one surviving commando.

Dinky was a mess. The entire front of his body was seared, black, bloody and blistered. Large chunks of flesh had been literally dragged off him in the high-powered slide to safety.

"Guess I should have slid you on your back instead of your front," Remo commented.

The commando's eyes rolled in opposite directions but seemed to focus for a moment on Remo.

"Can't even call you Dinky anymore, can I?" Remo said with a grimace. "I'll call you Ken, okay?"

"Kill me kill me kill me," Ken rasped.

"Oh, that's too good for ya."

"Jesus, where's your compassion?" blurted the arriving paramedic, who seemed unfazed by the extensive burns.

"Don't waste any compassion on this guy, uh, Shorley," Remo said reading her name tag.

"It's Shirley, moron, and this is a human being in terrible agony." She turned to her partner and started ordering up injectables.

"Your name tag says Shorley, Shorley, and this guy tried to murder a bunch of people with a submachine gun." He nodded at the efficient, quick procedures being performed by other paramedics over their blood-soaked gunshot victims. "I see four people with gunshot wounds and five people with sheets over their faces. That makes me care about this guy's suffering not at all."

Shirley yanked at her name tag, glared at it and swore savagely. "Okay, you're right about the name tag, but this man is not guilty until the court says he's guilty. Our human conscience obligates us to ease his suffering, so you just back the hell off, asshole!"

"Okay. See you, Shorley."

Shirley had been about to inject a massive dose of morphine into her patient when her hand came up empty. She looked on the floor. Her syringe couldn't have gone very far.... She swore and demanded another syringe of morphine.

"Don't *you* have the morphine?" her partner asked.

"I dropped it! Give me another!"

"What I mean is, don't you have all the morphine?

'Cause the kit's empty. Shit, everything's gone—all the painkillers."

Shirley knew—she *knew*—that the asshole smart aleck jerk had somehow just snatched all their morphine. That was so heartless. "This man is suffering! Give me something!"

"Well," her partner said, "we have this."

He handed her a single-dose packet of Tylenol, and it wasn't even Extra-Strength.

REMO FOUND Chiun standing in the hall near the blackened entrance to a men's room. No explanation was needed. Chiun had dispatched the gunners from the rear and tossed them into the men's room, then kept out the general public until the corpses blew up. Remo felt coldly despondent as he emptied the contents of several single-dose dispensers of painkillers into the water fountain.

"You are finally quitting your nasty morphine habit, I see," Chiun commented.

"Can it!"

Chiun was silent while Remo poured out the morphine, rinsed the bottles, then stuffed them in the nearest garbage can. In silence, the two Masters of Sinanju left the building without being noticed. Their hotel was only six miles away, and they wordlessly agreed to walk it. The stagnant front that locked in the bad air over Denver had yet to move on, and Remo breathed dirty air. He felt the smog taint his lungs and trickle into his blood. There was no way to stop it from happening, and he felt dirtied by it.

"These assholes are not like us."

It was a full two minutes before Chiun said, "I agree."

"I thought maybe we should go easy on them. Let them take out some of the garbage before we plugged them up. But I saw a lot of dead people back there who weren't guilty of anything."

"It is not the reason Emperor Smith would give," Chiun said, "but I think it is a better reason—as long as we're being paid anyway."

"In a couple of hours we can go visit Ken in whatever burn unit they put him in," Remo said. "But he's probably a know-nothing grunt."

"Did you learn more about him than his name?" Chiun asked.

"I didn't even learn his name. I was calling him Dinky first."

"Why?" Chiun asked.

Remo explained and Chiun smirked.

"But then, you know, I decided dinky wasn't accurate anymore so I switched to Ken."

"Why? What is 'Ken'?"

Remo once again explained.

Chiun smirked again, and steered them in the direction of a toy store that was on the way to the hotel.

16

"Boudoir Fantasies," said a husky, sultry voice, "I'm Ursula."

"Ursula, give me Harold," Remo said, feeling unfriendly.

"We do not have anyone working here by that name," Ursula breathed. "Is he one of our customers? We have lots of men who have sensual, provocative portraits done by our professional photographers."

"I doubt Harold would go for that."

"Oh, yes! Here we go! We have a five-o'clock appointment for a Harold. He's booked the Tarzan studio."

"Can't be him," Remo insisted.

"The loincloth is silk with leopard spots," Ursula continued relentlessly.

"Picturing it makes my flesh crawl."

"We have a stuffed lion that the gentlemen can pose with."

"Ursula, I'm begging you."

"For an extra fee we can have one, two, or three topless jungle girls appear in the shot with him," she insisted. "Some of our males have the shots done in the nude themselves. Do you think your partner Harold—?"

Remo hung up the phone with superhuman speed, but not fast enough. The message was delivered. The images were in his head, branded there forever.

"I may not be able to look Smitty in the face ever again," he said.

"Can you not see that my program is on?" Chiun asked from in front of the television. "From this moment until the end of time, consider me unavailable for conversation under such circumstances."

The phone rang and Remo waited a full minute before picking it up. "Remo," Harold Smith demanded, "why did you not allow the screening system to complete its scan?"

"Smitty, your screening system is screwing with my head," Remo complained. "And every time I call, it wants me to talk longer than the time before."

"I think you're exaggerating."

"Uh-huh. And who comes up with the weird scenarios? Not you, I hope."

"No, they're completely randomly generated."

"Man, I hope you're not lying."

"Of course not. Why would I lie? What happened when you visited the hospital? Did you get anything useful out of the gunner from the courthouse?"

"No. He didn't know a thing."

"How certain are you of that?" Smith asked.

"Pretty sure. We asked nice and we asked not so nice. He was doped up and didn't have much to say. He never knew anyone outside his own cell. Why? Somebody kill him?"

"Yes."

Remo lowered the phone. "Oh my God, Little Father, they killed Kenny."

"Speak only at the commercial," Chiun said.

"We're both sick about it," Remo informed Smith. "We did get the name of the cell commander. They called him General Bernie. I think it was the guy who got away."

"Was General Bernie an American?"

"Yeah."

Remo heard the tapping of Smith's keyboard in Rye, New York. "There's no record of a General Bernie in any branch of the armed forces. Must be made up."

"That's what Ken said."

"Ken?"

"Also made up."

"Nothing about the leadership of the White Hand? Stated purpose? Full name of anybody in the ranks?"

"No, no and no. But the FBI had Ken's real name."

Smith sighed. "Jerome Reik. Special Forces, dishonorable discharge, no known political or organizational affiliations."

"So why'd somebody kill him?" Remo asked.

"Maybe just insurance, in case he happened to accidentally pick up some tidbit of intelligence during his time with the White Hand, and we're not even convinced that's the real name of the group," Smith said. "There have been white supremacist groups with similar names, but the FBI identified Latinos and African Americans among the dead from both the Chicago and Denver cells, so that's not a likely affiliation. I can tell you that the Denver police would like to have a word with you about Mr. Reik's unfortunate passing."

"We'll be sure to stop by the station."

"I assume you were the ones who left the child's doll with the patient? Does this have any significance?"

"Not that you want to know about."

"Fine. But the hospital staff remembered the visitor in the kimono," Smith said. "We may need to ask Master Chiun to wear less distinctive attire while on mission."

"What?" Chiun squeaked.

"Hear that? I think you have your answer."

"Maybe you can explain to Master Chiun why this would be beneficial," Smith suggested.

"Oh, no I can't. You're on your own on this one. So what do we do next?"

Smith sighed. "We're working on that."

"Should we just hang out here in Denver? The air is making us sick."

"Smog?"

"Yeah. Anything you can do about it? Maybe call in the Air Force to use its highly classified weather-making technology to blow Denver?"

There was a stony silence. "What Air Force weather-making technology?"

"So the Air Force *does* have weather-making technology! What'll you give me if I keep it to myself?"

"I never said—!"

"Joking, I'm just joking, Smitty. Listen, isn't there anybody else in the vicinity who's done some governmental corruption?"

"Of course," Smith said. "In Colorado alone there are hundreds of government workers at all levels who are likely involved in corruption of some kind or another."

"I mean high-profile," Remo said. "Somebody who's getting a lot of press or maybe would get a lot of press if they got gunned down."

"Hmm," Smith said.

"Come on, Smitty, I can't take being cooped up with Chiun and his *Excito Tomate* soap opera."

"Exciting Tomatoes?" asked Mark Smith as the call at the Rye end switched to speakerphone.

"It is *Excito Totalmente*, imbecile," Chiun said.

"How's it going in the salt mines, Junior?" Remo said. "Help out the old taskmaster, would you? We're trying to figure out what targets might be next in the Mile High City of Asphyxiation."

Mark Howard answered with an eerily familiar, "Hmm."

"There's got to be somebody," Remo insisted.

"We've considered it, Remo," Smith said. "We're doubtful they would even continue with the next strike after their run-in with you and Master Chiun."

"Think again," Remo replied. "These people have an

agenda. You said so yourself. They've got a long to-do list, and I'll wager the plasma-screen TV at the duplex that they're not going to slow down for a minute."

"Do not take that bet, Emperor—it is not his television to gamble with!" Chiun called.

"You said yourself the cell is probably been pared down to the single commanding officer, this General Bernie," Smith said. "Maybe he would carry on, but even so he would change his planned targets."

"Maybe not," Remo said as the latest commercial ended and the discordant wail of music heralded the return to the *Exciting Tomatoes* soap opera. The tomatoes in question, Remo gathered from trying not to listen, were four generations of superrich Mexican women. They were all ruthless. They could all spew tears at the drop of a hat. Every one of them, from the seventeen-year-old bimbette daughter to the fifty-five-year-old grand matriarch, possessed massive breasts. They wore a lot of halter tops to show off their massive breasts, and Remo was almost certain that most aristocratic Mexican grandmothers did not wear halter tops, especially to formal dinner parties.

"I bet Ken knew what the next hit was going to be," Remo decided out loud.

"Who's Ken?" Mark Howard asked.

"The guy who was in the burn unit. We questioned him, but he was too dosed up in the hospital to be helpful. I tried getting something out of him at the courthouse but there were complications. Maybe he said something to the paramedic who worked him. Can't hurt to ask."

The *Exciting Tomatoes* matriarch and her teenage descendant chose that moment to sob and embrace, and the cameraman widened his view so as not to miss a single bulge of their fronts coming together in a braless mash.

"Anything's better than staying in the room," Remo added.

THERE WAS A MAN JOGGING alongside the ambulance. He made a gesture with his hand and the paramedic in the passenger seat incredulously rolled down her window.

"Hi, Shorley."

"What the hell are you doing here?"

"Can we talk?" asked the jogger.

Shirley Feely shook her head. "Did you happen to notice we're on a call?" she asked sarcastically. "That loud noise is called a siren. And see the flashing lights?"

"Yeah, I know about these things," the stranger said, amazingly unwinded by his running. "Is it really an emergency or just one of those cat-stuck-in-a-tree calls?"

Shirley Feely decided that this guy ranked just below her dad as the world's biggest all-time asshole. She turned on her partner suddenly. "Why are you slowing down?"

"Well, that guy you're talking to," Keith Ostrowski said.

"Forget that asswipe and drive!"

Ostrowski was competent enough when it came to his job, and he drove them quickly to the scene of the call. The suburban ranch house was quiet when they arrived. For a second, as they came to a halt in the driveway, Shirley thought she glimpsed a flash of movement in the backyard between the houses.

The front door was unlocked. When they stepped inside they heard an old woman saying, "Why, thank you kindly. That is much better."

They found the old woman on the sunporch, relaxing into a reclining wooden chair. Remo Williams was pouring her a tall glass of lemonade from a frosty pitcher.

Keith Ostrowski frowned. "Isn't that the guy you were talking to?"

"Hi, Shorley," Remo said.

"What are you doing here?" she demanded.

"Helping out," Remo said. "Mrs. Butler fell. She couldn't get up."

"I threw my back out again. Oh, it hurt to high heaven!" said the elderly Mrs. Butler. "Remo gave me a little squeeze on the hip and behold! The pain was gone."

"This doesn't explain what you are doing here," Shirley insisted.

"I thought he was getting fresh with me at first." Mrs. Butler smiled. "You weren't getting fresh with me, were you, Remo?"

"No, ma'am, I sure wasn't."

"What if I asked nicely?"

"Mrs. Butler, you slay me!"

Mrs. Butler giggled, but Shirley Feely was not amused. "Mrs. Butler, I do not know who this man is, but I can tell you he certainly is not a trained paramedic."

"Oh, but he did a wonderful job. My back hasn't been so loose in years."

"Regardless, I'm going to have my partner check you out while I have a talk with Mr. Remo."

"I don't need to be checked out," Mrs. Butler insisted mildly.

"Now, Mrs. Butler, you listen to Shorley. She's the professional," Remo said.

"Whatever you say, Remo."

"My name is Shirley!"

"Oh, no, it's not, dear, just look at your embroidery," Mrs. Butler pointed out.

Shirley grabbed Remo's arm and dragged him into the tidy kitchen off the sunporch.

"Let's talk," Remo said.

"No, you listen! You cannot and will not interfere with me or my job, understand?"

"I fixed her back spasm," Remo protested. "You would have had her in a neck brace on a stretcher by now. Poor lady would have wasted the next week in a hospital bed."

"I don't believe for an instant that you actually helped that old woman."

"Remo! Look!" Mrs. Butler cried through the screen door. "I can touch my toes!" Keith Ostrowski was dancing around in a panic as the elderly woman bent at the waist and touched her toes. Remo applauded.

Keith managed to coerce her back to the chair, and Shirley glared at Remo.

"Your head is gonna explode, isn't it?" he asked.

"Listen to me," Shirley pronounced slowly. "I do not like people interfering with what I do."

"I can tell. You've got real control issues."

She belted him. He took it and smiled. "Feel better now?"

She backhanded him.

"Now?" he asked.

He took a third blow to the face. Shirley knew how to throw a punch.

"This helping you out?" he asked. "Uh-oh."

Too late he sensed the change. His assailant had suddenly stopped being mad, and she started being something else entirely. It had to have been all the hitting. She threw herself into the air and landed her pelvis on the front of his beige Chinos, wrapping her legs around his posterior and encircling his neck with her strong arms. She latched her mouth on to his.

She pulled away briefly. "You're an asshole."

"Your punches hurt less than your kissing."

"Brace yourself." She hurt him again.

On the porch, Mrs. Butler watched and sighed with envy. "Lucky little tramp."

"Yeah," Keith Ostrowski said.

"YOU," SAID THE NAKED PARAMEDIC, "are the worst person I ever met."

"Have you met a lot of people?" Remo asked.

"If I meet a hundred thousand people, I'll never meet anybody worse than you."

"Ha! I can prove you wrong within the hour—just come to my hotel."

Shirley's sour glare became baleful. "Your wife?"

"Naw. My trainer. You want unpleasant, he can deliver it in truckloads. He's mean, he's nasty and he's so old he makes Mrs. Butler look as fresh as butter."

Shirley considered that, then shook her head. "You're still worse. Look what you made me do—no old man could use me like you did."

"I think you're actually warming up to me."

"Remo, look around you!"

Remo looked around. "So?"

"We just did it in an ambulance! My ambulance!"

"It was your idea," he reminded her.

"I'm a professional paramedic! My behavior's been appalling! I let myself be coerced and manipulated."

"Listen, everybody makes mistakes. You had a little too much to drink, I was complimenting you all evening, sometimes those things lower your defenses."

She rose on her elbows and blinked at him. He was sitting on the gurney, trapped by her legs. "What are you talking about?" she asked. "We only started mashing lips a half hour ago."

"You'll feel better if you go with my version."

She considered it, then shook her head. "I'm ruined. Keith's the biggest gossip in the city. He'll have my reputation smeared before the shift ends."

"I'll talk to him." Remo wasn't sure how to handle this young lady, and he didn't want to push the wrong button, but he finally got to the point. "You know, I actually came here to talk to you about your patient yesterday."

Her mean face turned sad. "Died."

"Murdered."

"By you, if the story I heard is true. Lord knows I tried to stabilize him."

"All I did was get him away from the bomb the fastest way I knew how. And you did stabilize him. He was murdered in the hospital." She got up on her elbows again, which made her trim stomach wrinkle in a way Remo found quite cute. Her breasts had just enough heft to sway with the movement. That was nice, too. In fact, Shirley was an incredibly attractive young lady when she didn't scowl, which wasn't often. There were also flashes of niceness that leaked out during the rare moments she forgot to be horrid.

"How?" she demanded.

"Somebody put rubbing alcohol into his IV," Remo said.

She shuddered. "Jesus. That would have burned his circulatory system from the inside out."

"He never felt a thing," he assured her. "He was on so many pain meds I guarantee he never regained consciousness."

"Not many people you could kill that way," she said conversationally. "Most patients would feel the intoxicating effects or the pain and alert somebody. Actually, though, isopropyl alcohol's a pretty good murder weapon. It's clear and mixes with water, so it'll mix just as easily with whatever hydration solution they had in the IV. It's common enough, it's untraceable. Even the smell wouldn't be a big problem if it was inside a sealed IV bag, and who'd pay attention to a little alcohol smell in a hospital anyway? It's a wonder there are not a lot more hospital murders like this."

"This an area of interest?" Remo asked.

"Yeah, forensics. I wanna be a coroner. I've got two more years before I can start my internship."

"Congratulations."

She gave him an interested look. "Now, you I'd like to autopsy."

"I'm flattered."

"I mean, what's going on with your physiology, anyway? You chased this ambulance for miles, you give the old woman a massage that cures a crick in her back that's older than I am, and you use some sort of magic musk power to force me to have sex with you. I don't know what kind of sex that was, but it wasn't human sex. There's also yesterday's troublemaking. If half of what I heard really happened, then you must be some sort of freak of nature."

"I've been called—"

"Like, a missing link."

"Maybe just the opposite, like the next step in human evolution."

She sneered as she gave him a head-to-toe examination. Remo modestly covered himself with a tiny paper pillow.

"Missing link," she concluded definitively. "But fascinating."

"You're not autopsying me."

"Maybe just a little look-see? I can do it with just one cut, eight inches long. Here to here." She poked his stomach twice.

"That's more than eight inches, and anyway I'm not letting you. You would just be disappointed."

"Figures. You're such an asshole."

"Yeah."

She burned him with her evil eye for a half minute, then fidgeted. "Well?"

"Huh?"

"Aren't you going to take advantage of me again?"

"Not until you talk about your patient yesterday."

"Never! You'll have to beat it out of me."

Remo grimaced. "Nice try, Shorley, but I've reached my kink threshold."

"My name is not Shorley, you asshole!" She viciously slapped his face and shoulders until he yawned. "Oh, all right, dammit, I'll tell you what the burned guy said."

She told him everything she knew. It didn't take long. "Help you out?" she asked.

"Maybe," Remo said, thinking over what she had told him.

"Good enough for a little something extra this time?" she asked.

"No."

She sighed and fell back on the gurney. "Vanilla sex

sucks," she complained, although, in fact, she had just had the best sex of her life.

"Hey, we don't have to do it again."

"Don't even think of weaseling out now," Shirley snarled, her legs clamping around his waist. "You are such an arrogant shit."

"And you're a foul-mouthed little tramp."

He saw the gleam in her eyes become a radiance. "Yeah? What else am I?"

Remo sealed his lips and paid his debt, wondering if Mrs. Butler would mind if he used her shower for an hour or two.

17

The *White Hand Book* was very clear on the subject of the grassroots political campaign. It had to look grassroots, and spontaneous, no matter how carefully events were actually manipulated to organize it. One of the most important points: allow the grassroots campaign to name itself. A name that comes from the people carries a legacy, a history. That makes the name, and the campaign itself, more legitimate.

But what if the name sucked?

"What's wrong with the name?" asked Senate hopeful Jessica Wicker of South Dakota. "It says everything we want it to say."

There were various murmurs of agreement coming over the sophisticated telephone conferencing system. Orville Flicker had eleven of his disciples on the line, all recruited personally by him but strangers to one another.

Frederick Horne, mayoral hopeful in one of the South's biggest cities, was the one who came up with the name.

"Various 'Behavior Establishments' have been around these parts for years. It's a name people know," Horne drawled. "That's exactly what the book says to look for."

"Sounds like a country club," Flicker complained.

"'Morals and Ethics' belongs in the name, too," insisted Herbert Moule, who had an iron grip on the third-place position in a race for one of the most powerful governorships in the northwest. "Morals and ethics is what we're all about."

"I agree with all of you," Flicker said. "It's a good name, yes, but the acronym is awful."

"Who cares abut the acronym?" somebody asked.

"The book doesn't say anything about the acronym," Jessica Wicker pointed out.

Murmurs of agreement. Orville Flicker didn't dare disagree now.

Flicker's campaign had been built around a core of wisdom, and that core was the *White Hand Book*. It was their strategy, it was their guide, it was their step-by-step plan for changing the world.

Flicker was the one responsible for making it the bible of his campaign, and he knew that faith in the *White Hand Book* could not be compromised if the campaign was to succeed.

What he knew, and no one else knew, was that the *White Hand Book* was the product of an earlier age. Back in the days of the first moon landings and the breakup of the Beatles. Back then, the world had been less acronym-obsessed.

The *White Hand Book* was nothing more and nothing less than a lifetime of collected wisdom from one of the great public-relations geniuses of the twentieth century. Orville Flicker studied under the man in college, respecting him tremendously for his skills as a marketer but disgusted by his liberal politics. The old man, semiretired at that time, taught a few college classes and spent years working on his book. He claimed, and everyone in the business believed, that it would be the most comprehensive how-to manual ever on the manipulation of public opinion.

Flicker helped proofread the book in the final days of the professor's life, when the old man's hands were shaking and his eyes were clouded over.

The old professor died quietly. The pillow over his face was what kept it quiet. The old man's weak respiration was snuffed out as quick as a candle. Flicker hid the magnificent book in his car, knowing it was a masterpiece. He knew it was immensely valuable and powerful, and someday, he was not sure how, it would be vastly important to him.

He piled the notes and early drafts of the book in the old man's bedroom and started a fire, let it burn awhile, then called the police and fire department. He was quite distraught when they arrived.

"He said the book was no good and he was no good. He locked the door. He wouldn't let me in. By the time I broke the door lock the bedroom was full of flames— I think he's in there. Help him!"

Sure enough, the old man was in there, along with clouds of fluttering paper ash, but he was beyond help.

A great loss—both the man and his book—to the noble profession of marketing, advertising and public relations, the obits said.

Years and years later, Flicker retyped the professor's never-published masterpiece and called it the *White Hand Book*. He didn't claim it for himself, but he never told his followers exactly where it came from.

"Seems to me this name is just right, just what the book says it ought to be," said Horne.

Murmurs of agreement. It was as good as a unanimous vote. Flicker risked his own credibility if he fought them on it.

"Okay, all, after two years we finally have a name," Flicker announced, feigning enthusiasm. "We are now the Morals and Ethics Behavior Establishment!"

Cheers and applause from all over the nation.

"MAEBE! MAEBE!"

They started chanting ecstatically. Flicker joined in but felt silly.

"MAEBE! MAEBE! MAEBE!"

Well, Flicker thought, if it brings the Everyman to the polling place then it was a good enough, no matter how wishy-washy it sounded.

WILL THIS BE The Next Powerful Political Party? Maybe!

Mark Howard smirked. Maybe not, he thought.

Bunch of losers with some good PR. What in the world had possessed him to bring his morning paper to work? He had skimmed the sports pages and the comics. He rarely bothered reading the news. After all, he spent most of his workday catching up on current events from far more accurate sources.

He put the paper in the wastebasket and in that morning alone he sifted through more electronic intelligence than the entire CIA processed in the entire decade of the 1950s.

HAROLD W. SMITH SMELLED something bad. Outside his office he found Mark Howard and his secretary, Eileen Mikulka, looking into a paper sack.

"Mark brought us lunch, isn't that nice?" Mrs. Mikulka said brightly.

"Really?" Smith asked dubiously.

"Burritos," Mrs. Mikulka added, trying to sound pleased.

"From the convenience store," Mark Howard added, dubious himself.

"Oh," Howard Smith said. He didn't know what else to say.

"Very frugal, I'd say," Mrs. Mikulka said.

"They smell awful," Mark announced. "Not sure what I was thinking. You don't want to eat these."

"You were just being thoughtful," Mrs. Mikulka said.

"I guess," Mark Howard said, and rolled the paper sack tightly closed on his way back to his office. When the door closed Mrs. Mikulka gave her longtime employer a worried look.

"I hope Mr. Howard is feeling okay," she said, loading the statement with a question that Harold Smith couldn't answer.

"I hope so, as well," Smith answered, and returned to his office without further comment.

MARK HOWARD FELT preoccupied, distracted by his own distraction. What in the world had compelled him to go out to the local convenience store for a sack of microwaved burritos?

He tapped the keyboard, got the wrong results and searched again. What was he looking for, again?

He needed a cup of coffee and he needed to get that stinking sack of burritos out of his closet-sized office. The fumes were probably a health hazard.

Mrs. Mikulka gave him a murky smile. Mark Howard strolled downstairs and out the service entrance to the trash bins. He opened the sack and took out a burrito, tossing it into the big green container.

He took out a second burrito, tossed it in.

He took out the third burrito and looked at it, his mind wandering somewhere far away.

Then he asked himself a question that changed his entire day: why didn't he just throw in the entire burrito sack and be done with it?

He was acting strangely, and sometimes he was so

damn dense it took him a long time to realize he was acting strangely.

"I'm an idiot!"

He dropped the sack and opened the burrito, poking around with one finger in the mushy contents of the soggy flour tortilla. Then he looked at the wrapper, read the ingredients label.

He didn't know what he was looking for, but he was looking for something.

He didn't find it in the refried-bean-and-cheese filling and he hoped like hell he wouldn't have to go retrieving the first two burritos. There was nothing else in the sack except for the receipt.

Mark Howard grabbed the receipt and held it to the sky, trying to make out the faint printing from the convenience store cash register.

The first three items were all the same: "BURTO, FZN, BF&BN, $3.49."

He was an idiot. Only an idiot would throw away ten bucks on those inedible things.

The last item was NEWSPPR, and the price was a very reasonable $0.75.

Mark Howard wadded up the mess of the burrito and the paper bag and sent them flying into the trash bin, then yanked at the door, carrying the receipt.

"OH, HELLO AGAIN, Mark."

"Hiya, Mrs. Mikulka!" Mark Howard was running fast, and then he was gone with a slam of his door.

On his desk was a copy of the morning paper, in exactly the same place as the one he brought from home, and which still poked out of his garbage can. Only now did Mark remember actually buying the paper with the burritos and putting it on the desk when he reached he office, but he didn't know at the time why he was doing it.

The front-page headlines read Will This Be The Next Powerful Party? Maybe!

Mark slithered behind his desk and flipped up the screen, bringing it to life with his last collection of windows still there. That's right. He'd been searching for something, and the search results were all wrong. What was he was searching for again?

He backed up a few screens until he found the answer. It wasn't a word he knew. He certainly didn't remember typing it, but he had. The word was "MAEBE."

"MAYBE?" Harold Smith asked dubiously.

"It's an acronym," Mark said. "Morals and Ethics Behavior Establishment. MAEBE."

Smith had one more item to look dubious about. "Not a name to inspire confidence, either way," Smith said as he pulled up the bookmarked files sent to him from Howard's computer over the extremely small Folcroft digital network. He began reading an article about MAEBE from the online *Washington Post*, frowned again, and skimmed *The New York Times* article in seconds.

"Mark, this group is new. MAEBE did not even

exist until yesterday evening," Smith pointed out. "The murders we're looking at go back as long as eight months."

"I know." Mark Howard nodded, wearing a doubtful look himself. "I haven't figured it out yet—what I'm supposed to be seeing here. I just know I'm supposed to see something."

"Yes?" Smith said, noncommittally.

"You did ask me to come to you as soon as I experienced any events, Dr. Smith. Remember?"

"Of course, Mark," Smith said, and he made an effort to sound encouraging, despite his doubts.

Smith was a pragmatic man, with a view of the world that had a hard time fitting in the extraordinary. Smith knew that anything that looked unusual, bizarre, supernatural, usually had a mundane explanation if you probed below the surface. But he also knew, from experience, that nature and science had some exceptional tricks up their sleeves.

Mark Howard just might be one of those tricks. The young man possessed what some would have called extrasensory perception, but which Smith liked to think of in clinical terms such as precognizance.

Howard, like Smith, came to CURE by way of the CIA, where his ability helped solve a number of sticky intelligence issues, although no one had known about it then. His mental sensitivity had almost killed him, too, when he began working with Dr. Smith at Folcroft Sanitarium, within the mental reach of a comatose man who had his own unique mind powers, and who was one of CURE's most dangerous enemies.

Those events had taken a lot out of Mark Howard, and when he came back to work Smith had become even more interested in understanding the mechanics of what was going on in Mark's head. The trouble was, even Mark didn't understand it very well. His insights seemed to come out of the blue, without effort on his part. He couldn't make it happen, apparently, and often didn't recognize it when it did happen. Sometimes he realized he had been giving himself messages repeatedly for hours until they registered. Sometimes the message, or clue, or whatever it might be termed, slammed into him in a single stroke.

Mark Howard had usually been on his own when it came to deciphering the messages he was sending himself, and the young man was blessed was a genius of sorts in the investigative realm. He always figured out the message, eventually. Smith had asked him, with a twinge of embarrassment, to involve him when he received these messages. He hoped Mark didn't take it as an intrusion of his personal privacy.

Now the boy had brought the latest such message to Smith's attention, and he didn't want to make Mark regret it.

"Tell me what you know about this group," Smith said officiously.

"Until twenty-four hours ago they were just a bunch of independent political campaigns from across the country. Mostly far right, mostly with an anticorruption platform. From what I've seen these are all 'give the government back to the people' types and they're mostly long shots in their respective political races. It looks like Dr. Lamble started getting calls from across the nation yesterday supporting his controversial statements about Governor Bryant after the assassination. All these supporters realized they had a nationwide brotherhood in the making, and somebody floated out the idea of turning their local movements into a national political party."

Harold W. Smith frowned as he shifted the screen from one online media report to another. "I'm listening. Please continue."

"There was a flurry of activity, first local meetings, then state meetings, that resulted in the appointment of state-wide representatives with voting authority. There was an election held by all fifty representatives during an online voting system put together by one member's college-age son. They had themselves a new political party put together in time for dinner."

Smith nodded. "Organized by whom? Lamble?"

Mark Howard considered that. "Nobody, from what I read. Lamble's a top dog, but he's not being touted as the head man."

"That's the impression I get, too."

"But that can't be," Mark added. "Somebody had to handle the logistics. Somebody spearheaded the thing."

"Yes, that seems likely," Smith said, but didn't sound satisfied.

Mark fidgeted. "Maybe this is a dead end."

"No."

Mark looked at Smith. "Why not?"

"This defies logic," Dr. Smith looked at him briefly, tapping the desktop that hid his display. "I don't believe MAEBE is what it appears to be. A hundred, two hundred independent campaigns from coast to coast spontaneously allying themselves nationally? Groups that exist independently to promote a specific political agenda would not be quick to become just a small cog in a big new machine."

Mark was scanning his newspaper and nodding. "But MAEBE is not replacing any local agendas. Listen to this. 'A spokesman says the new political party will not serve as a coalition of independent forces driven by one overriding philosophy—bringing ethics and moral principals back into government.'"

"Sounds like they're doomed to failure from the outset," Smith remarked. "Some of their members have got to have extremist views—who'll decide what constitutes ethical and moral principles?"

"One of the new members is Al Scuttle," Howard remarked. "He's the independent who's already started campaigning hard for Bryant's job. Then there's the fact that Lamble's campaign manager served as spokesperson yesterday. I think we need to look into Lamble's political race."

"I just had the same thought. The other races as well. I wonder what we're going to find if we start cross-referencing our list of recent murders, with MAEBE races. Why don't you start on the West Coast and I'll start on the East. Let's see what we come up with."

Mark Howard jumped to his feet. "Dr. Smith, I've got a new routine that I think can get it done faster than our old searches."

Smith raised his eyebrows. "We need a database on MAEBE membership before we do anything else."

"The system can make it in real time," Howard said in a rush. "There will be press releases appearing on the wires and online media outlets across the country. I can set up a routine to index them and cross match them as they hit the Web and the wires. It'll take two minutes to get it started."

The sour-lemon, bloodless gray face of Dr. Harold W. Smith seemed to blossom in surprise. He had been hacking the global networks since Mark Howard was in diapers. Hell, he had almost single-handedly created a sort of global Internet years before the university researchers at Stamford University ever conceived of the unique idea to share data over telephone lines using their room-size, number-crunching computing machines. But he had never allowed himself to fall behind the state of the art in terms of data compilation or networking technology. Still, at this moment he didn't clearly understand how Mark Howard intended to create a cross-referencing applications when there was nothing yet to cross-reference to.

Mark Howard was more than a little surprised when

Harold W. Smith got up and gestured at the chair. "Please. I'd like to see how you go about it."

Mark Howard walked behind the desk and sat in Dr. Smith's chair. He put his fingers on the keyboard, tested their tactile response and suddenly he was quite comfortable.

He typed furiously fast, as if he were beating the commands out of the keys. Smith was disappointed when he saw where the young man was headed. The on-line edition of the *Runoff Gazette* from Runoff, New Mexico. It had to be a small town since Smith had never heard of it, and the newspaper didn't look like his first choice for vital intelligence.

Before Smith had time to ask about it, Howard had a second window open and brought up a script from the store of custom applications stored in the CURE mainframes. Howard sped through the code, typed in a few extra commands, then hit the return key.

He sat back, folded his arms, and smiled.

"Mark?"

"*Runoff Gazette*," the young assistant director said.

"I see that."

"The Folcroft Four are hacking it. The *Gazette's* got one of those systems to alert readers when there is an update. Lots of Web sites have them."

Smith was sure he was missing something. "So you're signing us up to get updates from the *Runoff Gazette*."

"Yeah. Yes. But the system isn't too secure and it's piggybacked on the *Gazette's* internal LAN, so I've got the Folcroft Four reprogramming the system to feed all electronic documentation generated in the newspaper offices into a hidden Web page." Mark looked up at his boss and saw the heavy lines of concern. "You see what I've done, Dr. Smith? I've got the newspaper server dumping all its content into Web pages only we know about, indexing it and sending us the results if and when they match our search terms. MAEBE. If somebody in the vicinity of Runoff, New Mexico, becomes a part of MAEBE, we'll get the news, official and unofficial."

"In Runoff, New Mexico?"

Mark Howard smiled, sat up, and his fingers snapped so viciously against the glass that Smith was sure the young man had to be bruising his fingertips. The screen filled with chaos.

"It multiplying," Mark explained. "The script can hack the systems used by ninety-five percent of the media outlets in the United States. They're all a lot alike. Thousands of them, and they'll all be doing CURE's work for it. We don't have to go to them. They send the intelligence we want to us as soon as it is generated."

Smith was getting that wide-open look on his face again as he watched the streaming data of successful hacks and plants of the invasive application. "Yes," he said. He sounded almost, but not quite, excited. "Mark, this could be a tremendous tool if it..." He looked embarrassed suddenly. "I mean, have you tested it? What kind of results are you getting?"

Mark grinned again, and Smith thought he looked

like a six-year-old boy who just rode a skateboard for the first time without falling off. With a few more frantic keyboard strokes, the windows vanished behind a new window displaying a digitized map of the country. There were three green dots on it.

"I haven't given the system a lot of parameters to rank the search results. It's basically looking for the word 'MAEBE' along with a reference to an independent political campaign that is nearby geographically. When it finds it, we get a green, and we can assume there's probably a campaigner in the vicinity that's joined the new party."

There were six greens on the screen now, and one of them changed to yellow.

"It's cross-referencing them to our list of suspicious deaths," Smith said. "That's a yellow?"

"Yes. There's also a check for a match between the victim in the death and the position the MAEBE party is campaigning for. If MAEBE is trying to fill a seat that is vacant because of a suspicious death, then we get an orange dot. That data is part of the self-search function being performed for us by the newspaper servers, but the Folcroft Four are also doing some searching on their own of the election committee records in all the local jurisdictions. I haven't got those systems to do our work for us. So there's a delay. But when the margin of error is low enough, we'll get an orange."

"Or two. Or five." Smith was as pleased as Mark Howard had ever seen him as he watched the United

States map sprinkle itself with green dots, some of which became yellow. Five, now six, were orange.

Another dot appeared. It didn't start out green like the others, then change to yellow and orange. It just appeared, scarlet and more brilliant than the others, as if a drop of bright blood had just plopped onto the desktop.

Mark Howard became stiff, leaning close to the red dot shining at the tip of West Texas.

Smith had been trying to figure it out. "What does red mean? Multiple murders?"

"It means no murder at all," Mark said. "Yet."

HAROLD W. SMITH WAS in his own chair again when Mrs. Mikulka entered.

"Are you feeling okay, Dr. Smith?" she asked, setting down the tray from the hospital cafeteria.

"Fine," Dr. Smith said.

"I bought you tea," she said, which, of course, was obvious. She looked at Mark Howard, sitting uncomfortably on the old couch in the rear of the office. "Oh, dear, is something wrong?"

"What?"

"Has someone died?"

Mark Howard looked up with hollow eyes and swallowed his first words, then said, "No, Mrs. Mikulka."

She didn't believe him for a moment, but she knew better than to probe, and she left the office and closed the door behind her, thinking to herself that the directors of Folcroft Sanitarium were just a little too paranoid when it came to the security of the place.

After twenty years she was getting a little sick of it all.

AS SOON AS THE DOOR closed behind his secretary, Dr. Smith touched the switch that brought the monitor back to life and looked at the map of the United States with a growing dread. His amazement and delight at Mark Howard's powerful new data collection tool was forgotten as the vivid results blossomed before their eyes.

Mark Howard stood at Smith's side and watched the screen as more colored spots appeared. Several greens, two or three yellows and maybe two hundred oranges. Two hundred murders that were tied, almost without doubt, to MAEBE.

But you could hardly make out the other colors for great bloody patches of red that covered the map, overlapping by the dozens, each a murder yet to happen, and to Mark Howard it looked like a portent of the murder of the nation itself.

18

Orville Flicker knew he shouldn't be in Topeka, Kansas, especially after the disaster in Denver.

He was still reeling from that—almost an entire cell wiped out in a single encounter, and this after countless hits had gone off without a single man lost.

Not that he hadn't planned for losses. Not one man in any cell knew Flicker by name. Those who met him in person, his cell generals, required personal recruitment and coaching. But it had always been performed in his disguise. Flicker was a master of disguise. After all, drama was his major at college until he switched to public relations.

So, sure, he was safe. He knew he was safe. No comebacks, as they called them in the Special Forces. The blow was strictly to his operational capabilities.

General Bernwick had trained an excellent team of mercenaries. Flicker had come to rely on Bernwick's cell for all his most dangerous assignments. Then, poof, they were gone.

Sure, they took most of their targets with them, and his people were scoring some big points using the whole messy affair.

Actually, it worked out pretty well from a PR point of view. This was the martyr factor that Flicker hadn't exploited quite as thoroughly as he should have.

Human beings felt some sort of instinct to feel sorry for dead people, even if those dead people were bad before they were dead. It was only through masterful manipulation of the media that Flicker's people had been able to nip that sympathy in the bud.

But if the people who killed the bad people got killed, too, then they could be cast as martyrs. Freedom fighters who gave their lives in the battle against oppression. Well, not oppression, maybe, but they were at least soldiers against immorality.

Flicker rolled the phrase around in his head. Soldiers Against Immorality. SAI. Not good but it would have been a hell of a lot better name than the one they'd come up with.

Warriors for Ethical Politics. No, that made WEP. How about Morality's Soldiers? No, you can't say MS. How about Warriors Allied Against Corruption? Hmm, that was WAAC. Maybe they could spell it with an explanation point. WAAC! Kind of silly, but at least it wasn't wishy-washy.

MAEBE, Jesus. Do we stand for what is right and good? MAEBE! Do we believe in the extermination of corruption? MAEBE!

Flicker caught himself. This wasn't a constructive

train of thought. Their name was MAEBE, and it was going to stay MAEBE. Someday, when their power was consolidated, when they were the dominant political party in the United States of America, then he'd look for an opportunity to change the name.

Right now, though, he had some lives to ruin.

That would make him feel better. By the end of the day, things would be back on track. Bernwick would have struck a very public and powerful blow for the cause. It would be pretty damn hard for the people to have sympathy for eight gang lords and a police chief who wholesaled them narcotics. Especially when he, Flicker, leaked the FBI report to the press. And he would still have Bernwick. The man was a good soldier and could exert control over a squadron of brainless thugs better than any other general in the White Hand.

Flicker was pondering this martyr angle. Maybe, when there was a questionable job to be performed, it made sense to *plan* on sacrificing some of his men as an insurance policy against public backlash.

After all, Flicker was a genius when it came to public relations, but no scientist or artisan achieved perfect results one hundred percent of the time. If and when he had some doubts as to the outcome, he could just throw in a little extra insurance by arranging for somebody on his side to die fighting.

But he'd have to think about this. He couldn't afford to lose good men. Like Bernwick. That maniac was irreplaceable. He couldn't risk Bernwick.

Bernwick should have called in by now, come to think of it.

Never mind. He couldn't afford that distraction. There were big things afoot in the volatile little town of Topeka.

Yes, it was a risk for him to be here. He couldn't afford to be seen, to be recognized, to be linked to the action. Not yet, anyway. But he simply couldn't pass up this opportunity to witness the White Hand wring the ugly neck of corruption.

"Can I help you?" asked the sprightly woman at the desk just inside the front doors of the restored Victorian mansion.

Flicker allowed his gaze to wander the vast parlor and the adjoining rooms.

"Just beautiful," he observed.

"It certainly is." She had the face of a grandmother, with the size and energy of a third-grader. "Prettiest campaign HQ I've ever had the pleasure to work in. The senator has it run as a bed-and-breakfast between elections."

Flicker smiled. "Have you worked in a lot of campaigns? I never have before, but I would like to join on with Senator Serval."

"Well, we're glad to have you! I'm Elly." She grabbed his hand and pumped it. "We're always looking for more bodies."

"I'm not sure what I have to offer," Flicker said, putting a nervous twitch in his voice. "I've got a little PR background."

"Well, we might be able to make use of you in that

department. Tonight, though, we're stapling signs and watching the debate."

"What debate?" Flicker asked.

Elly's laughter filled the bottom story of the mansion.

AN HOUR LATER he was helping to staple campaign signs. Now that he was ensconced, Flicker didn't feel at all out of place. Lucky for him the rest of the staff was engrossed in the debate that was showing on TVs in every room, so nobody wanted to strike up conversation.

The debate was critical for them. Their candidate, the larger-than-life Julius Serval, had opted out, but the outcome of the debate still might have a strong impact on his chances of winning the election.

The debate was among the underdogs, the trio of candidates running against Serval. One of the men was Gerald Cort, but he didn't stand a chance. Another candidate was Ed Kriidelfisk, considered a long shot until recently. The front-runner was Martina Jomarca, a professional politician who had held the Senate seat before.

She stood a chance against Julius Serval and, in fact, Jomarca and Serval had made careers for themselves trading off the Senate seat on an almost regular basis for twenty years. There were half-serious rumors that the pair were secretly lovers.

In fact, they both had their share of skeletons in the closet. If they were lovers, it would have been the least damaging secret for either of them.

For the first time in three campaigns, Martina Jomarca was seriously undermined by a campaigner other than Serval. Ed Kriidelfisk was a poor campaigner but he hired good researchers, and they had unearthed potentially damaging information about Ms. Jomarca's private life and the funny accounting kept during her second Senate run, back in the late 1980s.

It took awhile, but finally the debate reached the critical moment when Ed Kriidelfisk laid out his charges regarding Ms. Jomarca's fiscal anomalies.

"Mr. Kriidelfisk," she said, the picture of a poise and stateliness, "you have made this accusation again and again to the press, and so far the only evidence you have is that I took a weekend trip to Las Vegas in 1987. I believe it is only right and proper for you to come clean, once and for all. Show us your evidence or cease and desist with the false accusations."

"My accusations are *not* false," Ed Kriidelfisk shot back.

"Prove it."

"While I can't prove it yet—"

"You sound like a broken record, Mr. Kriidelfisk. If you do not have proof, I think it is in your best interest to withdraw your accusations."

There was an awkward moment, Flicker knew. One of his fellow sign staplers snickered. "Kriidelfisk is fucked."

Yeah. Fucked, indeed, thought Flicker with amusement. Ed Kriidelfisk didn't seem to know it, though, cool and comfortable, as if unaware he had pushed Jomarca too far. She was threatening to charge him with slander if he kept tossing out unproved charges. If he backed off, he'd look weak. It didn't take a political analyst to read the writing on the wall for the Kriidelfisk campaign, barring a miracle.

"I have proof," said a voice in the crowd at the high-school auditorium where the debate was being held.

"And you are...?" Ms. Jomarca.

"Just a citizen who is concerned with making sure the people know the truth about the people who want to represent them."

"Sure, you are," Ms. Jomarca said. "All right, let's see this proof."

"I don't have it with me," said the man in the audience. "It's a videotape."

"And I'll bet I know where it is," Jomarca said sarcastically. "With Mr. Kriidelfisk's evidence?"

"No," said the man in the audience, "I gave it to Channel 3. They are airing it now."

There was a murmur in the crowd at the debate, and in the campaign headquarters of Senator Julius Serval somebody shouted, "Quick! Channel 3!"

The TV in the parlor switched to Channel 3, and through the miracle of two-hundred-dollar electronics they still had the feed from the live debate going on in a smaller window in a bottom corner of the TV screen. The candidates were looking offstage, obviously also watching a television set tuned to Channel 3.

It was a camcorder videotape from inside an opulent but virtually empty casino. The legend in the corner

Get FREE BOOKS and a FREE GIFT when you play the...

LAS VEGAS
GAME

Just scratch off the gold box with a coin. Then check below to see the gifts you get!

YES! I have scratched off the gold Box. Please send me my **2 FREE BOOKS** and **gift for which I qualify.** I understand that I am under no obligation to purchase any books as explained on the back of this card.

FIRST NAME	LAST NAME

ADDRESS

APT.#	CITY

STATE/PROV.	ZIP/POSTAL CODE

7	7	7

Worth TWO FREE BOOKS plus a BONUS Mystery Gift!

Worth TWO FREE BOOKS!

TRY AGAIN!

Offer limited to one per household and not valid to current Gold Eagle® subscribers. All orders subject to approval.

◄ DETACH AND MAIL CARD TODAY! ▼

He'd used some pretty big shoulder-fired boom de-vices when he was a soldier, before he ever heard the word "Sinanju." Now he disdained such weaponry, but someone two doors down did not. That someone had just telescoped the fiberglass tube of a shoulder-fired grenade launcher, and the click was the sights and fir-ing trigger popping out. Remo went to watch.

He crept away quickly and circled, remaining unseen and coming up seconds later behind the man who was readying a second Light Antitank Weapon. The first disposable LAW was leaning against the abandoned house that was his cover. The man was alone and he was dressed in the now familiar blacksuit with the white gloves, now dirty, and the white ski mask, now dingy.

Two rockets seemed like overkill to Remo Williams, but who was he to argue? This guy really looked like he knew what he was doing and, let's face it, Remo was out of touch when it came to using firearms.

With both LAWs prepped the man crept out into the weedy mess of a backyard, putting himself in the open but giving him a clean shot at the house where Chief Roescher was having his boy's club meeting. The cop at the back door was examining his fingernails and didn't notice the danger. Remo moved into the open a few paces behind the shooter. He didn't want to miss any of the action.

The white-masked man put a LAW to his shoulder.

"Wait. Don't." Remo's mumble was drowned out by the whoosh of the LAW. The back-door cop looked up, startled, and watched death come right at him. The projectile missed his body by inches and tore through the soggy wall before it hit something inside that was solid enough to blow it. The back-door cop hadn't taken his first step. Chief Roescher and the gang lords never had a chance as the house blew apart in all directions in a way a tank on the battlefield never would have, and the mess of rotted timbers and curling shingles that had once been the roof collapsed on top of what was left.

"Stop," Remo said under his breath as the man in the white mask snatched up the second LAW. He fired it at all that was left of the house, obliterating the ruins, then dropped the tube and ran two steps before the solid earth was no longer under his feet.

"Nice shooting," Remo commented.

The white-masked man was a pro. He wasted no time with surprise before launching into a series of moves designed to extricate himself. They would have worked on any other assailant, but they didn't work on Remo.

"I thought the second one was kind of overkill, though," Remo said as he walked with his prisoner into the train yard and over the tracks. The masked man kicked at Remo's chest, missed, then lost his cool and started wiggling and twisting frantically.

"Stop that," Remo shook the shooter vigorously, nearly rendering him unconscious. Then he ripped the man's blacksuit at the shoulder, looking for a wound. He found it, a big mass of bloody bandages applied over the spot where his wooden missile had impaled it just before the quick escape from the courtroom yes-

terday. "You're a dedicated employee, I'll hand it to you, going to work today even feeling under the weather."

The ground in the vacant train yard was contaminated with train oil and fuel. When Remo put a few rusting boxcars behind them they couldn't see the dilapidated neighborhood any longer, just a plume of black smoke climbing into the blue sky. Remo plucked off the mask, his prisoner too dazed to resist.

"White's not a good color for this kind of work, you know? It's all dirty." He dropped the mask, then removed the gloves, as well, and ripped the front of the blacksuit open at the chest.

"No dog tags?"

"That would be stupid," his prisoner answered.

"Well, depends on your point of view. See, now that I've heard you talk I know you're an American. I also know you're military. So Upstairs is going to want a positive ID on you. If you had dog tags, I could have taken those. Instead, I have to give them your fingerprints."

"Won't do you any good. I'm a dead man anyway."

Remo scowled, then gingerly sniffed the air in front of the prisoner. "You took something, huh?"

"I saw you working yesterday, remember? Didn't want to take any chances. What if you showed up again and took off all my hardware? Had to have another last resort."

Remo considered that, then nodded. "But if I didn't show up you could take an antidote, right?"

"Yeah." The prisoner grimaced ruefully. "What are you, anyway, some sort of freaky Special Forces experiment?"

"Yeah. I eat steroids for breakfast every day," Remo answered, then began patting down the blacksuit. The man began to fight again, but Remo found the place where a tiny capsule was sewn into the lining of the suit. He slashed the fabric and poked the pill into the back of his prisoner's throat, then held his mouth closed until the pill was gone.

"Son of a bitch!" the man gasped.

"Okay, now we've got all the time in the world, so talk while we walk." Remo heard the approach of sirens behind them and began carrying his prisoner into a gully that meandered downhill and under an overpass.

"Boris Bernwick. U.S. Army, retired."

"I give two shits, Boris. I've learned enough about you in the last five minutes to know you are definitely not the brains behind this little operation. Those are the people I want to know about. Who, why, where, when."

"I'm telling you nothin'," Bernwick growled.

"Let's hold hands," Remo said, and grasped the dangling soldier by the wrist, inserting his finger into one special pressure point that made the soldier whine like a beagle.

"Well?" Remo asked.

Boris Bernwick, for the first time in decades, began to cry.

"Hurts!"

"What about this?"

"Hurts more!"

"And this?"

"Hurts hurts hurts hurts okay hurts hurts!"

Remo decreased the pressure slightly. "I'm taking you back to 'hurts more' so you can answer, but if you want to get down to 'hurts' again, you're going to have to earn it."

"What about 'no hurts at all'?" Bernwick pleaded.

"That," Remo said, "you're *really* gonna have to earn."

Boris Bernwick tried hard for more than ten minutes to earn "no hurts."

"I'm not impressed with your effort, Boris," Remo said finally.

"That's all I know!" Boris sobbed, knowing he had become something pathetic.

"I believe you, Boris," Remo said.

"So do I get 'no hurts'? I really want 'no hurts.'"

Remo nodded. "Okay."

"Thank you thank you thank you."

"In fact, you're never going to have hurts ever again."

"Oh," Boris said, seeing the light. Then, as blackness engulfed him so swiftly he didn't even know how it happened, he wondered about the afterlife. Because there were some who said the afterlife, for the bad people, had a lot of hurting in it.

20

The man in the T-shirt came into the shop whistling a Grateful Dead song about a narcotized locomotive conductor. Helen Lendon thought he looked like a very nice young man. He slapped a Visa card on the counter and went about his business.

First he selected a black permanent marker from the display. Then he took a ream of white paper from the shelf and opened it, extracted a sheet and went to the counter where customers did their form filling.

Helen Lendon would watch them in the security mirrors. She wasn't the kind to poke her nose in other people's business, but she didn't want anything unsavory going on in her Mail Boxes & More store.

Somehow the young man with the marker managed to position himself so that she couldn't see what he was doing. He took something out of his pocket, did something with the marker, did something with the sheet of paper, then put whatever it was back in his pocket.

He capped the marker and took the sheet of paper to

the fax machine. He poked and positioned the paper in various places, and Helen Lendon asked him more than once if he needed assistance. He said no. Finally he had the paper in the right place and looked across the shop. Helen Lendon nodded. He smiled with satisfaction and picked up the phone on the fax machine, then pressed the buttons as he shifted his weight, and Helen Lendon couldn't see what numbers the young man was dialing.

But she heard him speaking into the phone. "Blah, blah, blah," he said quite clearly. "Carrots and peas, carrots and peas." This went on for almost a minute.

"Hiya. It's about time," he said then. "Got a fax for you. No, I already pressed a button. I don't want to press another button. Send? How do you know there's a button that says Send? Even I know there's different kinds of fax machines. Oh, wait, there is a button called Send. So I press it, then what? You sure? Okay, here goes."

The young man pressed the Send button, then watched the page feed through the fax machine and slide out into the bottom tray.

The machine beeped.

"Aw, hell!"

"No, that's what it's supposed to do," Helen called out to him assuredly. "That means it's done. Look at the display." A few seconds later she clarified, "The display on the fax machine."

"Oh." He glared at the display, then shrugged and shredded the sheet of paper so fast Helen couldn't quite believe her eyes. The shreds fluttered into the wastebasket.

The young man charged it all to his Visa, the paper and the marker and the fax call, which Helen's computer claimed had gone to the Solomon Islands. The man didn't want to take the paper or the marker with him. "Don't write things down very often," he explained.

When he was gone, Helen Lendon's curiosity got the better of her and she poked around in the wastebasket. Not one tiny sliver of paper had missed it. She found a sliver with some black on it and peered at it intensely for a moment, then gasped. It was a fragment of a black fingerprint.

But the man hadn't sent his own fingerprint. That meant the thing in his pocket...

Helen Lendon let the little scrap of paper flutter away. This time it missed the wastebasket.

21

"Get it?" Remo asked on the pay phone in the hotel lobby.

"It came through fine," Harold Smith answered. "I hope you used discretion disposing of the finger."

"Yeah, I tossed it," Remo said, taking the finger out of the pocket of his Chinos and flicking it into the brass trash can with a sand-filled ashtray on top. The ashtray had been recently cleaned and molded into the stylized S that was the hotel chain logo. "Learn anything?"

"Nothing he hadn't already told you," Smith admitted. "He was who he said he was, of course. It looks as if his body has already been discovered near the explosion site." Smith sighed. "I really wish you would have stopped him from firing those missiles, Remo."

"I begged and pleaded," Remo said. "Anyway, it's done and this city's a better place because of it."

"The police department is in chaos," Smith said sourly. "The federal investigation is in tatters. It will take them months to sort out the mess."

"Can't be worse than leaving Chief Roescher in charge."

"Yes, it can. Chief Roescher was corrupt, but he was at least keeping the system running."

"He was a murderer and a drug dealer."

"Remo, CURE doesn't go after men like Chief Roescher. He was already under investigation. He would have been removed from the system eventually."

"Hey, Smitty, since when are you on the bad guys' side?"

"I am not. I am on the side of peace and order. Do you realize that this country is starting to fray at the edges? There is instability in Pueblo just as there is instability in Governor Bryant's state and in Old Crick, Iowa."

"They'll get over it."

"That's just the tip of the iceberg, Remo, and there are a hundred other places like them."

"They're isolated."

"No. The reverberations are starting to be felt. The instability could easily escalate. We can see the beginnings of governmental breakdown. Once it happens, it may happen again, and then we'll see a chain reaction."

"Then what? Apocalypse? We leave ourselves open for an invasion by the Soviet Union?"

"Joke if you like, Remo. What might actually occur is mob action. When the structure disintegrates, it unleashes all kinds of societal elements capable of creating unrest."

"All right, Smitty, I apologize. I won't let it happen again. Now, what do we do next?"

"We're trying to select a logical series of targets, but all the other cells have been inactive too long to pinpoint them. Once we know where they are, we can postulate other targets in the vicinity, based on our new database of likely hits. Until then we just wait."

"What about the information we got from Boris on the leader? The guy who recruited him?"

"The name was fake and the description was not helpful. All we have is Bernwick's assertion that the man was a press agent. That's not terribly helpful. There are hundreds of press agents in the ranks of the new political party."

"Uh-huh. But who's the head press agent in charge?"

Harold Smith sighed. "If we only knew."

BY THE TIME HE REACHED the hotel room the plans had changed. Chiun's chests were stacked neatly near the door. "The Emperor says we must leave immediately. There is no time for a bellhop."

"When did he call?" Remo demanded. "I just talked to him in the lobby."

"So I was informed," Chiun sniffed. "What has taken you so long to come from there?"

"It was three minutes ago."

"Were you dawdling over the filthy magazines in the gift shop?"

"This place is too classy to have dirty magazines in the gift shop," Remo said. "Where we going?"

"Topeka."

"Are you joking?"

"Why?" Chiun demanded.

"Seems like kind of a sleepy place to do murdering, is all."

Chiun squinted. "But there really is such a place as a Topeka?"

"Well, yeah. It's in Nebraska. Or Idaho. One of those states that everybody always forgets about."

Chiun nodded. "Good. I believed at first that the Emperor was committing a practical foolery upon me."

"But why we going to Topeka?"

"No time to talk! If you had arrived in time, you could have spoken to the Emperor yourself, instead of reducing me to handling your travel arrangements." Chiun pointed at his chests. "Bring those." Chiun was out the door.

22

"Ah," Chiun said appreciatively as they slipped through the front door into the vast old home in Topeka, which, they had been surprised to learn, was in the state called Kansas. Remo wasn't sure if he'd ever been to Kansas— he'd certainly forgotten about it if he had. In fact he wasn't sure if he had ever actually believed, before today, that Kansas was a real place and not a fictional land of monochrome misery invented for the opening scenes of *The Wizard of Oz*.

There was nothing monochrome about Senator Serval's home, which was one of the original great houses of the city and had never been allowed to fall into disrepair. The Serval family fortune had remained steady enough over the generations to maintain the home as a showcase, and now the home was a city icon.

"Makes my brain hurt," Remo complained. "What's with all the doodads and swirlies and embellishes?"

"They give the decor a richness, even if they are not

to my taste," Chiun said. "You simpletons have no taste."

"This place puts the 'oh my God' in 'gaudy,'" Remo said.

"Grendel had a better eye for home decor," Chiun said dismissively.

"You mean Gollum?"

"I mean Grendel."

Remo stared at Chiun, uncomprehending, then grinned. "*Beowulf.*"

"You are truly learned."

"Thank the nuns who learned me."

Chiun turned away in disdain, roaming silently through the lower levels of the opulent home of the wealthy political pretender. In truth, this overindulgence of European-inspired gimmickry was not to his taste, but it was a contrast to his own home. Chiun was weary of the drab residence he shared with Remo in Connecticut. It was flavorless. There was no artistry to it. Just bland walls, no balanced spaces. When he sat in that dwelling and reached out with his senses, he found just hollow gray air.

Some new home was needed that would be worthy of housing a Master of Sinanju Emeritus, one that was appealing to his discriminating eye, invigorating to his refined sensibilities. But the choices in this land of white culture were severely limited.

Not a castle. Chiun was once lord of a true castle, in

the city of beans and bad drivers, and that beloved dwelling was destroyed in flames. The memory galled him. Chiun would not want a new home so big and grand it reminded him of Castle Sinanju.

One thing he had learned was that he didn't need so much space. His possessions, at least here in this ugly land of America, were few. Even this large house decorated in the style of the Victorian era was too large and too—stationary.

Chiun had begun to consider the potential of a home that was mobile. He would have scoffed at the idea at one time, but he had recently seen examples of such dwellings. Some moved upon the water and some moved upon land. Were he and Remo not constantly traveling anyway?

Remo was the proverbial pale pig in the ointment. Chiun sensed that his ungrateful protégé would be unhappy with such a home, and when Remo disliked something he tended to bawl endlessly like a sick goat or a sick pig.

Remo came down from his search of the second and third levels of the home, keeping utterly silent despite the century-old wooden stairway he trod upon. "King Victoria and his concubine are fast asleep."

"Emperor Smith said this senator's wife is in Europe," Chiun remarked.

"Hope she finishes her business and comes home early." Remo grinned.

"Maybe that is her arriving now."

Someone was approaching the great Serval mansion, coming on foot, through the darkness, bearing gifts.

GENERAL WILLIAM CHATTO didn't feel very much like a general at the moment, sneaking through the shrubs in a funny-looking outfit. He felt like a burglar.

Truth was he had never really been a general. Or even a colonel or a major or, well, the truth was he'd been a staff sergeant when they kicked him out of the U.S. Army.

But, what the hell, they wanted to call him a general they could call him a general, as long as they paid him. It was just that they had these expectations that Chatto possessed leadership abilities and when the time came, he had to admit, he obviously didn't.

"Come on, you guys!"

"Hey, you think you can do any better, you carry the bitch!"

"That's insubordination, Baldwin," Chatto said stiffly.

"Fuck you, General."

"Shh! Shh! Shh!" Even as he was hushing his troops Chatto was thinking that a real general would never say "Shh!" to his men. "I want you to keep your voices down."

"I want you to get the fuck out of my face," Baldwin said, throwing down his burden, which was the front half of a drugged and unconscious middle-aged woman. The soldier with the rear half of candidate Martina Jo-

marca had no intention of carrying the burden on his own, so he dropped the rest of her.

The harsh exchange between Chatto and Baldwin was satisfied when Baldwin agreed to keep quiet and Chatto agreed to treat Baldwin as an equal.

Baldwin was sure real generals didn't treat their subordinates as equals.

His only relief was that they were nearly at the house, when he knew his men would fall in line, even Baldwin. They were all soldiers, and they were all paid well for their skills. None of them was stupid enough to allow their egos or their attitudes to get in the way of mission success.

In near silence they picked the back-door lock and entered one of the most famous homes in Topeka. The alarm system was a joke and was disabled with a pair of needlenosed pliers, then they fanned out through the lower level of the home, just to be sure there was nobody on the premises they hadn't planned on. Recessed lighting in every room of the house made the search easy, and proved that the lower level was empty except for hundreds of recently completed campaign signs.

They took their positions on the second level and then the stealthiest pair continued to the third floor and made a careful search. They accomplished it with only the tiniest of squeaks on the old wooden floors.

Chatto breathed more easily when the pair descended and gave him the thumbs-up.

Nothing left to do now except a little cold-blooded

murder. Chatto had the knife. It was from the kitchen of Martina Jomarca. As the mercenaries crept into the senator's bedroom, Jomarca's drugged, unconscious, whiskey-drenched body was placed in a chair by the window. On the bed was a barely legal campaign worker huddled up in the armpit of the snoring senator. That little piece of sweetmeat was in for a nasty shock when she woke up. But it would be nastier for the old biddy in the chair. As for the senator...

The teenager had to be neutralized first. Chatto brought the handle of the knife down hard, but the knife never seemed to reach the girl's skull. His hand got stuck.

His hand wouldn't move because somebody was holding his wrist.

"Tsk-tsk," said the little scrap of a man who had to be half Chatto's weight, and maybe four times his age and a Chinaman to boot!

Then the little old Chinaman broke Chatto's wrist.

There was a commotion in the hallway, followed by a burst of gunfire. The senator woke up bellowing and the teenager shot to her feet, dancing on the bed naked except for the cheerleader skirt bunched up around her waist.

Chatto staggered across the bedroom, landing in the limp lap of Martina Jomarca, but then the pain became a mechanism to focus his thoughts. He pushed himself up and groped with his good hand for the mini-Uzi on its shoulder strap. The senator barked in fear, and the cheerleader scrambled behind a chest of drawers.

Chatto found Baldwin and another soldier on the floor, facedown and toes up. He stepped over them and in the hallway witnessed what seemed to be a dozen specters flashing like shadows among his men, who fired their weapons crazily.

Before Chatto could issue a command that would grab their attention, his men were finished. The last one to die was Steve, the one who insisted they call him by his SEAL nickname, Scorpion. Scorpion was kneeling outside the bedroom with his eyes wide, his trousers soiled and his throat showing a tiny red cut encircling it.

Steve the Scorpion had to have died in a state of nearly perfect balance, but when he finally fell over his head rolled right off and came to a halt at Chatto's feet.

"Who are you guys?" Chatto demanded, surprised to find just two attackers in the hall.

"I'm the karate kid, and that's Miyagi," said the slender figure.

"Pah!" answered the tiny Asian.

"Old man, you broke my fucking wrist," Chatto said, waving the mini-Uzi threateningly at the pair.

"Had I known what you did with it, I would have broken something else."

Chatto knew there was something wrong here, but he couldn't figure out what it was. The two in the expansive landing didn't seem to care that they had a submachine gun targeting their guts. The little Asian was an inscrutable mass of wrinkles in the dim light. He had

his hands in the sleeves of his geisha dress, for crying out loud. The taller man...

Chatto couldn't see his face, really, but somehow he could see the eyes. It was like he was looking at pin-pricks of death light.

Who were they? Were they even human? Because Chatto had seen them in action and it wasn't normal.

"Answer the question!"

"What was the question again?" asked the man with the dead eyes.

"Who are you!"

"I'm James. He's Jinx."

"What is Jinx?" the little Asian demanded of the tall dark figure.

"Shut the fuck up!" Chatto shouted. He hurt like hell. "One more smart-ass answer, and I'm gonna make somebody into dog meat."

"It is possible Remo would make acceptable dog meat," the Asian said. "He has certainly proved to be without value in most other capacities."

"And it's true you wouldn't make an appetizer fit for a Chihuahua," the tall man said, to Chatto's dismay. His world had made sense until about ninety seconds ago.

"You pieces of shit—"

"Not going well, is it, buddy?" the tall man asked sympathetically, stepping up and taking the mini-Uzi out of Chatto's hands so easily and casually that Chatto had to make a real effort to be surprised. He was even

more surprised when he saw that the mini-Uzi he had threatened them with had a corkscrew barrel. Now when had *that* happened?

"So, what's up? What's going on? Why're you here? You fans of the senator?"

The dark figure nodded at the bedroom, where Chatto heard the baritone sobbing of the senator and the comforting murmurs of the cheerleader.

"I'm not telling you—"

"Yeah, heard it a million times," the tall figure said. "And then I go like this—" Chatto felt his earlobe get pinched "—and then you go like this, 'Ouch ouch please stop I'll tell you everything ouch ouch.'"

And that's exactly how it happened.

"He couldn't tell us a thing, Smitty, except that Serval and Jomarca were definitely their big targets in the area. The other targets were little and middle-sized fish in the greater Topeka area," Remo reported from a phone booth on a street corner in a more urban part of town. "Who would have thought there was so much corruption in Topeka?"

"That's irrelevant now, with the cell destroyed," Smith said.

"I mean, half the elected officials in this state spend their free time with hookers and/or attending white-supremacist organization meetings."

"It doesn't matter, Remo," Dr. Smith insisted. "You neutralized the cell. Those people are no longer targets."

"Get this, Smitty, the majority leader in the state senate? He's a compulsive shoplifter! And he steals nothing except frozen meat!"

23

"Remo, please."

"Hey, don't get mad at me, I'm not making this shit up."

"I don't care! Can we please address matters of importance?"

"Yeah. Sure. But you won't top my frozen-meat story."

MARK HOWARD WAS watching his map of the United States of America and feeling despondent.

So many electronic dots. Each one indicated corruption of one kind or another among the public officials. And there were hundreds of dots.

Some were as minor as the doughnut-eater in Chicago, while others were vast and sophisticated systems of extortion or theft that involved many people, including some of the highest ranking tax-paid personnel.

This was not some Third World nation where payoffs were a part of the culture, where graft was simply standard operating procedure, where politicians were underpaid to the point where they had no choice but to take bribes to survive.

This was America, one of the world's richest nations. Where politicians were supposedly accountable to the voters.

So why was there so much underhandedness? Was it all for money? Was it all for power? Did power always result in corruption, as the old cliché said?

No, he knew that wasn't true. He had delved into many of these accusations and found that many were just that—accusations, without foundation. The targets weren't necessarily guilty, but there had to have been some publicity that led the population to believe they might be.

For the most part, the murder victims had been shown, after they died, to have in fact been guilty of their crimes, but without more intense scrutiny, they couldn't be absolutely sure that the evidence was genuine. And they didn't have time for that now.

All they had time to do was sit and sift through the hundreds of potential targets and look for the likeliest first strikes—or wait for the Folcroft Four to point out a strike as it occurred.

Mark Howard heard the tiny electronic tone that brought his attention to the map again, where one of the red lights was blinking. He began pounding commands into the keyboard, brought up the details and snatched at the phone.

"Mark here," he said, knowing Dr. Smith was on the line with Remo. "Sorry to interrupt. We've got a flagged incident in San Francisco."

"I see it," Dr. Smith responded quickly, bringing up Mark's quickly organized window of data about the event. He would see it on his own screen just as Mark did—and see the possible implications of the attack. If it was an attack. "Remo, I'm ordering an Air Force transport for you. How soon can you get to the airport?"

"Like I know," Remo responded. "I have no clue where it even is. You tell me, Smitty."

There was a moment of furious keystrokes, then Smith announced, "Twenty minutes from where you are now if you find immediate transport."

"Should I find immediate transport?"

"We need you in California as fast as possible, Remo, if we're going to stop further attacks."

"I'll get a cab. Here, Chiun wants to talk to you."

Mark was barely listening as he read the details of the first attack. The indications of corruption for San Francisco were many and tightly spaced. How in the world were they going to pick out the likely next target? It could be any of them.

"Dr. Smith. Prince Howard." It was Master Chiun, using his most melodious voice, which was usually reserved for preparing them for the asking of special favors.

"Master Chiun," Dr. Smith said brusquely, "there is no time to talk now. You and Remo must get to California immediately."

"I understand many important events are afoot, Emperor," Chiun practically sang. "But there is a matter equally important of which we must speak."

"No time now, Master Chiun," Dr. Smith insisted.

"Ah, but now is the optimal time," Chiun replied, but the beautiful, songlike quality of his demurring voice was shattered by a raucous mechanical screech.

"What in the lord's name was that?" Dr. Smith asked.

Chiun sighed in disgust. "Remo is holding a cab."

"Do you mean hailing a cab?" Smith asked.

"No, I do not mean that," Chiun said.

"WHO ARE YOU JOKERS?" asked the air force officer who was the highest ranking officer on duty.

"Schneiders and Kurosawa. Glad to meet you but we're in a hurry."

"What the hell kind of an ID is this?" the major barked. "Says here you're from the DOJ, Mr. Schneiders."

"He's Schneiders," said the dark-haired Caucasian man, pointing a thumb at the tiny Asian.

"Sure, you are."

"Kurosawa is a Japanese name, and I am most certainly *not* Japanese," declared the Asian.

His partner added, "Like I said, we're in a hurry."

"How come I never heard of you?"

"Dunno. We're supposed to be meeting a liaison with General Norton."

"Oh, really?" The officer leaned against the guard post windowsill, and he threw a smile and a wink at the guard inside. The guard moved his hand discreetly to the control that would call for more backup. This pair might be packing who knew what. Hell, the little Asian named Schneiders might have explosives under that robe of his. This was only a small military terminal at the Topeka airport, but who knew who might want to take it out.

"Did not the emperor handle this?" the Asian demanded of his taller partner.

"He always does."

"You have forgotten a password perhaps?" the little

man said. "You have failed to approach the correct entranceway to this outpost? Think, Remo! In what way have you failed?"

The major was stiff now. The clown act had gone into full gear, and his instincts told him it was a distraction from the real action—any second now something big would get sprung on him. A busload of America haters, probably, and might be from anywhere. France, Germany, and four out of any five Asian, Middle Eastern or South American nations held grudges against the U.S.

"Major Wylkes!" came a call from behind him, along with a rush of fast-moving vehicles. Wylkes spun fast, realized he'd just turned his back on the intruders and spun back, only to find Schneiders and Kurosawa standing motionless, watching his antics curiously. Then Wylkes realized who he had just seen coming at him in a big hurry in a jeep and he spun back again. The vehicle came to a hard stop beside the guard shack. General Norton stepped out quickly and snatched the IDs out of Major Wylkes's hand.

"Mr. Kurosawa?" the general addressed the small Asian man.

Before the Asian could respond, the tall man said, "I'm Kurosawa. He's Schneiders."

"General Norton. There appears to have been a lapse in communication. My assistant did not realize you would be arriving this quickly. We came as fast as we could, but..."

The general nodded disapprovingly at the jeep. His driver was a stone-faced statue, but a young officer in the back seat was staring at the floor like a fourth-grader being shamed by the teacher.

The Asian shook his head, clucking gently. "I sympathize, General," he said. "A competent lackey is a rare thing indeed."

The barrel-chested general laughed quietly. "Isn't that the truth? Let me know if you ever find one."

"I shall, but do not stop breathing in anticipation of my call," said the small Asian, apparently delighted with himself, and then he gave a sharp, disapproving look at the dark man called Kurosawa.

The general ushered the pair of oddballs into his jeep. The general's assistant was ordered out to make room for them.

"Could you have the suits brings the trunks, General?" the dark one asked.

"Suits?" the general grunted.

"Blacksuits." The younger one pointed up, down, around.

"I don't understand," the general grumbled.

The younger man stood in his seat, leaned out, and his arm seemed to reach an impossibly far distance to extract a Special Forces commando who had slithered on the scene in response to Major Wylkes's silent alarm. The commando spluttered, but realized he was facing a general and went rigid when he was lowered to his feet.

"Oh," the general said, as surprised as the commando, and he and Major Wylkes stared at one another for a long moment, knowing they would never, ever speak of this incident again. "Yes, Wylkes, have the trunks brought to E-pad. Now."

"Yes, General."

"But no scratches!" declared the old Asian, Schneiders, as the jeep rumbled off.

THERE WERE THREE CREW on the small military jet. It was used to transport top bureaucratic brass and visiting foreign VIPs around the country, so it was outfitted like a passenger jet for wealthy businessmen. The cabin had a communications system designed for civvies, which meant no complicated protocols. It was almost as simple as a regular telephone.

"Doesn't work," said the dark-haired man.

"What number are you trying to dial?" asked the helpful Air Force officer who served as steward.

"Can't tell ya. Have to kill ya."

"I can get you an outside line again and you can try dialing yourself one more time."

The dark-haired man shrugged. "No, thanks. They'll call me. I'll wait."

The steward explained that the aircraft was one of the most highly secure in the world, with a dynamically shifting communications array so that it communicated with the world on varying wavelengths and frequencies and even different technologies, shifting frequently and unpredictably, and there was no way somebody was going to know how to dial *in*...

The phone rang. The steward picked it up, then handed it to Remo, face reddening.

"Agent Kurosawa here."

"Your ETA is seventy minutes," Smith said without greeting. "We've narrowed the possible number of follow-up targets to thirty-one."

"Whoa. What're we supposed to do about that?" Remo asked.

"Canvass as many as possible," Smith answered dryly. "We can only hope we'll get lucky."

"We're developing a patrol itinerary that should have you reconnoitering the maximum number of targets in the least time," Mark Howard added. "Are you seeing the map?"

Remo looked for help from Chiun, who stared into space with his hands in his sleeves as if his thoughts floated in another universe, but Remo knew he heard every word. Chiun nodded briefly at the wall behind the conference table, where a small panel was embedded. The steward was well-trained in security protocol and knew enough to not be in the compartment, so Remo had only himself to rely on. He jabbed at the words at the bottom of the screen, then at the tiny pictures above the words, and the screen came to life with a computer image.

"We see it," Remo reported, grinning with self-satisfaction. Anyway, he saw something that looked like a map of San Francisco.

"Less than two hours ago a board of elections judge was murdered in a Greek restaurant in San Francisco—

that's the red icon," Smith reported. "From that central location, we foresee a number of possible targets, the blue icons."

"Hold on," Remo said. "An election official? Like one of nice retired folks in the neighborhood who makes sure you stick the ballot in the box right-side up?"

"Only the first move by the local cell," Smith assured him. "They always strike a number of targets, and they always include some local figures in the mix. It's their way of connecting with the people on the street."

"The locals who get axed are always corrupt?" Remo asked.

"There is always a high-profile accusation of corruption," Mark Howard said.

"So somebody can always say he or she was a crook and got what was coming to him," Remo finished. "But you think some of the accusations are false, Junior?"

"They have to be," Mark Howard said. "There are so many victims, such a wide range of crimes, there's no way that even CURE resources could find a definitive answer on all of them."

Remo considered that, feeling grim. "Tell me about the election judge," he said.

"She's of no consequence now," Smith said. "We need to think about the next target."

"Tell me about her."

"Remo—"

"You have a date, Smitty? You said we have more than an hour, so tell me about the election judge."

There was a pause, then Mark Howard began reading from his screen. "Eleanor George, age seventy-seven, lifelong resident of San Francisco and a prominent society figure. Family has had money for generations and she married more of it. Husband died in 1979, and she began putting her money into facilities to help unmarried mothers. Her centers provided housing, education and job training, that kind of thing. Very outspoken about getting out the vote, and she served as an election judge for twenty years."

Remo considered that. He felt Chiun looking at him. "She's a real troublemaker. Got what she deserved, that's for sure."

"She was accused of vote fraud," Howard added. "Says here one of the other judges turned her in."

"Her heinous crime was?" Remo asked, knowing he wasn't going to like the answer.

"She drove some of the women from her shelters to the polling place," Howard said. "If you're a judge, that's against the rules."

"I see." Remo did see.

"She never got the chance to enter a plea, but in several interviews she admitted doing it. She even said she'd done it in past elections."

"Which undermines the entire electoral process, and so on, and so on," Remo added. "Okay, so what about MAEBE? Who gets a big assist now that this election thrower is out of the picture?"

"Nobody," said Mark Howard.

"Yeah, somebody," Remo agreed.

"We've investigated that angle," Smith said. "Mrs. George was never one to espouse any candidate. She had an agenda, but it doesn't look like she made her views about the coming elections public."

"What about the MAEBE candidates in San Francisco?" Remo asked. "She wouldn't have voted for them, would she? So could this mean MAEBE will put in its own judges?"

"Remo, this is a dead end," Smith insisted. "Mrs. George was simply a convenient target for the local cell. She's just one more name they can add to their list when and if they decide to publicize their efforts to clean up the corruption. There's not much to be learned from her murder."

"She influenced elections," Remo said.

"Indirectly."

"But in a big way, in her section of the city, right?"

"Perhaps."

"Who's the alderman or whatever that's going to be less likely to win if Mrs. George isn't there to get her unmarried mothers to the polling place?"

After a moment Mark Howard said, "There's a Melanie Satz who has been a supporter of Ms. George's causes, and she's running for the state House of Representatives seat in that district," Howard said. "The incumbent state representative is Bruce Griffin, and he's ahead by a lot of points. The MAEBE candidate is Dr. Robin Eomer, a dental surgeon and Baptist minister."

"What kind of skeleton does Griffin have in the closet?" Remo asked.

"None, far as I can tell," Howard said.

"Look harder."

"Remo—"

"Humor me, Smitty."

"I'm seeing a DUI arrest from 1990, but it was thrown out—no conviction."

"Is he connected?"

"I don't know."

"Look!"

The silence was tense. The only sound coming over the phone was from Mark Howard's keyboard.

"What do you know," Howard said quietly. "There was a cover-up. Griffin killed somebody. The judge was later convicted of taking bribes for innocent pleas, but nobody ever connected him to Griffin before—until today. There's a *San Francisco Journal* article for tomorrow's paper about the conspiracy, and the local TV is going to break it on their evening news."

"Then Griffin's dead meat and it's a race between the boring old Melanie Satz and her out-of-fashion cause to help working mothers, versus the candidate from the wonderful new Party for the People," Remo said.

"Hmm," said Smith. "You may be on to something, Remo."

"Aw, Smitty," Remo said, "you know it's embarassin' when you start gushing all over."

24

Orville Flicker was afraid. Worse than that, he was nervous, and he was acting jittery, and that absolutely wouldn't do, especially tonight of all nights.

Flicker couldn't understand it. His White Hand had been doing its work for months, cleaning up the bureaucracy of the United States at every level, removing one despicable public servant after another from the government payrolls. There had never been a major hitch, not one, and subtle support was growing here and there across the nation. Everything was going exactly as planned.

Now, of all times, as the White Hand began its most important phase of operations and Flicker's political organization became a juggernaut, everything started going wrong. In just days there was catastrophe after catastrophe. The Midwest cell, wiped out at the Bryant assassination. The Continental Divide cell demolished, with only Boris Bernwick surviving and escaping—

only to be found dismembered near the scene of the bombing of the drug-lord police chief.

Somebody knew a lot more than they should about the White Hand. The question was, how much did they know about the sponsors of the White Hand?

That was just one of a number of reasons why the big announcement should not happen tonight, but they didn't matter. The stage was set, the expectation level of the nation and the party had been primed to the perfect level. The announcement had to come now, tonight, without delay. Everybody was ready and waiting for the steamroller of events that had brought the MAEBE political party into existence to continue rolling, inexorably, flattening the competition.

Nothing could be allowed to interfere with the momentum that Flicker's carefully orchestrated series of "spontaneous" events had generated. MAEBE had to have unfaltering momentum. There could be no time for the individual parties in this eclectic mix of rightwingers to stop and discuss this course of events.

Discussion, contemplation, a true interchange of ideas—anything along those lines would bring this thundering herd to a dusty halt. If there was one lesson Flicker learned from years of politics, it was that discussion murdered progress.

MAEBE was born when a bunch of small, roly-poly snowballs got nudged into one another at just the right moment to create an avalanche, and if anybody slowed the avalanche it would simply crumble to pieces again.

Flicker had to keep the avalanche careening downhill. It had to be perfectly clear to every one of these minor campaigns that there was no time for negotiations. If they insisted on stopping and talking things over, they'd end up left behind, talking to themselves.

Today, the dramatic events that brought these various entities together to form MAEBE had to now be upstaged by anther dramatic event, and the event had to come now.

In one short hour, Orville Flicker would be raised up from comparative obscurity among the ranks of top MAEBE brass and, humble but determined, accept the nomination of his party as its candidate for President of the United States of America.

But Orville Flicker was frightened. He had never once shown discomfort in all his years as press secretary to the state governor who then became President. Even at the press conference after his firing by that same back-stabbing, narrow-minded President he showed nothing but self-control and iron resolve.

But all these past performances had been leading up to today, and in every public appearance he made from now on he had to be better than ever. So what to do about this stage fright?

What if exposing himself now was a fatal mistake? Somebody had come incredibly close to nabbing Flicker. He had been sitting inside that Victorian monstrosity in Topeka just hours before someone was there to intercept his White Hand cell charged with assassinating that adulterous swine Julius Serval.

The newspaper accounts were confusing. The reports Flicker received from his FBI sources were more credible and yet more unbelievable.

There was an angry pounding on the door and a sudden barrage of shouting. Ed Kriidelfisk shoved the door open and squirmed around Cleo, which was no small achievement.

"Flicker, you fucker!"

"Mr. Kriidelfisk!" Cleo snapped. "You will not use such language in this home."

"Go to hell," Kriidelfisk said. "You fucked up, Flicker."

"Mr. Kriidelfisk, this is your last warning!" Cleo Reubens exhorted, drawing back her heavy shoulder and making sledgehammers out of her meaty fists.

"Tell the linebacker to get the fuck out," Kriidelfisk growled.

"You're showing your ugly side, Mr. Kriidelfisk," Flicker said, mustering his cool.

"Tell the ugly old broad to get out now, or I press 7."

He held up his cell phone. The color display showed little tropical fishes swimming around in an aquarium.

Flicker felt his pores open up and his body temperature skyrocketed, but he showed only calm composure when he asked. "All right, Mr. Kriidelfisk, I'll bite. Who will you reach if you press seven?"

Kriidelfisk's lower lip curled over his chin. "CNN."

Orville Flicker stifled his hiss of indignation, and he had to force himself to nod.

"Mrs. Reubens," Flicker said finally, "please leave us."

Cleo Reubens left the office, closing the door behind her, hard.

The Flicker house was a large, contemporary home in a clubhouse development in Dallas. The home was huge, and most of Flicker's neighbors were large families with a well-planned social agenda. Flicker had turned most of the house into the headquarters for MAEBE, before MAEBE had its name. Mrs. Reubens had been his housekeeper and had begun handling bodyguard and secretarial duties when the need arose—like now, when Noah Kohd was out arranging the press conference. She was a good soul, and not to be underestimated. She didn't like poor behavior, and she had never known her employer, the good Mr. Flicker, to tolerate profanity in his household. Why he would do so now was beyond her understanding.

Orville Flicker dredged up a stall tactic from his early days and strolled to the wall, adjusting the air-conditioning to its lowest setting. The chill might make Kriidelfisk less comfortable and ease some of Flicker's unbecoming perspiration.

Kriidelfisk wasn't going to allow him the dignity of a thoughtful silence.

"What the fuck happened, Flicker?"

"I'm trying to find out myself."

"You fucked me over! I'm out!"

"Not necessarily, Ed."

"Not necessarily? Serval gives this speech this morning that makes him look like a hero and a victim all at the same time! He feels so sorry for Ms. Jomarca, and he'll sponsor a gambling addiction support bill in her name when he's reelected! No mention of the cheer-leader, says the gunman were all hired by Jomarca. His popularity ratings have gone up ten points since the morning news, and the worst part is they aren't even mentioning my name! I don't even exist! I thought you were supposed to be some sort of a political whiz kid, Orville. You mean to tell me you're so out of touch you can't tell I'm fucked?"

Flicker nodded, trying to come up with an angle to spin this on. He had not expected Kriidelfisk to show up at his house, and now he knew why he had not been able to reach the MAEBE candidate at home all morn-ing. Flicker's prepared appeasement deal was clearly in-adequate now, but what was the right way to go? What was the right message to give a mutineer? Should he re-ward the man for his insubordination and threats of ex-tortion? Or should he...?

"Do you have anything to say for yourself, Flicker, you idiot?"

Orville Flicker smiled. It was the confident smile again. He had just decided the perfect way to handle this backstabbing, foulmouthed Benedict Arnold.

"Mr. Edward Kriidelfisk, you are a man of deep convictions."

"I don't need your crap, Flicker."

"But you do need a job, Mr. Kriidelfisk, and in fifty minutes I'm beginning my campaign for the presidency."

Kriidelfisk waited to see where this was headed.

"I need a vice president, Mr. Kriidelfisk."

The independent politician from Kansas chewed on that. He said cautiously, "Are you saying you want me to be your running mate?"

"We had planned to hold off on declaring a vice presidential nominee. We didn't want it to look as if we planned it. But the series of events of the past twenty-four hours were pure happenstance in the eyes of the public. You're the right man who came along at the right time, through the quirks of fate."

Kriidelfisk nodded, a new light gleaming in his eyes. "Yeah. It's perfect."

"Will you take the job?"

"Yes, certainly, Mr. Flicker!" Kriidelfisk said, relearning his manners in an instant. "I'll be honored to stand at your side."

"There is no better man for this role, Mr. Kriidelfisk," Flicker said, standing up smoothly. They shook hands formally.

"Thank you, sir."

Flicker checked his watch. "We're short on time. Let's get you to wardrobe."

25

The Air Force officer couldn't wait for his passengers to leave. They gave him the heebie-jeebies.

They were killers. He knew it from looking at them. Especially the younger one. He could swear that guy had pupils shaped like skulls.

The small man was Korean. He had told the steward that much during their conversation, which was nothing short of an interrogation.

"I'm sorry, sir, I just don't know," the steward had said. "You would need to ask the Air Force. They're the ones who maintain this aircraft."

"This is not like most Air Force jets," the Korean had said accusingly.

"We use it to transport visiting dignitaries. Heads of state, foreign diplomats, those kinds of people," the steward explained for the fourth or fifth time.

"If one were to choose to dwell in such a craft, would there be a large staff required?"

"I don't really know, sir."

"There would be a pilot needed."

"Yes. And a copilot."

"I would need no copilot," the Korean man said disdainfully. "One pilot is sufficient."

"I think there are FAA regulations about that," the steward suggested.

The Korean was extremely suspicious. "And the FAA, they are likely to come about often, demanding compliance?"

The Air Force officer said, "Uh, well, probably."

"Bah!" the Korean exploded. "This is a nation of nuisances! Permits and officials and pencil-pushing fools! It is no wonder some men of wisdom see the need to disembowel the bureaucracy!"

This was an alarming and vaguely threatening display of temper and the Air Force officer wished he hadn't heard it, since it was probably something he wasn't supposed to know anyway. He tried to look noncommittal.

The Korean finally stopped staring at him and said, "Fine. I will acquiesce to this demand for a copilot, but only if he will handle janitorial services, as well."

"I do not know what the FAA would have to say about that, sir."

"Let them say whatever they like. I will never pay for a pilot who does not pilot unless he serves some useful function."

The steward wished his copilot would announce the beginning of their descent or that a sudden thunderstorm would break out or that the rudder would sheer off—anything to save him from the terrible old man.

While he was thinking it, his wish came true. The Korean was gone.

He poked his head out of the galley and saw that the Korean had somehow, in under a second, made his way to the far end of the cabin and snatched the phone out of the hands of the white man, who was some sort of servant or indentured assistant, from what the Korean had said.

"EMPEROR SMITH, I crave a moment of your time," Chiun announced into the phone.

"I'm sorry Master Chiun, but not right now. We may have a new investigative trail and we must have it thoroughly explored before you and Remo land in San Francisco."

"This is quite important, Dr. Smith."

"Now is simply not a good time, Master Chiun."

Remo went to a seat near the front and reclined his seat. "Do not disturb," he told the steward when the young officer peered out of the galley. "I'm napping."

"We'll be landing in less than twenty minutes, sir."

"En. Ay. Ping. Napping. Understood?"

"Yes, sir."

Remo closed his eyes and couldn't help but overhear the awkward conversation behind him.

"Please hang up, Emperor Smith."

"Pardon me?" Dr. Smith asked.

"If you will not afford me the time to discuss the matter, then I must discuss it with other parties. Please hang up, then you may begin your very urgent business and I will go about mine."

"What other parties will you be discussing this with, Master Chiun?" Smith asked.

"I am not at liberty to say."

"What is the nature of this business?"

"If you are not ready to commence with a full discussion of this matter, then I must keep it confidential, Emperor."

Chiun waited. He was very good at waiting. Smith was also skilled in this regard. But Smith was a child next to the manipulative skills of Chiun.

"Master Chiun," Smith said finally, "our current situation requires all my concentration. If we can delay this discussion just a little while longer, I will give it my full attention."

Chiun was silent.

"That is my promise to you," Smith added formally.

"Very well," Chiun said imperiously, and hung up.

26

Bruce Griffin threw up some more and watched it swirl down the drain in the running water. Just like my career, he thought, and grabbed the phone from his pocket on the first ring.

"It's Clayton."

Griffin's heart started pounding. He hadn't expected the old newshound to return his call. They weren't exactly friends.

"Clayton, you've got to hear me out," Griffin said. "I know we can make a deal. You have got to kill that story!"

"No deals, Bruce. You know I don't work that way."

"Bullshit! Just tell me how much."

"I'm not selling out," Clayton said.

"Like you've never killed a story for cash," Griffin said, sneering. "I know for a fact you're retiring on your payoffs from the Scarpessi Family."

"I think we're done talking, Bruce," Clayton said.

"Clayton, wait!"

But he was talking to himself.

Bruce Griffin swore and stared at the phone, thinking fast. Clayton had clearly not been ready to deal, so why had he bothered to return the call?

Because his phone was bugged? Yes, he was trying to prove to somebody that he wasn't playing dirty pool. Maybe, Griffin thought, he could get the newspaper editor to talk in private and there would still be time to kill the story.

ADAM CLAYTON WAS pacing his office when he spotted a familiar figure coming at a half jog across the sidewalk eight stories below.

Stupid bastard. Clayton dragged on his jacket and headed for the door, taking the stairs to avoid running into the state representative. He got down to the fourth floor before he changed his mind. He had to at least warn this poor slob that he was on somebody's hit list.

Clayton raced back to the eighth floor and spotted Griffin fidgeting outside his office, demanding answers from the receptionist. Clayton got his attention with a wave and Griffin came fast to the door to the stairs. Griffin started to whine, but Clayton cut him off with a quick set of instructions.

Ten minutes later they rendezvoused and were sitting side by side at the counter at D-Burgers, a 1950s-style diner that had been around so many years that the worn-down look was no longer artificial.

"Griffin, you gotta cut some sort of a deal with me,"

Clayton pleaded after the waitress poured them steaming hot coffee that was older than her current wad of gum.

"No deals."

"You gotta—"

"Shut up and listen, asshole," Clayton said. "You got worse problems than you know. Somebody is going to try to kill you. Tonight, maybe. Not until the story is out, anyway."

The state representative stared at the political editor of one of the largest newspapers in the city of San Francisco.

Clayton glanced in his direction, then stared into the black gruel in his cup as he scalded his lips on it. "Don't look at me—we don't know each other," Clayton growled.

Griffin looked into his own cup and Clayton risked a glance. "You look like shit."

It was no exaggeration. Clayton's hair was disheveled and crusted with something. There were stains on his crooked, wrinkled tie, which was now soaked at the bottom in very bitter coffee. And there was a smell. The state representative had been driving the porcelain school bus.

"What'd you expect when I find out my life is about to be ruined?" Griffin demanded. "What do you mean somebody is going to try to kill me?"

"Kill. Murder. Bang bang. What's not to understand?"

"But why?"

Clayton shrugged and filled his mouth with more black liquid.

Griffin was looking at him again. "You know why," he stated. "Tell me why."

"I don't know."

"Yeah, you do."

"Just tell me. Is it revenge, 'cause of the guy that died in the accident?"

Clayton laughed. "Is that what you call it? An accident? You drank a fifth of bourbon and decide to go for a drive, and it's an accident when somebody gets squashed at a crosswalk?"

"That's the reason?"

"No, asshole, it's not revenge." Clayton realized he and Griffin were now having a very public conversation. Shit. All he wanted to do was warn the guy! "Listen, I'm doing you a favor by telling you to get the fuck out of town now 'cause somebody is going to try to make you dead. What you do with this advice is up to you, but my part is done."

Clayton tossed some bills on the counter and walked back to the office, fast. His old wing tips had new soles that made satisfying clops on the sidewalk and people got out of his way.

Why did he have to be the one to figure this out? How come some other schmuck couldn't have been the one to connect the dots? Why him?

It was the story of a lifetime, sure, but it was a story that no reporter could break, because he'd be dead before he wrote it.

Whoever these guys were, they had to be the toughest sons of bitches who ever got together to represent the people of the United States of America. But sure as shittin' they had done it, and from coast-to-coast, anybody who got in their way was getting carefully executed.

What made them so damn hard to spot was that these guys killed about ten times more people than was necessary for their immediate goals. So they needed to off a city planner in Baton Rouge, they would kill a few cops, a sheriff, a small-town mayor and assorted others while they were at it. It helped obfuscate their real intention and it helped clean up the scum.

Because they had two goals: one was to get their people elected, and the other was to clean out a lot of the dirty-handed public officials.

Adam Clayton received a phone tip that opened up Bruce Griffin's sordid past. Clayton got one of his best political reporters to do the research, and pretty soon the entire ugly affair was exposed.

Clayton had the story ready that morning, and everybody was getting excited. Ruining somebody's career was always a big rush. The promotional spots would start running in prime time.

But something was bothering Clayton about the anonymous tip. He looked into it, looked at some of the other killings that had been going on. The connections were being made. Who's Killing The City Slackers? was the headline in Indianapolis. But nobody guessed how far the murder spree extended.

Oh, maybe some of the federals had figured it out, but they weren't going public with it yet.

Clayton figured it out over his salami sandwich at

lunchtime and pretty soon he knew who was sponsoring the killers.

There had to be a lot of killers. Groups of them, working across the country, and then with a jolt Clayton made the connection between the killing spree and the murder, that very morning, of Mrs. George.

Soon more people would die in this city. Anybody whose salary came from the taxpayers and who had been accused of some sort of underhanded business was in deadly peril. The list was pretty damn long, and as soon as Clayton's exposé ran on tonight's TV news and in tomorrow's paper, Representative Bruce Griffin would be on the list, too. Clayton would have helped murder him.

MAEBE. What the hell kind of name was that for a political party anyway? Sounded like a neighborhood watch committee or something. And yet, whoever pulled the strings over at MAEBE had to be the coldest, most heartless son of a bitch who ever ran for public office.

And that was saying something.

27

Perry Rhinebeck was following in the footsteps of the greatest press secretary of all time, Orville Flicker. It was an honor and a privilege, and he was going to pull it off perfectly. He felt cool as a cucumber as he worked the press and the crowd of supporters.

"As you know, we've only just created our national organizational structure in the past twenty-four hours, so things are a little chaotic," he said, giving a smile that made him look happily disheveled when in fact he was put together more neatly than a mannequin in a formal-wear display window. "But we're on a roll! We're now represented across the nation, with state leadership elected in all fifty states. Through this leadership we held our nominating elections for a presidential candidate in the last twenty-four hours. The results, I might add, were nearly unanimous."

The crowd was in the palm of his hand. He played them perfectly.

"We've moved fast," he said, moving away from the

moment of tension. "We've moved tremendously fast. But the support we've received from across the nation tells us this is the right thing to do. We're taking the high ground. The people of this nation want leaders of uncompromised integrity and ethical fortitude. That is why we're seeing so much violence against the freeloaders and liars and villains who run our towns, our states and our nation. The message is clear and the message is this—now is the time to cut out the diseased parasites and replace them with new, healthy, untainted flesh. It is the time for MAEBE."

"Maybe not!" shouted someone in the crowd.

Perry Rhinebeck smiled and waved at the man. The people watching the news conference at home couldn't see him being dragged out. "Of course, maybe not," Rhinebeck admitted. "It seems unbelievable that a political party could have come into existence on a national level in something like two days, but we did it. The people of America practically *willed* MAEBE into existence. If their will remains strong, MAEBE will be here for the long run."

And with that, Perry Rhinebeck finally announced the name of the presidential nominee.

IN HIS OFFICE in Rye, New York, Dr. Harold W. Smith nodded to himself, very slightly, as he heard the name of the presidential nominee of MAEBE.

Mark Howard entered a moment later.

"Orville Flicker," Howard said.

"It makes perfect sense, doesn't it?" Smith asked.

"It does. It sure does."

IN HIS OFFICE on the eighth floor, overlooking San Francisco, political editor Adam Clayton nodded.

"Orville fucking Flicker."

One of the secretaries entered a minute later and he was still nodding.

"Orville fucking Flicker!" he said to her.

"Exciting, isn't it?" she asked, clearly enthralled by it all.

"Exciting?" Clayton demanded. "You think stabbing old women is exciting? You think shooting a man four times in the heart is exciting? You think twisting a lamp cord around the neck of a young prostitute until her throat is crushed and her tongue turns black is exciting?"

The secretary left in a hurry.

"I didn't think so," Clayton grumbled, and he sucked on his flask. The bourbon was gone. Where had all that bourbon gone?

Didn't matter. He fished around in the file drawer of his desk and found a fresh bottle of bourbon and started making it be all gone, too.

Between swigs he said the name again like an awful profanity. "Orville Flicker. Orville Fucking Flicker."

"WHO'S ORVILLE FLICKER?" Remo asked.

Chiun looked at him, a mixture of disgust and pity.

"The little space alien from the final season of *The*

Flintstones wasn't named Orville Flicker, was he?" Remo asked.

"You are saying deliberately stupid things," Chiun accused.

"Just trying to meet your expectations."

"You do not need to put in the extra effort. Just act natural."

28

"What's with the look?" Remo asked.

"I am watching out for more careless dumping of my precious trunks." Chiun had been eyeing him suspiciously since they picked up the luggage.

"I'll whistle if I feel the need to throw them around anymore," Remo said. "See that guy?"

"You are trying to distract me?"

"No, just making an observation. Look at that guy."

Chiun glanced to the left, then returned his gaze to the trunks balanced, perfectly, on Remo's shoulders. "He is just another white man in a monkey suit. What of him?"

"Business traveler. See how he manages to pack all his paperwork and probably a laptop and a few changes of clothes into that one bag? And then he carries it on and never has to wait for the luggage to arrive. Plus, he doesn't have to have an argument with the security people at every airport when he checks his luggage. Isn't that cool?"

"I do not see your point."

"My point is, if that guy can travel with just a carryon, why can't you?"

Chiun sniffed. "Are you not weary of trying to convince me of this?"

"Not as tired as I am of carrying your trunks."

"I am a Master of Sinanju. I cannot travel with a carryon."

"Hello? I'm one of those, you know. All I carry around with me is a change of clothes and an extra pair of shoes."

"You dress in underwear. If you were a woman, you would have spent the last twenty-odd years globetrotting in lingerie. This is not a style I wish to emulate. What are we doing in San Francisco?"

"You heard Smith. We're looking for the next MAEBE cell."

"I don't like this city," Chiun announced.

"You've only just started complaining, if I guess right."

Chiun's suspicious squint became flinty. "Meaning what?"

"Meaning our first stop is in Japantown."

"Ach!" Chiun waved at the air as if to ward off a disgusting stench. "Now you'll be telling me our next stop is in Chinatown."

"Lord, I hope not," Remo said. "For Chinatown's sake."

REMO PARKED the rental in a no-parking zone and Chiun's disgust mounted exponentially. Remo vaulted out of the car and slammed the door before the old Korean could express himself, circled around the complaining parking meter reader and entered the Japantown Lenny's. The always-open chain of family restaurants had hundreds of outlets that looked exactly the same, but the franchise in Japantown, San Francisco, was an original. Vast open ceiling with a hanging fabric and wood-frame artwork and a menu that included sashimi as well as the usual UltraMelt line of roasted sandwiches. The smell of unfresh fish mixed with the usual fried-cheese odor.

"Revolting," Chiun said, standing at Remo's elbow. "Incidentally, the young woman on the sidewalk has threatened to kick you in the behind."

"What?" Remo asked absently as he scanned the clientele.

"Give you the boot."

"Oh. Let her."

"Like I would try to stop anyone from putting a shoe in your huge, pale backside?"

Remo saw Adam Clayton. Not that he recognized the man, but he was distinguishable enough among the booths occupied by mostly elderly Japanese men involved in animated discussion.

"You Remo Uberstock?"

"I suppose so," Remo said, breathing shallowly. Clayton's breath was eighty proof. Clayton was the man behind the exposé on Griffin that would be teased on the evening news and run tomorrow in the newspaper.

Smith had arranged for Remo and Chiun to meet with the man, and Clayton had hinted over the phone that he had his own hypotheses, quite accurate ones, about MAEBE and the killings.

"Your friend is attracting attention," Clayton pointed out.

"No killing, Moses," Remo pleaded, trying to usher Chiun into the booth first. No such luck. Getting locked in the back of the both would have slowed down Chiun not at all anyway.

"Where's Griffin?"

"I don't know," Clayton said. "Hopefully he's got the hell out of San Fran. I told him MAEBE was after him. I told him he was dead meat. I don't think he bought it, though. He was too worried about his career going down the tubes."

"His political aspirations don't count for much when he's dead," Remo said.

"He thought I was full of shit, like I had bought into some sort of a conspiracy theory. But I've been covering politics for thirty years, and I know what a legitimate conspiracy smells like."

"He knows nothing of smells, or he would not have us meet with him in a place that smells like Japanese people," Chiun complained in Korean.

"Japanese people don't smell bad," Remo replied, also in Korean, the one language besides English in which he was fluent—and he had learned it purely by accident.

"You, too, are odor-ignorant, else you would be plagued with self-loathing."

"Where would Griffin be if he were still in San Francisco?"

Clayton shrugged, sipping his tea. "At home boozing or puking, or maybe at BCN trying to stop the commercials."

"The commercials?" Remo asked.

"See, once BCN starts airing the promo spots for the seven-o'clock news, there is no way they pull it. They're committed. They look like idiots if they run the spots, then don't run the piece. And once they run the piece, there's no way the paper will pull the story out of the morning paper 'cause then *we'll* look like idiots."

"So why'd he come to you in the first place?"

"It's our story," Clayton said. "I could stop it by coming up with some sort of rationale like one of our sources changed his story, something like that. That's what Griffin thought, anyway. Truth is, then I'd look like an idiot and the story would run anyway because there are three or four reporters who helped put it all together and they're the ones with the sources, not me."

"Say Griffin left the city. Where'd he go?"

"Beats me," the editor said. "I don't know him socially. I don't even like the bastard. I just didn't want to see him killed. He's a bastard, but he doesn't deserve to die."

Another person who did not deserve to die was the obstinate middle-aged Japanese man in a loose tie. He was making loud jokes in Japanese and had his three companions laughing. Remo didn't need to understand the language to know the object of their ridicule.

"I'll handle it," he announced.

"You? You'll give them more reason to laugh," Chiun said.

"Just watch me. Excuse me, Clayton."

Remo stood, strolled to the booth holding the amused Japanese and bowed low, looking the joker right in the eye.

"Master of Sinanju," Remo said quietly.

Whatever the obnoxious office man had expected Remo to say, that wasn't it. His face went blank.

Remo went back to his own booth.

Behind him he heard one of the Japanese men ask the office worker what had been said. The office worker told him.

"What does that mean?"

"Sinanju!" hissed one of the other men in the booth. "Master of Sinanju?"

There was more whispering. The elderly Japanese were the first to start leaving. They were whispering among themselves, repeating "Sinanju!" Most of the younger men and women didn't understand what was happening, but they knew a mob action when they saw one. The crowd of elderly Japanese was soon followed by a thickening mob of younger people and a steady murmur of fearful voices.

Remo took his seat in the booth. "You know who might know where Griffin would go to if he were to leave town?"

Clayton was stunned by the abrupt and nearly silent stampede for the door, and he tried to drag his attention back to Remo unsuccessfully until, a half minute later, the evacuation was complete. Aside from a young woman in the rear, too busy with her toddler triplets to notice anything else, the place was empty of customers. The waitress at the counter was standing holding her order pad and her pen, trying to understand what had just happened. A waitress emerged from the kitchen with a round tray full of plates of noodles and stopped cold. She stared at the ceiling, looking for signs of crumbling masonry from a tremor she had obviously been too preoccupied to feel, but the building was intact and there was no movement under her feet.

But her customers had clearly fled. She began putting the noodles on the table in front of the triplets. "On the house," she explained.

"Friends? Lovers? Spouses? Griffin have any?" Remo persisted.

The editor finally heard him. "Executive assistant," he said. "And occasional concubine. Nadine Hannover. Try his office."

"Thanks." The waitress still had one wide bowl of noodles to dispose of, and Remo summoned her with a glance. She slid the noodles in front of Clayton, but she never took her eyes off Remo Williams as he slid out of the booth and gave her a warm smile. Even with her long, jet-black hair braided under her Lenny's visor and her face flushed from hours of waiting tables, she was a very attractive young woman. Remo's elbow hurt suddenly.

"Let us go from this place, horny goat!" Chiun barked.

"In a second," Remo said. "Least I can do is buy lunch for our friendly journalist." He handed one of his slips of currency to the waitress. "Keep the change."

"It's a one," she said, but a sultry smile was coming to her lips by degrees, like a slow glow.

"Oh. Here."

"That's a hundred," she observed.

"Okay."

There was a sound like an asp about to strike, and Remo's elbow hurt a lot more. He went with Chiun to the rental car.

"She was cute," he pointed out, mostly because he knew it would get a reaction.

"She was Japanese!"

"I like Japanese."

"You would sully the pure bloodline of Sinanju with—with Japanese?"

"I said she was cute, I didn't say I was going to father children with her," Remo said. The meter maid was still there, hands on her hips and a smile on her face. A crew of city workers had just finished clamping on the heavy steel device that locked a wheel and made the car undrivable. Remo tapped it along the seams, and the two halves collapsed to the pavement. He extracted the half that was under the rental car and handed it to the meter maid. She sputtered.

On the opposite side of the street a gathering of Japanese onlookers gasped and murmured among themselves.

"Sinanju!"

"It is true!"

"Congratulations," Chiun said. "The legend of Sinanju only grows in stature under the mastership of Remo the Traffic Scofflaw."

THEY REACHED the fifteenth floor of the BCN Building, with its commanding view of the Golden Gate Bridge. "Seems to me I recall one of the Masters had a Japanese wife," Remo said.

"Who?" Chiun demanded irritably.

"I'm trying to remember...."

"I mean who are we here to see, idiot." Chiun turned his attention to the woman at the crescent receptionist's desk. "Forgive my son. He is an idiot."

"News director. Guy name Bang." Remo pulled out an ID badge wallet for the receptionist's benefit. "FBI."

"A father-and-son FBI team? I don't believe it."

"And yet you broadcast a television program last season based on that premise," Chiun pointed out.

"Nobody bought that, either," the receptionist said. "That's why we replaced it with *Odd Couples who Shack Up*."

"He's not really my dad," Remo said. "He's just old,

and, you know." He twirled his finger in the vicinity of his ear.

"He's crazy and old and he dresses like that and they let him in the FBI?"

"Yeah, can you believe it?"

"Shh!" She was busy jotting it all down on a tiny square sticky note. "Series about crazy old Jap cross-dresser (R. Machio dead yet?) and hunk (Keanu dead yet?), FBI team..." Remo read Bang's name and office number off a small laminated map next to her, and they went to find him while she finished her concept.

"HE WAS HERE." News Director Bang chuckled. "Man, was he a mess! All wrinkled up and he smelled offal. Get it? Offal?"

Remo thought that, however much of a mess Griffin had been, he couldn't compare to Bang, who perspired profusely just from the effort of walking out of the production room.

"He couldn't talk you out of running the promos, I take it?"

"Naw. Besides, the tapes are already in New York, for running nationwide. They're promoting the story now, coast-to-coast. Too late to stop it, even if he had met my price." Bang chortled.

"Any idea where he went?" Remo was getting extremely bored chasing California State Representative Griffin.

"Naw."

"What is this?" Chiun asked, pointing to the muted television screen in the small room outside the video production studio.

"That's live." Banks chuckled. "MAEBE."

"Maybe it is live?" Chiun asked.

"MAEBE. That's MAEBE. That guy there is from MAEBE."

"It's live?" Remo demanded, not trusting the Live! banner in the top left corner of the display.

"Press conference. See that guy? He's gonna be the next President of the United States of America. Maybe!" Banks huge torso never stopped its amused jiggling.

"We know him," Remo said. "Don't we?"

"He used to serve under the presidential pretender," Chiun said. "He was the official glad-hander until he fell from favor."

"That's Orville Flicker. Used to be the President's press secretary. Remember the whole big controversy about the Office of Religious Activities?" Banks asked.

"No," Remo said.

"Excuse my son," Chiun explained.

"Yeah, I'm an idiot, so what about this guy and the office of God Activities?"

"When he was press secretary for the President, he came out one day and told the media that the President had decided to make the Office of Religious Activities a cabinet-level position and would have a say in all major executive decision-making," Banks said, clearly delighted by it all. "Don't know how you missed it—

the Democrats went bonkers! The separation-of-church-and-state people started screaming from sea to shining sea. Man, it was wild for, like, three hours, and then the President comes on and says it was just a big lie and Orville Flicker made it up! And that made everybody even more nuts! Half the people thought the President put Flicker up to it just to judge the public reaction. But he swore up and down it was all Flicker's doing and next thing you know, Flicker's out of a job."

Remo was trying to catch up. He hadn't heard a word about this, but, then, the only TV he got to see was Spanish-language melodramas and even that wasn't by choice. "Okay, but what is he doing on TV now?"

"He's the MAEBE nominee for president, if you can believe that."

Remo looked at Chiun questioningly. Chiun shook his head. "I cannot explain this. I find *everything* about this nation's process of leader-choosing to be baffling."

"Here's the really bizarre part," Bang said. "He just might do it."

"No way," Remo said, watching the tall, scrawny man in the nerd glasses speak to the crowd.

"Yes way." Bang had stopped laughing. "I know shit about politics but I know popular opinion, and this MAEBE bunch has got a rocket engine strapped to it in the popularity poles. If they keep climbing like they have been, and if they can hold on to a good chunk of it, then that fuck Flicker'll do what Ross Perot only dreamed of."

Remo briefly considered what it would be like to have the skinny PR guy calling CURE's shots. "Not good," he announced.

"Not good at all," Bang agreed, and now his flabby face was a bulldog frown. "They're so right wing they'll outlaw half the lifestyles in San Francisco. No ifs, ands or maybes."

29

"I believe now would be an excellent time to call Emperor Smith," Chiun said.

"First things first." The tires squealed and Remo steered the rental car around a knot of fist-shaking pedestrians, ignoring them and putting his foot down as far as it would go.

"This is unwise."

"Everything I do is unwise, isn't it?" Remo felt the sinking of his entrails as the car shot over a rise and momentarily defeated gravity. The long street went straight downhill, with a number of rises designed to slow traffic that otherwise would have had a three-mile mountainside slide into the sea.

"When I said unwise I was being kind," Chiun insisted as they roared into the next rise.

"You? Kind?" They went over. "Never!"

The tires never left the pavement but the car was almost weightless for a few seconds, then descended heavily and the underside hit with a brief crunch.

"You'll kill the both of us!"

"What would the world be like without you?"

"Why are we in such a hurry? The killers will still be there when we get there."

"I don't want to take any chances!"

"If this meets your definition of 'not taking chances'—"

They went up again. They came down again.

"Pieces of the car are being left behind," Chiun shouted over the suddenly loud engine noise.

"They can't be too important. It's still going," Remo insisted.

"Have you considered they might be important if and when you decide to stop?"

Chiun was a master of balance, among other things, and he adjusted his body perfectly as the car dipped, roared and soared. Then it came down, and down, and kissed the pavement with a spray of sparks and a ripping of plastic body parts.

"I had daylight under them wheels that time, Little Father!"

"You're a lunatic!"

"You're a grouch. And you're supposed to be watching the street numbers. What are we at?"

"We're in the thirty-eight hundreds."

The tires squeaked and kept squeaking for ten seconds. The rental car, a three-week-old Saturn that had no future except to provide parts to other Saturns, skidded and vibrated and shuddered to an ugly stop.

Remo found himself alone in the front seat. He jumped out and discovered Chiun waiting twenty paces behind him.

"I had no desire to be a part of your spectacular finale."

"There's Griffin's headquarters," Remo said, jogging by Chiun fast. "Come on."

They heard the choked sound, not a scream, more like a sob that other ears would not have heard. It came from behind the glass of the storefront that had the legend Bruce Griffin, California State Representative.

Remo stopped. Chiun was surprised. Not that it made him falter as he, too, came to an immediate halt. He simply didn't understand what Remo was doing.

"Little Father, nobody dies. Got it? Nobody dies."

Chiun didn't get a chance to respond before Remo was bolting for the door and twisting off the door latch.

The metal knob made a short protest, but Remo didn't care. He slipped inside, finding himself in an empty reception area illuminated only by the light through the window. An eight-foot portable office wall blocked off the rest of the office. The sobbing came from behind it, as did the alarmed voices of people who wondered about the sound of the lock ripping apart. Remo went up and over the wall as if it were waist high and landed silently in the midst of the killing floor.

The sobbing sound came out of the woman on the

floor, but it was the last sound she was ever to make. Her gaze froze, surprised—Remo Williams's arrival was the last thing she would ever see. A face-up corpse sprawled beside her had once been a middle-aged man, and nearby was a police officer, sprawled on his face on the desk. Their throats had been cut.

"Messy," Remo commented to the trio prepared to spring on the intruder who would come in around the room divider. They all turned fast, fumbling into one another.

"Messy," Remo told the one who still wore his white mask. The others had removed the masks but still wore the now-familiar blacksuits and white gloves.

The man triggered the Uzi, but by the time the brain command reached his fingers the Uzi had gone missing. He relocated it as the hand grip inserted in his mouth, and the stock and barrel were bent around his head, tight.

The gunner's skull was wearing a new kind of hood, but it was steel and it was one size smaller than his head and part of it was gagging him. He clawed at the curled Uzi, then felt himself shoved. He slammed into the wall and crumpled, semiconscious.

Remo snatched the guns out of the hands of the other pair and shoved one man fast enough to spin him to the floor, which kept him occupied while Remo created handcuffs for his partner. The Uzi stock bent easily enough around the gunner's wrists, and the gunner stared at the results as his partner was lifted from the floor and given similar treatment.

CHIUN COULD HAVE BEEN a colorful ghost, for he seemed to glide rather than run, and the long skirts of his kimono hid most of his knobby legs. To the pair of blacksuited, white-hooded killers he came out of nowhere to appear in the narrow alley behind the politician's headquarters.

"Stop right there, Grandpa." Two machine guns pointed at his stomach.

"I am sorry, gentlemen."

"Sorry for what?"

"That I cannot kill you right away. You see, there is a pale piece of a pig's ear who has become quite bossy of late. If I kill you now, I will be forced to endure his complaints for days."

The gunners snorted through their white masks. "A batty old chink."

Chiun smiled. "Come with me, please."

He floated into their midst like a swan floating on the surface of a still pond, but came so fast they didn't have time to squeeze their triggers. The weapons lifted out of the gunners' hands and slid into the hands of the old man as if he had the assistance of invisible spirits. A moment later the four pieces of the two Uzis dropped to the pavement, and the gunners became prisoners of the old Asian man in the most embarrassing manner possible.

He was holding on to their earlobes, though the tiny

little man had to reach above his head to grasp them. The gunners felt hundreds of muscles clench in a head-to-toe spasm of agony.

"Please accompany me inside so that you may meet the pale piece of a pig's ear about which I was telling you."

The gunners felt as if they were in a state of living rigor mortis, but the pressure on their earlobes decreased, just slightly, and they were able to walk where the little man led them. He guided them to the narrow rear doorway to the politician's office, which stood open. The little man went through, but the gunners went into the brick wall on either side of the door.

"You are being uncooperative," Chiun admonished the two. "I may have to kill you after all."

The gunners found themselves maneuvered through the door, walking sideways. The pain emanating from the earlobes was so mind-boggling they didn't even notice the shattered facial bones.

THE FIVE THUGS WERE lined up on the floor, where they could stare at their handiwork. The man was the state representative Griffin. The woman was his assistant. The cop was just some cop who happened to get nosy at the wrong time.

"I want answers, I want them now and I want no dicking around. Who's your boss?"

There was stony-faced silence from the killers.

Remo moved from one man to another. He twisted

the Uzis a little tighter, and he pinched the wrists of the paralyzed pair from the alley.

The thrashing and screaming went on and on, and for the five killers their lives could be divided into two halves: the time before the pain and the time of pain.

"Raise your hand if you want me to make it stop," Remo called.

There were no words in all the screaming and shouting, and the only one of them physically capable of raising his hand was the one with the Uzi skull clamp. He managed to stop trying to pry the thing off long enough to shove his hand in the air.

"Okay," Remo said, and he loosened the Uzi just enough. The others also received a temporary reprieve. "Who's the leader of this band of idiots?"

"General Kough. Him in the middle."

"Okay, Kough, I'll ask you. Who do you take your orders from?"

"I never knew his real name," gasped the one named Kough.

"This is why you had me waste time not killing them? So you could ask them questions they cannot answer?" Chiun stood behind the line-up, irritated.

"You never know. Kough was never told the man's name, but that doesn't mean he can't make an intelligent guess. What about it, Kough? Ever have a hint about who your boss was?"

"No."

"Sure?"

General Kough wasn't exactly general material by most Army standards. He was whining. "Maybe!"

"Ah," Remo said. "Maybe?"

"Orville Flicker," the general admitted. "I heard his name a couple of times when I was on the phone with him, and once, when we met in person, his beard fell off. I got a good look at his face and I thought I recognized him. And he said we were a part of the great new movement in American politics. Then, when I saw him on TV today, I knew it was the same guy."

Remo grinned at Chiun. "See, Little Father? Now we're getting somewhere."

"So get on with it."

"Anything else you'd like to add?" Remo asked the general.

"I know a target—not one of our targets but another one. A big one."

"Let's hear it."

"I want a guarantee. I don't get killed."

Chiun frowned at the idea.

"We're assassins, pal. You want to make us look bad?"

"That's the deal—take it or leave it."

30

"I took the deal," Remo reported.

"Did you honor it?" Mark Howard asked hesitantly.

"Course. He'll live."

"Meaning?"

"Accident. He'll be a deaf-and-dumb quadriplegic. But he'll live. Better than he gave the senator and his assistant and some poor cop who happened to be in the neighborhood." A moment later Remo added, "Hello?"

"I'm still here," Mark said, feeling slightly queasy. He was no stranger to violence, but still, the ease with which the CURE enforcement arm did its job could be disturbing. "Give me the list of targets he provided before his accident."

There was rustle of the phone and a female voice in the background said something in a stilted voice like a badly acted hussy from a 1950s movie. "Sorry. Stewardess," Remo said. "Here's the list."

Mark Howard tapped out the names provided by Remo, and was disconcerted at the lack of activity on the screen. The Folcroft Four, the mainframes in the basement that handled the vast data-crunching activities for CURE, should have automatically sought out all available information on the names. It was a function they performed as a matter of course for any intelligence entered by Howard or Smith. Full profiles of the first names should have been assembling in background windows even as Howard was finishing entering the last of them.

Then he realized that the names were some of the names he had expected to see on the list, but so badly mangled, mispronounced and transposed that the ID routine wasn't matching them to their actual names. Howard sighed and rekeyed the names he recognized. Gerhard Slippers became Gerald Cypress, the mayor of one of the wealthiest coastal cities between San Francisco and Los Angeles. Lizette Gambino became Elizabeth Gamby, a high-profile judge in the Federal Circuit Court, based in Sacramento. Some of the others fell in place, but a couple of the names would take research to decipher. "Remo, I wish you would be more careful when gathering intelligence," Mark Howard said.

"Hi, Smitty."

"That was me talking. Mark."

"Are you the one with circulation or without? I can't keep you two straight anymore."

"This Dick Lard. Is there any chance the name was actually Richard Ladd?" Howard asked.

"Uh, maybe," Remo said uncertainly.

"Yes," said the high-pitched voice of Master Chiun in the background. Howard could never quite get used to the fact that whatever he said on the phone to either of them would be heard by the other if he was within a city block.

"Maybe I'll have Master Chiun begin reporting on your intelligence gathering," Howard sniped.

"I am not a clerk!" Chiun snapped.

"Hey, he's the one who makes me take down all my notes in Hangul characters anyway," Remo said. "I'm supposed to be learning better writing skills and English doesn't count."

"It would be extremely helpful if you would use English on those rare occasions that you gather information in the field," Howard said irritably.

"All right, Smitty, don't have a cow. Oh, sorry. It's Smitty the Poorer I'm talking to, isn't it?"

The toughest part of his job, Mark Howard decided for the umpteenth time, was staying on the mission track when dealing with Remo. And Chiun, for that matter. If he ever left CURE, he would be prepared to teach eight-graders.

The name Humbert Coleslaw, the last one on the list, clicked in Mark's head. "Herbert Whiteslaw."

"Remo Williams, actually."

"I'll call you back."

Mark Howard clicked off the connection to the aircraft phone and began frantically calling up everything he had on Senator Herbert Whiteslaw, D-CA.

A senator from California was important enough a

character, but Whiteslaw seemed an unlikely target for MAEBE. He wasn't up for reelection. There was no MAEBE candidate vying for his post. If MAEBE murdered him, the governor of the state would appoint a successor to fill his term and it wasn't too likely the successor would be from MAEBE.

But something was bothering Mark Howard about the name. It wasn't some psychic radio waves from space aliens, either. Some connection was there, something he couldn't quite get.

Then he got it.

"THAT WAS the greatest moment of my life!" Ed Kriidelfisk cried happily. "Those people loved us!"

"They did," Orville Flicker agreed, in the best of spirits. "We're going to make it, Ed. We're going to the top."

"Yes, sir! Nothing is going to stop us now. Man, what a great day!"

"It's only going to get better."

They sipped their champagne and rode in silence, basking in the glow of the press event. Buoyed by spiraling popularity, the MAEBE nomination for President had been greeted with wild applause. Even Ed Kriidelfisk, when he was introduced as man running for vice president alongside Flicker, was given a warm ovation, even if nobody knew who he was.

Flicker had made sure that everybody knew who Kriidelfisk was before the press conference was over, listing Kriidelfisk's long list of achievements and emphasizing his dedication to the cause of what was right and good. Kriidelfisk came across as a living saint.

"Where we headed?" Kriidelfisk asked as Kohd, Flicker's emotionless assistant, steered the long limousine off the highway and onto a side road.

"Into the pages of history." Flicker smiled and toasted Kriidelfisk, who wasn't sure what that meant and didn't really care. He'd go wherever Flicker wanted to take him.

When the car stopped in the middle of nowhere and the guns commenced firing, Ed Kriidelfisk had only a moment to realize that he had chosen the wrong set of coattails to ride upon.

"That's what you get, you blackmailing bastard," Flicker told Ed just before the cops arrived. Ed was beyond hearing.

Kohd held a sliver of glass and examined Flicker's face. "Where would you like it?"

Flicker traced a line across his jaw, where the scar wouldn't be visible all the time, wouldn't be repulsive, but where it could be brought into view with a proud lift of his head.

Kohd nodded and inserted the glass.

Dr. Harold W. Smith was taking a walk.

Every fiber in his being told him it was somehow wrong to be doing this thing, but his assistant, and his secretary, had ganged up on him, berated him, browbeat him and nagged him. Worse, they had pummeled him with logic.

"You need exercise," Mark Howard said.

"A walk at lunchtime does me a world of good," Mrs. Mikulka chimed in.

"You'll work better," Howard insisted.

Smith tried to downplay the advantages, but Howard fired back with encyclopedic research showing the link between exercise and improved mental performance.

"The last thing I have time to do in the middle of a crisis is go play eighteen holes," Smith had declared, hoping that would be the end of it and knowing it would not.

"Who said anything about playing golf?" Mark said. "You just need to walk."

"We have lovely grounds," Mrs. Mikulka said with a smile.

Smith wanted to reply that he had, in fact, seen the grounds of Folcroft a time or two in his several decades as director of the sanitarium. He had only one argument left to make, and, with the same gentle smile, Mrs. Mikulka shot that one down, too, before he even uttered it. "Besides, there's nothing that can happen that Mark can't handle while you're out."

Skillfully done, Smith thought. His secretary had challenged Smith to deny Mark's competency, which he could not do.

So Dr. Smith went for a walk, and he went the next day, and every day for a week.

His walks were enjoyable, he found. His legs felt a little stretched and sore and that was enjoyable, too. The fresh air felt good. He returned to the office reinvigorated.

But this day he returned to the office and found Mark

Howard waiting for him with a serious concern etched on his young face, and Smith knew the walks were a huge mistake. Not one, but two events occurred while he was gone, both requiring his attention.

"You should have paged me, Mark," he insisted.

Mark shook his head. "That would not have accomplished anything."

"I could have been at work on this sooner."

"Ten minutes sooner. And I was already at work on it. The Orville Flicker thing is still breaking. He says gunmen attacked the car not long after the press conference, drove them off the main highway and tried to gun them down. Ed Kriidelfisk was killed, Flicker was slightly injured."

"Kriidelfisk was the VP nominee," Smith considered aloud.

"But they must have been gunning for Flicker."

"Why?"

Howard stalled. "I am not sure. Lots of people have reasons."

Smith wasn't satisfied, but switched to the more immediate concern. "Where are Remo and Chiun headed?"

"They were en route to La Guardia. I'm having the plane land in D.C."

Smith looked at him.

"That is what you would have done," Mark explained.

Smith realized that it was. More alarming, however, was the realization that, in fact, CURE could get along without him for twenty minutes each afternoon. Not just get along, Mark Howard could actually function, make decisions, make *progress* without Smith. The concept had been dawning on him slowly in recent months, but it hit him now with extra force, and he wasn't quite sure how he felt about it.

He neatly tucked the thought into the endless file drawers in his mind and began going over the machinations Mark Howard had put in place to deviate the New York-bound flight to a landing in Washington, D.C.

31

"I fail to understand why this elected pretender is of consequence. To us, or to those with ambitions to the throne of the puppet President," Chiun said.

"Don't look at me. Junior started going on and on about committees in the Senate and I don't know what all," Remo said. "I gather this bunch of MAEBEs had got far-reaching plans to exercise control of Senate committees."

Chiun's parchment brow wrinkled. "For what purpose?"

"Make things happen." Remo shrugged. "They have to send a law through a committee of senators before it can go on to the floor and be voted by all the senators, I guess."

Chiun's eyes were hard with suspicion.

"I'm not making this up," Remo said.

"The big bunch of lawmakers deliberately divides itself into smaller bunches of lawmakers to vote on laws before the big bunch votes on laws?"

"I think that's how it works," Remo said, steering the SUV through D.C. traffic.

"You're a liar, Remo Williams!"

"I'm not lying."

"You can't be telling the truth. It is ridiculous!"

"It's the political system, I guess."

"It is not a system but a bureaucratic morass!"

"Can't disagree with you there."

"This nation never ceases to amaze me with its stupidity. Even the Chinese have a less convoluted government—and I am beginning to think one with a smaller population of degenerates, thieves, and bribe-takers."

"Also, there's some bad blood between Senator Coleslaw and Flicker," Remo said. "Believe it or not, that guy had a lot of power when he was press secretary. I guess he was a thorn in the senator's side and vice versa. Senator Coleslaw—"

"Whiteslaw," Chiun corrected.

"Senator Whatsislaw told the press he's gonna introduce a bill that will change the elections process just enough to roadblock MAEBE."

Remo parked the car eight doors down from the canopy over the sidewalk that advertised Daryl's On Durham Street.

"Why would the other senators allow the upstarts into their committees?" Chiun demanded, not letting up on the earlier ludicrousness.

"Guess they'd have to if there were enough MAEBEs," Remo said. "Otherwise, the MAEBEs would fight everything the Democraps and Republi-craps did. I guess it's a part of the checks and balances."

After a long moment, Chiun shook his ancient skull shortly. "Fah! This democratic system is even more asi-nine than even I had imagined, or your knowledge is flawed, or both."

"Never said I was an expert," Remo answered, his concentration on the faces of the guests entering and leaving the restaurant. "I'm basing all this on what I re-member from high-school civics class."

"What is amazing is that you've blundered along like this and not been annihilated after 230 years."

"Sometimes it seems that long to me, too, Little Fa-ther," Remo answered mechanically.

"Not you, this nation of yours."

"Uh-huh."

"It needs a leader—and not one of those clownlike elected pretenders."

"They're not all that bad."

"Name a good one—from your lifetime!"

Remo was watching the restaurant.

"Well?" Chiun demanded.

"I'll think of one eventually."

"You thinking about anything could take another presidential pretender's term. Meanwhile I shall take ac-tion to preserve and enhance this undeserving nation," Chiun announced quietly.

"Not the marketing campaign again?"

Chiun said nothing, and Remo wasn't sure if it was

in his best interest to get involved or steer clear. He saw a huge truckload of annoyance spilled on either road he decided to go down, and he had other worries. "There's Senator Whatlaw."

"Whiteslaw," Chiun corrected impatiently.

"Real effective bunch of Secret Service he's got working with him," Remo noted. He turned to glimpse an armored stretch limo approaching from behind their rental. The senator's ride was a rolling cliché of black paint and dark windows. The driver was a stony-faced Secret Service agent in dark glasses and an earpiece.

Remo frowned.

Chiun glanced at him, then returned to watching the entourage as the agent performed a quick electronic scan of the interior and a pair of agents circled the limo in opposite directions with their handheld devices.

"What is bothering you?"

"I don't know," Remo said.

"The driver?"

"I don't think so."

Chiun was the one frowning now. For all his berating of his pupil, Chiun knew that, in fact, Remo had the second-sharpest set of eyes on Earth. Sometimes sharp eyes, and other heightened senses, picked up minuscule scraps of information that were difficult to identify immediately.

"Was there something wrong with the car?" Chiun demanded.

"Maybe, Little Father."

Remo watched the driver go through a high-level security check. Although the driver was likely a part of the same Secret Service group and well-known to the others, he was still questioned and required to provide his fingerprint. If the driver checked out, and if he was worth his paycheck, he would have stayed in the car and alert while the senator was inside having lunch. It was unlikely the car could have been sabotaged.

"Even if there was a trap their tricorders should find a bomb or anything," Remo remarked.

"Fah!" Chiun said. He had little faith in technology of any kind.

What was it? Remo couldn't put his finger on what was itching him. Had there been something wrong when he glimpsed the driver?

The limo pulled into traffic and Remo followed at a distance. The plan was to make their presence known to the senator when he was at his office, then hang out and watch what happened.

Remo was now worried about what would happen before they even reached the office. He kept seeing the brief video clip of the Senator's limo replay in his head. What was wrong with that picture?

Remo Williams knew he was no mental giant, but he also was pretty sure he wasn't the dull blade that certain over-the-hill Koreans said he was. He never claimed to have a photographic memory. But he kept seeing that glimpse. The driver. Damn—every time he pictured the driver again, the man morphed a little more into Tommy Lee Jones from the *Men In Black* movie poster.

He gave up on the driver.

Only then did he remember the car.

What kind of car was that? A Lincoln? What kind of an ornament had been on the reinforced grille? Now, hadn't that ornament been a little too blobby to make a good car company insignia?

"Shit!"

"Done thinking?" Chiun asked.

"Me done thinking. Now me go driving."

"Not again," Chiun protested, but Remo stomped on the gas and sent the rental swerving through the heaving D.C. traffic. He closed only half the distance to the limo when the traffic locked him in.

"There is something to be said for urban congestion," Chiun commented.

"There's something on the grille," Remo said, holding up his fingers in a loop the size of a quarter. "Like maybe a plastique button or something like that."

"Even I know a thing so small cannot boom the senator through the hard shell of the car," Chiun said.

"I don't get it, either, but it's something." Remo lifted his upper body out of the rental to see over the stopped traffic. The senator's limo was near the front of the line at a traffic light. Nobody else seemed interested—federal government limos were a dime a dozen on the streets of D.C.

The traffic was heavy. Remo knew he wasn't going to catch up to the senator anytime soon in his SUV.

"Come on." He got out and began weaving through the stopped cars, skimming over the pavement, keeping himself out of sight while attempting to monitor the limousine and every other car and pedestrian in the vicinity, looking for someone who was also interested in the senator. He wondered if he was overreacting. What if the blob on the grille of the limousine turned out to be mud? Or pigeon fudge? Chiun would never let him hear the end of it.

Damn! He hated this sneaking-around kind of stuff.

The light changed and traffic began flowing. Remo followed on foot, ignoring the honking behind him from the drivers stuck behind his rental. Chiun was on the streets, as well, glimpsed like a phantom's shadow on the far side of the street as they glided after the limo, off the main artery and onto a four-lane street lined on both sides with storefronts. Traffic was much lighter and the curbs were solid with parked vehicles.

Good place for an ambush, Remo thought, and a moment later the ambush commenced.

It was a smelly affair. There was a brief flash of light from the front end of the limo, then Remo smelled smoke, and the smoke became noxious. He slowed his breathing as the vapor turned into airborne acid.

He saw the plan now. Of course it didn't need to be a big explosive. Just enough to flush out the prey. The limousine screeched to a stop and doors burst open on both sides. Remo rushed into the street and grabbed the hacking Secret Service agent who had collapsed half in, half out. Remo dragged him free of the limo and sent him rolling across the sidewalk. Pedestrians were fleeing the gas on foot.

Remo inserted himself in the limo and found a pile of bodies on the floor, three choking agents atop the choking senator.

Remo had enough breath for a quick sarcastic comment. "Good plan," he told the agents as he shoved them off. "Suffocate the man when he's already short on breathable air."

The white sedan slowed alongside the open limo doors as Remo unearthed the senator. The driver's window opened. Remo saw a man in black, with a white ski mask and a white hood. The man smiled and dropped something on the pavement.

Remo might have had time to extricate himself from the car and get to the grenade—but not without shoving agents out of his way with deadly force, he decided. Instead he twisted himself and the senator out of the open door on the opposite side, and he felt the pressure waves coming at him. Too fast. There had to have been a one-second fuse on the device. There was no time to get himself and the others to real safety.

The blast engulfed them.

32

The senator from California found himself on the sidewalk, finally able to breathe again despite the smoke from the limo.

"My feet hurt."

"I bet they do."

"What happened?"

"They tricked you into opening the doors. If you'd have kept them closed, the grenade wouldn't have hurt anybody."

Senator Herbert Whiteslaw's feet hurt so much he had to see what was wrong with them, despite the vivid scene in front of him. He looked down, was dizzy for a moment and found himself looking at two black things in an inflatable children's swimming pool. The black things were his feet. He was sitting on a plastic chair in front of a small hardware store. The glass storefront had blown inward and left the kiddie pool undamaged.

"Sorry. I didn't have time to get you fully under cover."

"Who are you?" the senator asked the man who, he realized, had just departed, fast.

The man was back in a moment with a Secret Service agent. The agent was burned, as well, more extensively but not seriously, it seemed. The agent rolled his eyes in relief when the man sat him down in the children's pool.

"Who are you?" the senator asked again.

The man was gone again. The senator remembered dark eyes. Not the eyes of a man who saved people, when he thought about it, but cruel eyes. Appearances were deceiving, he decided, and by then the man was back again. The driver in his arms, who was a massive brute of an agent who had chosen the service after his pro wrestling career fizzled, was being carried without effort. His body was limp and his suit was smoldering.

"Is he dead?" the senator asked.

"No, just bonked his head." The ex-wrestler was placed in the pool with his head leaning against the inflated palm tree that emerged from one end.

"Don't let him drown," the man instructed the other agent and the senator. On the next trip he carried another limp figure, burned superficially across his entire back. When he was placed in the kiddie pool the water sloshed out over the top.

"We'll need another pool," the conscious agent observed stupidly.

"No, we won't," said Remo.

"There's more agents," the agent insisted.

"There's not," Remo said. "Not anymore."

HE'D DONE all he could. Remo strolled down to the end of the block, ignoring the senator's questions, to where the white sedan was parked. There were crowds a few hundred feet away, but the rumors of a gas attack were keeping them at a distance for now. Sirens were approaching.

"What do we have here?" Remo asked.

"A nothing," Chiun explained. "A worm or a snail or some other low level of life-form."

Chiun stood alongside the car, which had a dead man in the passenger seat and a wide-eyed paralyzed man at the wheel. The paralyzed man sought mercy from Remo Williams.

"He is the boom dropper," Chiun explained, not looking at the driver.

"And the sidekick?"

"He is the foul talker. You should have heard his language."

"I won't swear, I swear," the driver whined.

"Hope you've got something to tell me," Remo said, "such, as, where's the rest of the guys?"

"Guys?"

"You know. The guys. Your buds. The rest of the gang. We've shut down White Hand cells in Chicago and Colorado and San Fran and those losers in Kansas. There's always a bunch of you."

"There was just the two of us for the D.C. job."

"Bulldookey."

"It isn't bulldookey," the driver cried, rolling his eyes like a beaten dog.

"Little Father, did you hear what he just said?"

"Yes."

"I said bulldookey! Just like you!"

"I'm allowed."

"It's not a swear word!"

"It means 'motherfucker' in Korean," Remo explained.

The driver's head was flopping around in panic and he even made an attempt to shift the car into Drive with his teeth, which toppled him on the steering wheel.

"Company's coming," Remo pointed out as the first squad car came around the corner, siren screaming, and braked fast. The officers jumped out of the vehicle and aimed their weapons at Remo and Chiun.

"Don't shoot. They saved us." It was the senator on the lawn chair. The cops got a good look at the blackened bodies in the kiddie pool and they boggled.

"I shall kill this one and we may be on our way," Chiun announced for the driver's benefit. The driver, now trapped in place staring at the remains of his former partner, started talking.

THE COPS TRIED to figure out what to do, until the Secret Service arrived and tried to figure out what to do, but the Service looked more intimidating during their decision-making process. Finally the ambulances began pouring in and the EMTs more or less took over, stabilizing the burn victims. The Walter Reed ambulance took the senator, with two high-ranking Secret Service agents insisting on coming along. The phone call came in as soon as the doors closed.

"Spacey," answered the more senior agent, then he nodded to his partner. "HSCC with the CO."

"Okay."

For the HSCC—High Security Conference Call— the two agents dialed their phones into a security system that took them through the highest level of electronic screening and encryption. When it was all done their commanding agent was back on the line.

"Agent Spacey, Agent Nor?"

"Yes, sir."

"The next voice you hear will be the President's. Understood?"

"Yes, sir."

The next voice they heard was the President's, and the President gave a very strange set of instructions.

It would have been a big joke except for two things. One, Secret Service agents never, ever joked. Two, the encryption of the phone call was reserved for the highest-security concerns.

They looked at each other. This was a waste of effort since Secret Service agents never, ever showed emotion and, if they accidentally one day showed a twinge of emotion in the call of duty, the sunglasses were there to mask it.

Then Spacey and Nor looked around the interior of the ambulance. It was a big ambulance, but still crowded with the senator, the EMT and the two agents. The President had said there was someone else there. Well, he was the President, but it seemed unlikely that there would be a fifth person present without their knowing.

"Here I am," said the fifth man, who now stood at Spacey's elbow.

Spacey and Nor were so surprised that their expressions betrayed it. Spacey's eyebrow twitched. Nor blinked three times very fast.

"Whoa, guys, don't get all freaked out on me now," said the fifth man. "I don't think the commander in chief is done commanding."

Spacey and Nor put the phones back to their ears and, exercising their extensive training, managed to regain their emotionless demeanor.

"Yes, sir. Sir? Yes, sir."

The senator opened his eyes when the agent tapped his shoulder. "For you, Senator Whiteslaw," Spacey explained. "It's the President."

Whiteslaw took Spacey's cell phone. Nor handed his to the fifth man, whom the senator was surprised to see, and was more surprised to recognize.

"Yes, Mr. President," he answered, distracted by the dark-eyed, dark-haired man.

"Wait a moment, Senator," the President said.

"Here," Spacey called to the driver, and the ambulance pulled to the curb. Spacey and Nor opened the rear doors, which finally alerted the EMT to the strange go-ings-on and dragged his attention away from the elec-tronic displays that were constantly taking the senator's vitals. The EMT saw sunlight streaming in.

"What in blazes are you doing?"

"Going to get drunk and forget the whole thing," Spacey reported in a monotone.

"As ordered," Nor tacked on

"You're coming with us," Spacey added.

"You were *ordered* to get drunk?" the EMT demanded.

"As were you."

"Bye," said Remo Williams as the EMT was man-handled out of the ambulance.

"Bennigans? *This* is where you Secrets go when you wanna get schnockered?" the EMT cried. "That ex-plains a lot!"

The doors slammed and the ambulance started moving again. Senator Whiteslaw got on the mobile phone.

"Yes, Mr. President?"

Remo was supposed to be in on the call, but he and mobile phones were sworn enemies. This phone had a little TV screen that showed an animated scene of au-tumn leaves—he wouldn't begin to know how to make the thing work. He gingerly put the phone through the slot in the wall-mounted container labeled Danger Of Biological Contamination.

The senator was getting flustered. "You must be jok-ing, Mr. President."

Remo had his opinions about the current man in the White House, but he didn't think of the guy as a joker. When he thought of joking presidents he thought of that Democrat two-termer from the 1990s. Now *that* guy came up with some real knee-slappers.

"Of course, Mr. President," the senator said. "Yes. Of course."

The senator hung up, and his gaze turned to the dark-eyed man. "Your name is Remo, and I guess you saved my life only to put it in jeopardy again."

"Nothing personal, Senator."

"Think you can keep me from dying twice in one day?"

"I'll do my best."

"How good is that?"

Remo shrugged.

But Whiteslaw already knew, because he had seen Remo in action, and it was something he would never, ever forget. Another interesting factoid, a guess but almost a certainty, was that saving lives was not what Remo was trained for. Quite the contrary.

Which made the man whose name was Remo a very interesting person indeed.

33

The blue phone rang, and Smith put it on speaker for Mark's benefit. The two executive-level employees of CURE had been discussing strategy, and getting nowhere.

"Remo?"

"Good afternoon, Emperor Smith," sang the lilting voice from the speaker. It was a voice like a cherry blossom floating on the breeze. Smith instinctively distracted it.

"Yes, Master Chiun, is there a problem?"

"Of course not, Emperor. This undertaking is well in hand."

Smith knew Chiun was likely uninformed as to what the undertaking actually was, and likely didn't care outside his own duties in the matter. How he could therefore assure them that it was "well in hand"...?

"I have a matter to discuss with you. I hear the young Prince Regent with you—it is good for you both to listen to my proposal."

Mark smirked. He hadn't said a word. Could Chiun hear him breathing over the phone? Or had he simply assumed from the sound of the speakerphone that Smith had company?

"Master Chiun, you are en route to the senator's office, are you not?" Smith asked. "You must be about to arrive. I don't know if this is the best time to discuss unrelated matters."

"One moment, Emperor," Chiun said pleasantly. They heard the phone become muffled, and Chiun was speaking to someone else. "Driver! How soon do we arrive at the bureaucrat's lair?"

A woman's voice said, "I have a name, you—" There was a yelp. Smith closed his eyes. The woman said, "ETA six minutes, sir."

"The hospital chauffeur reports we are still twelve minutes from our destination, Emperor," Chiun said into the phone, the embodiment of graciousness. "There is time for this, and you must agree we have delayed it long enough."

Smith frowned, and realized that Chiun had been attempting to draw him into this conversation in the past few days. Not exactly a long time. "Proceed, Master Chiun," Dr. Smith said reluctantly, hoping this wasn't going to be a ploy to renegotiate their contract.

"It is in regards to the current assignment."

"It is?" Smith asked. "How?"

"Pertaining to this upstart alliance of politicians and their hired killers—it is my belief that they pose a unique threat to CURE."

Smith didn't know what to make of this. Why hadn't Chiun made this clear to him from the outset? What did Chiun know? "Please explain, Master Chiun."

"It is possible that this mob of MAEBEs could lead ultimately to the demise of our organization," Chiun restated.

"How?"

"Through superior marketing, good Emperor."

Smith said, "Marketing?"

"But I have devised a scheme to halt the hemorrhaging."

"What hemorrhaging and marketing are you referring to?"

"I have retained the services of a wonderful public-relations agent from the Windbag City."

"You did what?" Smith asked, aghast.

"She was the artisan who promoted the campaign by the late Governor Bryant to empty the jails for his own profit," Chiun explained with delight, while Smith's gray face became as pale as corpse flesh. Mark Howard hoped the old doctor wasn't about to have a heart attack. "She's a drunkard, of course, but obviously a genius. Look at the fairy tale that was connived in the state of Chicago—and this young genius convinced the people to believe it all. When her role in perpetrating this magnificent lie becomes known, her services will be in great demand—you must hire her at once or she will be snatched up by the tobacco makers."

Mark saw a slight tinge of healthy gray return to Dr.

Smith's flesh and he said cautiously, "So you have not hired her, Master Chiun?"

"I wired her funds to hold the option on her services. The option does expire soon, however."

Smith typed as he said, almost gently, "And what does she know at this point about the public-relations campaign you have devised?"

"Nothing. I will not put my trust in her until she is contracted to us—what if our competitor were to hire her and learn our intentions?"

"What competitor?" Smith demanded.

"As I explained, Emperor, I refer to this organization, MAEBE." Chiun's polite patience was waning. "These upstarts are doing what we do, are they not, flushing out the human waste in the governmental plumbing? Unlike us, they have elaborate plans to publicize their achievements and grow rich on the currency of public accolades. We must beat them to the punchball. You must come out of the closet, reveal yourself to the world, advertise your great successes. You will become magnificent in the eyes of the people, and this popularity will enable you to effortlessly take the Eagle Throne at last!"

Smith was simply staring at the speakerphone, and Mark Howard could see the man trying to organize the long list of responses he might have made to Chiun's sales pitch.

"Master Chiun," Dr. Smith began.

"Yes."

Mark Howard got to his feet. Smith looked at him. Howard paced the office fast.

"Master Chiun, I will consider your proposal," Smith said. "Say nothing to this marketing agent until I have issued my decree."

It was just the right response, noncommittal but enough to cut off the conversation, then and there.

"Proceed with the current assignment and report in when completed. I shall ponder the options."

"Yes, Emperor!" Chiun replied, clearly delighted.

Smith cut the line.

"What is it?" he asked Howard.

"Public relations. That's the angle we need. We have to beat them at their own game."

"Pardon me?"

"The whole MAEBE strategy is to take the high ground, while the White Hand wipes out corruption, right?" Howard asked. "But Chiun is right—it's all just a marketing campaign. They're creating an image for themselves. Let's ruin that image."

Smith frowned. "MAEBE politicians are riding on the public controversy created by White Hand activities without actually taking responsibility for them. I don't know that we have evidence enough to convince the public of MAEBE's culpability. What if we released our proof and the public didn't buy it, Mark? There would be a backlash, and MAEBE would come out ahead."

Mark nodded. "I agree. MAEBE has been too careful to keep its political and terrorist arms separate. But

I'm not talking about the White Hand at all. I'm suggesting we target the politicians."

"You want CURE to run negative campaign ads?" Smith asked incredulously.

"I want us to do what we always do—dig up dirt. Only we dig it up on the MAEBE candidates. They can't be as clean as they claim. If we find a closet skeleton that needs some extra dirt, we can massage it, make it look worse than it is."

"Lie?"

"Why not?"

"We'd be taking the low ground."

"Compared to letting Remo and Chiun kill them off one by one and risk making martyrs out of them?"

Smith nodded shortly. "You're right. Let's do it. Start putting together some press releases and incriminating evidence."

Howard grinned. "I'm on it."

Smith didn't smile. "I hope you're not going to charge me what Chiun is paying his PR agent in Chicago, just for a retainer." Smith tapped the screen. Mark leaned in to see the amount that Chiun had advanced on one of his alias credit cards, which were covered by the CURE operating budget.

"Criminy," Howard said. "I don't make that in a year."

He left for his own office.

34

"What is this place?" Chiun demanded as the ambulance rolled to a stop.

"The Old S.O.B.," the ambulance driver said, then caught herself as the child-sized Korean became as stern as a gathering thunderstorm. "That's what they call the building," she explained hastily. "The Old S.O.B."

Chiun did not know whether to believe her. He lowered the window, and the nearest of the ridiculous army of Secret Service agents tried not to respond to him.

"Please do not say you are attempting to look like mere pedestrians," Chiun announced stridently, so that he could be heard by everyone within fifty paces. "You are all quite inept at passing yourselves off as anything other than Secret Service agents."

The nearby agent was in a panic of indecision. The orders had been odd enough—offer protection for the arriving senator but under no circumstances interfere with him or any who accompanied him.

The agent decided anything was better than allowing the old man to continue blowing their cover. "Yes, sir, how can I assist you?" He spoke out of the side of his mouth, sidling up to the ambulance as if he were merely another pedestrian in a trench coat, wing tips, sunglasses and a radio earpiece.

"What is this building called?"

"It's the Russell Building," the agent answered, confused.

"I see," the old man said, his voice as brittle as ice.

"Wait!" the woman at the wheel called. "Tell him the nickname!"

Now the agent was more confused.

"Most everybody just calls it the Old Senate Office Building," said Senator Whiteslaw himself as he and a thin man emerged from the rear of the ambulance, which seemed to have opened in virtual silence. "They call it the Old S.O.B. for short."

"I see," the Asian man repeated, and stepped out of the ambulance cab with a last, cold glare at the driver.

Remo was holding the senator by the shoulder. Whiteslaw was getting his first close-up look at the small Asian figure who had accompanied his strange new bodyguard, Remo. The Asian looked as if he predated the Wright brothers, but he didn't show any sign of infirmity.

The old Asian proved his fitness by putting his scrawny, ancient arms around Whiteslaw's middle and lifting him, apparently without effort. Between the young assassin, and the old one—yes, Whiteslaw was convinced this one was an assassin as well—they had him almost completely off his feet and perfectly balanced. Whiteslaw went through the motions of walking; the truth was that if he put any more weight on the soles of his feet he would scream in pain. His soles had taken the brunt of the blast and ignited the leather of his shoes. Only Remo's quick action had snuffed them out.

The attack had put the media on alert. They had never dreamed the senator would put in a show at his office, but there were production crews working the steps anyway, getting reaction from other senators and their staff and trying to get more facts behind the blossoming rumors.

When the news crews saw the victim of the attack himself arriving back at work less than an hour after the attack, obviously wounded, his feet covered in hastily applied bandage wads and perched on the shoulders of two oddly dressed assistants, there were cries of journalistic ecstasy.

Two camera crews stampeded toward the senator, the correspondents and cameramen pushing and shoving one another until both crews ended up in a brawl in the gutter. They were closely followed by two more crews who were just as ambitious but marginally less self-destructive.

"Start rolling now," screeched a waif of a woman in a brilliant orange jacket three sizes too large. Her camera operator started up the camera while he was running, and he stumbled on a sidewalk crack. The waif wailed. The cameraman fumbled the heavy unit and saved himself from collapse by steering into one of the thirty or so pedestrians who just happened to all be wearing trench coats, sunglasses and radio earpieces. The pedestrian pretended the brutal collision hadn't happened and hobbled away whistling, apparently admiring the architecture, while the cameraman started taping.

The correspondent composed herself, then spoke in a deadly serious cockney accent. "This is Sandra Chattersworthy at the Old Senate Building—"

"This is Derek Mueller in Washington D.C.," boomed the correspondent from a competing crew, drowning out the tiny woman. "Here on the steps of the Old Senate Office Building a brave man, Senator Herbert Whiteslaw—"

That was as far as he got before the small woman ran up and screeched at his chest, directly into his handheld microphone. The cameraman ripped off his headset and nearly lost his equipment as he danced with his hands to his ears.

"British bitch!" bellowed the big correspondent.

"American swine!"

"Hello? Hello? Oh, God, I'm deaf!" The mortified cameraman looked as if he were trying to crush his own head.

"Shut up and start shooting!"

The cameraman didn't hear him.

The big-mouthed correspondent roared in frustration and manhandled the camera off his debilitated cameraman, shoving it at a man in a trench coat who just happened to be standing around.

"Point this in my direction for thirty seconds and I'll pay you a thousand dollars."

The man in the trench coat pretended not to see him. "Asshole!"

"I'll do it." A passing construction worker, with a mortar trowel dangling from a loop on his overalls, took the camera. "Thousand bucks, right?"

"Yes, just start shooting—oh, shit!" The correspondent had lost his subject matter. The wounded senator had not stood around and waited. He was near to entering the Old S.O.B., and the limey pixie with the fingernails-on-chalkboard voice was doing her report!

"Come on!" The correspondent went at the British woman in a crouch, changed his mind at the last second and steered into her equipment assistant. The man made a croak of dismay as he toppled, his video camera landing hard enough to produce several shattering sounds.

"You miserable worm!"

Orville Flicker watched it all, live, his own cameraman getting it all on a digital camcorder with an uplink through a mobile broadband connection. Flicker's cameraman was just some kid from a community college, hired for a one-time job and instructed to keep his distance. Still, the banshee voice of the tiny British woman came through clear enough to vibrate Flicker's water glass.

Despite the screaming, the big correspondent positioned himself where the slow-moving senator would pass within the shot. The blue-collar man in the overalls jogged up and pointed the camera.

"Where did that son of a bitch come from?" Flicker demanded.

His assistant, Noah Kohd, talking on two mobile phones at once, started to answer.

"Shush!" Flicker said. "Where the hell is Rubin?"

"On his—" Kohd said.

"Oh, no." Flicker turned up the sound on one of the news feeds. "We're going live now to the our correspondent at the Old Senate Office Building...."

"This will ruin everything," Flicker complained through grinding teeth. "Whiteslaw can't be a media darling—he can't!"

"Under control, sir," Kohd said.

"Under control? Under control?" Flicker felt the pressure in his head become so great he thought his skull would open up violently.

"There, sir," Kohd said.

On the screen from his own video feed, Kohd saw the bricklayer with the video camera sprint away, taking the camera with him. The little British woman brayed viciously and hysterically. The big correspondent stood there for a long moment, not believing what he was seeing, then burst into sobs.

"In your miserable American face!" the British woman shrieked.

The sobbing man snatched her up by the neck while the senator and his escort entered the building unhurriedly. The Secret Service agents stood around acting as if there were nothing out of the ordinary taking place.

Flicker couldn't believe his luck. "Thank you, God," he breathed, going limp into a leather chair. They had just avoided a catastrophe.

"I hired him," Kohd said simply, nodding at the video feed. "The bricklayer. Paid him ten grand to disrupt the reporting."

Flicker nodded. "I see. Good move."

"No problem." Kohd was calm, unsmiling. He was always calm and unsmiling, one hundred percent of the time. He could have been a Secret Service agent.

Kohd was darn competent, as well. If tape of Whiteslaw hobbling bravely into his office had made it onto the networks, the senator would have become a hero. That would make him untouchable; killing a hero only strengthened the hero's cause.

Whiteslaw had gone from a thorn in the side of Orville Flicker to a poison pill. He was the man who could neuter MAEBE.

He had to die and he had to die today—before people started liking him for all the wrong reasons.

"Where's Rubin?"

"En route," Kohd said.

"Why wasn't he there to intercept Whiteslaw?"

"Rush-hour traffic. He'll be there in ten. They'll be staged for an assault within fifteen. Mr. Flicker?" Kohd nodded at one of the monitors, where the senator's ugly face floated over the left shoulder of a female news anchor.

Flicker unmuted it. The anchor was a blond, benign woman whom Flicker knew from his White House days.

She had failed to succumb to his charms. When he was President, that bitch would be one of the first to go on the blacklist.

She started talking about a press conference.

"...on the steps of the Old Senate Office Building in one hour."

"Those bastards. They're taunting me."

"Sir?" Kohd asked. He had just one phone against his head, which was about as much attention as he ever gave anyone.

"Look at all those Secrets around there. They didn't lift a finger. This whole scene was staged to draw us out. We didn't bite so they'll try it again, in the same damn place, just to make it convenient."

"Perhaps, sir. Another wrinkle has come to our attention, sir. The pair that escorted the senator inside? They match the descriptions we have from our losses in recent days. Chicago, Colorado, San Fran and today."

Orville Flicker became very nervous then, and began going back and forth over the video, which he had saved to his hard drive. He had been so worried about the reporters he had not paid much attention to the senator.

Over and over he replayed the footage of Senator Herbert Whiteslaw being assisted from the ambulance and walking slowly through the media turmoil and into the building. The senator's face was perfectly focused through much of the footage, and yet the faces of the men on either side of him were a blur the entire time.

"Electronic interference?" Flicker asked.

Kohd shook his head. "Creating a perfectly localized visual distortion? Never heard of such a thing."

"But it could be, right?"

"I'd say you're grasping at straws, but what else could it be?" Kohd clearly believed it *was* something else.

Flicker shook his head slightly, his insides growing colder. He was thinking back to the chaos he had witnessed at the Governor Bryant assassination. There were men who moved like flickering light, neutralizing his sniper and every other man in his Midwest cell in just seconds. Flicker was taunted on the radio by someone, and then there had been the glimpse of a brightly colored wraith drifting across the auditorium, searching for him. Could the wraith had been a man in a kimono, of all things?

Of course it could. Once you accepted the notion of a human being who floated with the speed of a shadow, why not put him in a kimono?

Even without a visible face it was clear enough on the video feed that one of the men assisting the wounded senator was a man in a long, golden robe with multicolored stitching. The other man was dressed just as unexpectedly, when you considered that he should have been a Secret Service agent. The man was in a T-shirt, of all things, and casual slacks.

Just minutes ago the worst enemy to his future had been a senator with an old grudge and a new bill. Now it was something new—these two.

"They are very special agents of some kind," Flicker said. "How come I never knew about them? The President told me almost everything."

"Maybe the President doesn't know about them himself."

"They've got presidential backing now. You've got to throw a hell of a lot of weight around to get the Service to fall in line. Only the President's got that kind of muscle. Unless—they're Secrets themselves."

"Considering the duty they're pulling, that makes sense," Kohd stated. "A clandestine branch specifically for protecting the politicians in high-risk security situations. But their purview must include investigative duties. And assassination."

"Yes," Flicker said, staring at the blur of a face on a bizarre, short body in its colorful robe. The hands of the man were in focus, and they were wrinkled with age.

"Assassination is illegal," Kohd added. He was feeling uncomfortable. Flicker didn't notice. Kohd was uncomfortable because of the look he was seeing on his boss's face—a sort of excitement. Kohd added, "If they are what we think, these men represent an officially sanctioned but blatantly unconstitutional federal entity."

"Almost certainly with presidential knowledge and backing," Flicker said, smiling like a teenaged boy watching his girlfriend get naked. "They're my ace in the hole."

"Sir?" Kohd wasn't following and wasn't sure he wanted to.

"Call the airport. We're going to D.C."

35

Harold Smith lifted the red phone. "Yes, sir?"

"Smith, I just got a call from my old press manager, Orville Flicker," said the President of the United States.

"Really?"

"He's on his way to D.C."

"I see."

"He'd like to meet with me. He made some veiled threats."

"Such as?"

"He said he knows about my assassins, Smith. Says he'd like to talk it over before he goes public."

"I see."

"Excuse me, are you listening? If that little twerp exposes CURE, I'm finished! My administration will experience the fastest impeachment of all time!"

"It's under control, Mr. President. We know what evidence he has, and it's useless."

"But he knows something, Smith," the President insisted. "He might use it. He knows how to get attention."

"He knows nothing, Mr. President," Dr. Smith assured him. "Mr. Flicker is only making an educated guess, and he will not use it. After tonight, I believe, he will have no credibility left."

Smith, without a second thought, hung up on the President and replayed the videotape on his screen. Mark Howard had just finished working with a digital video stream they had intercepted feeding into the Flicker residence in Dallas.

Mark's changes were expertly done. Smith couldn't see the editing.

Still, there was much about this exercise that made him feel grim, and angry.

36

"I dig your threads, man," Remo said with genuine pleasure.

"Fah!" Chiun snapped.

"But it's the shades what make the suit."

"Leave me be, idiot!"

The senator was looking from one to the other, unable to come to terms with this pair of, well, whatever they were. They had squabbled like siblings ever since the old one was informed he needed to dress like an agent from the Service.

"Never! Not for all the gold under Fort Knox!"

The young one, Remo, finally convinced the old one to wear a dark suit jacket and dark glasses over his robe, which was obviously a traditional Asian garment of some kind.

"How will I see the projectiles with my vision obscured?" the old man demanded.

"You can take them off as soon as we get to the

podium," Remo told him. "Nobody will be looking at you then, anyway."

The senator had his doubts about that. The old man, whose name he couldn't quite get his tongue around, was an unusual sight, and the jacket didn't disguise much of his unusualness. Everything else aside, he was a head shorter than any Service agent in history.

"We're ten minutes late—we ready or not?" demanded the senator's executive assistant, who served as his press secretary.

"I'm ready," Remo declared, folding his hands in front of him in a standard Service pose. "You ready, Little Father?"

The Asian made the sound of a striking cobra.

"He's ready," Remo told the assistant.

"I was asking the senator!"

"Oh. You ready, Senator?"

"Yes," he said to Remo, caught himself and said "Yes," to his assistant. She went to announce him, muttering.

"You must fire that woman," the Asian man instructed Whiteslaw. "She called us names."

"She'd divorce me if I fired her."

They emerged from the front doors of the Old S.O.B. The media was everywhere. The public cheered the elected official who had been attacked so heroically.

The senator was still being supported by the men as he walked, and they transported him with minimal fuss and without effort, as far as he could tell. They were scanning the crowd, and the sunglasses were lifted off their eyes the moment that all three of them came to stop at the oversized podium.

Whiteslaw was sweating under thick armor, but his head was entirely exposed. He still didn't quite understand how he was supposed to be protected in the event of a head shot from a sniper. He hoped he wasn't going to regret this....

Before the senator even opened his mouth the first shot was fired. Whiteslaw's first indication was when his vision was obscured. Somebody had put a big piece of metal in front of his face and before he could think it over there was a heavy metallic crunch, followed a second later by the sound of the shot.

Somebody had just fired a sniper rifle, right at his head, and the one called Remo had shielded him with a piece of armor plating that looked as if it had been literally ripped from under the body panels of one of the Service's armored cars. There were pieces of the electronic door latch dangling from it.

Next thing the senator knew, he was stuffed into the podium's hollow and the inch-thick steel door was slammed in his face. He was in darkness.

RUBIN SWORE. Of all the dumb luck. They had to have guessed the sniper would fire the moment the Senator was in place, which meant they knew that the intent was to keep Whiteslaw from appearing on the media. Well, so far the news had nothing more than a few shots of him walking to the microphone, but the man was still alive, and conveniently trapped by his own bodyguards inside the armored shell of the podium.

General Rubin smirked at the foolishness of that act. The podium would be Senator Whiteslaw's coffin.

"Move in," he snapped into his radio and saw his four men push through the crowds of onlookers. Their attack came only heartbeats after the failed sniper bullet, and the Service was too slow. In fact, the Service seemed to be keeping to the fringes.

The pair in the middle were the ones who mattered, anyway. Rubin didn't know who they were, but according to his boss their deaths were just as important as that of the senator. Thanks to the new hardware his men was using, their deaths were a sure thing. No more machine guns. They had sawed-off combat shotguns, with a wide, deadly spread.

Rubin's men shoved their way into the open and targeted the podium pair, but for some reason there were no sounds of gunfire. Where were the shotgun blasts?

General Rubin of the White Hand had an unobscured view of the action. What he saw was the pair from the podium moving among his men like darting birds, snatching shotguns like worms. The shotguns clattered on the walkway and, like worms, they were now curved and bent. Useless.

The gunners were going for their backup weapons, but were demolished before they freed any of them. Rubin saw the light, impossibly swift strokes and didn't trust his own eyes. It was too swift, like flashes of sunlight. The collapse of his four men was slow by comparison, and their precise wounds left Rubin with no doubts that they were dead.

How had this all gone so wrong so fast? Who were these two?

Whoever they were, they had no real cover. They wouldn't escape a sniper.

"Morton, take them out," Rubin said into his radio.

At that moment the pair turned and looked right at him, as if they had heard his voice.

"I'LL GET THAT GUY." Remo spotted the man who was coordinating the attack. He was ensconced in a portable electronic sound booth, where the media had been required to stage its retransmitting equipment. Equipment trucks had not been allowed anywhere near the press conference.

Remo stepped around an incoming .357 sniper round that would have disemboweled him. The bullet chopped a hole in the pavement and sent concrete shards raining against the armored podium that protected the senator from California.

"The long-range boomer must be eradicated first," Chiun declared. "Draw his fire."

Chiun vanished as the next sniper shot passed through the spot where his body had been, continuing into the building facade.

Missed one old S.O.B. and tagged another, Remo thought as he retreated, maneuvering away from the screaming crowds who had the good sense to panic and flee. The Secret Service agents were also taking cover in flocks. Orders were shouted. Agents started moving out. They could not have been less relevant to the goings-on.

Remo dodged more rounds, trying to look lucky instead of deliberate, but the man who was coordinating the attack knew something was going on. Remo was trapped where he was. He had to keep the sniper's attention until Chiun neutralized him, but he wouldn't want to lose the one doing the supervising.

The man in the equipment booth bolted, knocking a pair of cowering equipment operators into their equipment. Dammit, where was Chiun?

Remo's gaze shifted back to the nearby rooftop where the sniper crouched. A rainbow of gold swept across the roof and pounced on the gunman's position, then Chiun stood and waved. The gunner was history. The crowd could now panic in peace, without risk of taking sniper rounds.

Remo ran fast, vaulting over a concrete barricade and glimpsing the fleeing man, but the electronics booth blew apart before he touched down. He felt it coming and rolled, exhaling, absorbing the blast as it rolled overhead, then springing to his feet again. A glance showed him four or five bodies in the booth, but the real goal of the explosive was to ensure no further transmissions came from this place.

Remo Williams was sick and tired of it all. Perception and promotion and how leaders were marketed to the gullible masses. What sort of a sick bunch of idiots allowed their nation to roll on the rails of advertising in lieu of common sense? What had they come to when it was okay to blow up a handful of people to keep the wrong fucking commercial off the fucking television?

"You!"

He had his victim by the arm before the man even knew it, and Remo stopped. The man kept running and almost tore his own arm out by the socket.

"Let go of me!" General Rubin cried.

"I hate television," Remo told him.

"What?"

"Commercials and propaganda and promotions and sound bites and all that crap. I hate it!"

"Fine! Let go of me!"

Remo removed the 9 mm handgun from his victim's hand and squeezed the muzzle closed before dropping it. "I don't care if it's the nightly news. I don't care if it's the *Exciting Tomatoes*. It's all the same bullshit."

The man found his combat knife, finally, and tried to cut off the wrist of the hand, like an iron vise, that held him. Remo took the knife away, snapped it, dropped it. "Magazines, too. Billboards. Whatever. It's all crap and so are you."

"I'm not in marketing!" Rubin promised.

"Sure, you are. You just killed five innocent men, just to keep the competitor's commercial from going on the boob tube. You know what that makes you?"

"I'm just a soldier. Okay, I'm a murderer! Arrest me!"

"You're worse than a murderer," Remo told him, a

savage grimace on his face, a deadly cold in his eyes.
"You are an advertising executive."

"I'm not!"

"Do you know what I do to advertising executives?"

"I don't know and I don't want to know!"

"But I want to show you."

Remo showed General Rubin exactly what he did to
advertising executives.

37

"Hi, Smitty. Where's this guy Orville Flicker at right now?"

"Why do you ask?" Smith asked.

"I'm going to go kill him."

"We can't kill him. It will make him a martyr. We need to put an end to this movement entirely."

"You said that before. Now he's gone and wiped out a bunch more innocent people. Just some dopey techies standing around fiddling with their electronics. How many more people have got to get killed before it's enough?"

"Remo, Flicker may be just the tip of the iceberg. What if there are five more men capable of organizing the White Hand?"

"I'll kill them, too."

"Eventually, but first you'll have strengthened MAEBE by turning Flicker into a saint. The White Hand's activities will be further legitimized."

"Then what, Smitty? What do we do?"

"We're fighting back."

"Yeah, and a lot of good it's doing."

"Not you and Chiun," Smith said calmly. "Mark and I are playing the MAEBE game."

Remo frowned at Chiun, who was standing outside the phone booth watching the dirty wisps of smoke drifting up from the blast site in front of the Old Senate Office Building, three miles away from where they stood. Chiun shrugged in answer to the unasked question.

"We don't get it," Remo said.

"We're countermarketing," Smith said. "We're creating negative publicity for MAEBE. We're tarnishing their halos."

"You gonna save lives using press releases? I don't think so."

"Remo, I need you to understand what MAEBE is— a house of cards propped up on an image of purity. The public thinks MAEBE is squeaky clean while all around is corruption and unethical behavior. Do you see?"

"No."

"Their popularity skyrocketed in days, but if the public perception is ruined, then their popularity will fall just as fast. Think of MAEBE is a one-legged stool. We're starting to chip away at the leg, and we don't have to cut deep before it will collapse under its own weight."

REMO HUNG UP, irritably. Plastic chips scattered at his feet.

"Another phone assassinated by Remo, Destroyer of Public Utility Property."

"Shut up, Chiun." Remo marched into the street.

"Where are you off to?" Chiun asked, irked at having to catch up. Catching up was undignified.

Remo nodded at the Circuit City store in the nearby strip mall. "Going to watch some TV."

Dunklin County, Missouri

GEORGETTE REDSTONE looked at the printout. "It's a wire transfer."

"It's for ten grand," said her advertising manager.

"Is it legit?" Redstone asked.

"Yeah, I called First National. The money's in our account right now. They want us to start running it as soon as possible. You want to see the commercial?"

Georgette Redstone nodded. "This is too good to be true. Is it a white-power group or something?"

"It's a negative ad, for sure, but nothing out of bounds," said her ad manager. "Nothing we can't air."

Georgette knew her ad manager well enough to take his assessment with a grain of salt. The man would do anything to sell commercial time.

The wire transfer had come unexpectedly. In fact, nobody at the tiny rural television station had known about their good fortune until an e-mail arrived ordering the advertising time and asking the station to download the video from a remote server.

The commercial certainly wasn't well produced. The

narrator sounded digitized and cold. The graphics were second-rate. What Georgette Redstone found most intriguing about the ad was its subject matter.

"It's a negative ad about MAEBE?" she asked when it ended.

"Why not?" asked her advertising manager.

"I never heard anybody say anything bad about them before, that's all."

"George, it's ten grand for five one-minute spots," her ad sales manager said. "That's four times our rate. We can't turn this down."

Georgette shrugged. "Who's turning it down? Go run it."

THE AD RAN at the top of the hour in the rural southern counties of Missouri. Not many people were watching the local station in the middle of the afternoon, but Henry Nimby was one of them.

He was trying to come up with a local story for the following day's paper. He always tried to devote his front page to something local—otherwise, why buy a local paper? But not a lot happened around Dunklin County, and so far his top story was about the revived controversy about the use of Peanuts as the mascot for the Washington Carver High School teams. There was nothing racial about it, as some locals insisted. Black or white, seventeen-year-old football players did not enjoy being called Peanuts.

In protest the entire student body had adopted the

derogatory version of the nickname that had been used against them for years. They were calling themselves the Penises.

An interesting turn of events, Nimby thought, but the story lost a lot of its impact since he could not actually use the new, unofficial nickname in print. He couldn't even print it "p***s" or he'd have every grandmother in three counties calling to complain.

Without the story, though, he had an empty front page—until his good friend Georgette from the TV outlet called with a heads-up." Just watch and see," Georgette said. "In fifteen minutes you'll have tomorrow's front page, and you'll owe me a steak dinner."

Nimby was doubtful.

The commercial started out grainy and green, an image taken through night-vision enhancement, but the audio was good. You could hear every word, and just in case there were white captions at the bottom of the screen.

The police officer had his back to the camera, but the other one was recognizable, if you knew the guy. Everybody around these parts knew the guy. It was Joe Ronfeldt, running for one of the federal house seats.

"That's all I got," Joe said.

"Five thousand ain't enough to erase a DUI," said the voice of the faceless police officer. "I know you got a nice campaign fund going, Joe."

"Where do you think the five G came from? I can't take out any more. No way to hide it. I'm audited, you know."

There was an audible sigh. "Fine. I'll do it for five Gs. Call it my civic contribution."

The image froze on the face of Joe Ronfeldt, while the other half of the screen scrolled down to show a photocopy of the arrest report. It was a close-up, so you could read the report clearly and the image scrolled to show it all. "Two months ago he was arrested while driving under the influence, but the arrest report vanished from the police files," said the dramatic but digitized voice-over. "He is MAEBE Candidate Joe Ronfeldt. What else is he hiding?"

Henry Nimby had his front page, and it was well worth the price of a steak dinner for his good friend Georgette Redstone.

Portland, Oregon

"YOU RUN THAT AD one more time, and I'll sue you into bankruptcy," Andy Harris shouted.

"It's a political ad, Mr. Harris," said the station manager at the local ABC affiliate. "We're not responsible for the content."

"You are if it's untrue," Harris insisted.

"If it is untrue, then you can take steps to stop us from airing it."

"That will take days!" Harris said. "I'll be finished!"

"Mr. Harris," she said coolly, "maybe you should have thought of that before you snorted cocaine in front of a camcorder."

Harris slammed the phone. Smart-ass bitch.

Funny thing was, in all the times he'd used coke, he couldn't remember ever doing lines where somebody could have taped him. He was always careful. Also, he couldn't place the location he had just seen in the TV commercial. Somebody's living room that he didn't recognize.

But that sure was him, no denying it, bent over an ugly coffee table and vacuuming up white powder through a rolled-up five-dollar bill, then falling back on the couch with a wasted grin on his face. "BLEEP-ing good blow man!" He spoke right to the guy with the camcorder.

Bad judgment, Andy, he said to himself. He couldn't remember any of this. It really *must* have been some kick-ass blow. Well, there had been blackouts when he got into some good blow....

The phone rang and he closed his eyes as he picked it up. Please don't be Linda. Please don't be Linda.

It was Linda.

"I hope it was a good party, Andy, because it just cost you everything you have."

"Linda—"

"Your campaign, your deaconship and me. It's all gone. I hope it was a really fun party."

"Wait, Linda!"

She was gone.

"Who'd have thought drugs could fuck up your life so fast?" Andy asked his schnauzer. Andy didn't know what else to do, so he fished the little plastic bag out from behind his washing machine and started to cut a line.

The dog watched, happily wagging its tail, because it knew that as soon as its master did this odd thing, they would go out together and share a big sack of sliders.

Cleveland, Ohio

"I'M SCREWED," said the judge as the commercial faded and the station anchor came on, showing the same commercial and reporting it as news.

"You sure are," said the other judge.

"I never should have gone with MAEBE."

"What you never should have done," the other judge said unkindly, "is sleep with that girl. What is she, twenty?"

The judge didn't need to answer the question because the news anchor was telling them all about the student, an unidentified seventh-grader from Lincoln Junior High.

"You make me sick," said the other judge, and left the chambers.

More of the same would be coming his way, the judge knew. So much for reelection. He'd probably be disbarred. Maybe incarcerated. If he stayed out of jail—a big if—he had only one career option left.

He hated teaching, but it had its advantages. Just

think of all the bubble-headed young coeds who'd do anything for a passing grade.

Washington, D.C.

"DONALD LAMBLE SCORED a huge lift in the polls when he came out with controversial negative comments against the recently slain Governor Bryant," said the network anchor on the TV screen. "Lamble is also a key figure in the newly formed Morals and Ethics Behavior Establishment, the political party that came virtually out of nowhere to unite independent political candidates across the country. The revelation last hour has already sent Lamble's popularity plummeting. Preliminary BCN polls show him at his lowest level ever."

The anchor disappeared, and the screen showed a photocopy of student transcripts from Hemming Community College in Grievance, Minnesota.

"The revelation came this afternoon when newspapers and television stations throughout Lamble's state received couriered copies of Mr. Lamble's community college transcripts and student ID card," said the anchor's voice-over. "The transcripts show Mr. Lamble received poor-to-failing grades in all his classes except horticulture—this in the same semester in which he publicly claimed to have received a doctorate in political science from Montgomery College, a small private college near Minneapolis. Montgomery College, however, looks as if it was an invention, as no evidence has emerged to prove it ever even existed."

"That dude is out of work," said a teenager browsing the flat-screen TVs.

"I guess so," said Remo Williams.

"It has been a bad, bad day for the Morals and Ethics Behavior Establishment," commented the BCN commentator, a man known to rejoice in the misery of others. "Riding to the heights of glory on their claims of purity and incorruptibility, this party of newcomers has had mud splattered on its white dress. The previously unknown Truth-Be-Told Organization has hit MAEBE hard, across the country, leveling accusations of immoral, unethical and illegal behavior on the part of fourteen MAEBE politicians and counting. In every case, TU-TO backed up its claims with evidence that is difficult to refute. The result is a whip-snap backlash against the party that placed itself on a pedestal. The question now is will negative publicity spillover and adversely affect the entire party in the long term?"

"Sure as shittin' will," the teenager said. "Those guys are screwed!"

"I guess so," said Remo Williams, and he was smiling. "Come on, Little Father."

"The program has only just started," Chiun complained, his face inches from a nearby high-definition display.

"Hey, it's the *Exciting Tomatoes*!" said the teenager. "I don't know what those babes are always cryin' about, but they got some fabulous racks, huh?"

The teenager didn't notice the old Korean wasn't answering him.

"I mean, you ever see a grandma whose got 'em lifted way up like that? In a halter top, no less!"

The teenager was so engrossed in the *Exciting Tomatoes* he didn't see the fingernails that almost decapitated him or the hand that stopped it from happening. Remo led Chiun toward the entrance, but the phones started ringing as he went by the mobile phone display. All the phones.

"Aw, crap." Remo grabbed one of them, opened it, poked it and handed it to the salesperson. He opened a second one and was about to poke a button when Chiun barked, "Just talk, imbecile!"

"Hello?" Remo said to the phone.

"Remo, it's me."

"I kinda guessed that, Smitty. I gotta hand it to you and the little prince—nice smear campaign you've got going on."

"However, the time has come to take care of Flicker in the manner you suggested earlier."

Remo's mood was improving all the time. "What about the martyrdom problem?" he asked.

"That will not be a problem at all," said Harold W. Smith.

38

Orville Flicker felt his aircraft come to a halt and the engine noise dropped and died. He was back in D.C. He arrived not in a moment of victory, but in a moment of desperation.

Every ten minutes on this long flight there had come another slap in the face. It started with a small-time MAEBE state representative in Missouri and snow-balled from there.

The worst thing about it was the skill with which the campaign was executed. Whoever these people were, this Truth-Be-Told Organization, they knew just how to strike at MAEBE with effectively damning marketing.

"But there wasn't a video camera in the hotel room!" the judge from Cleveland protested when Flicker called. "That hotel didn't have shag carpeting!"

"Doesn't matter," Flicker responded.

"Of course it matters if the evidence is faked. It won't take much to prove it."

"It will take too much to prove it. Too much time and

too much publicity. The fact is, you nailed a junior high school girl. That will come out."

"Not necessarily," the judge insisted.

"It will. It already has. Look at the television."

"What channel?"

Flicker hung up on the judge. Didn't matter what channel. Pretty soon it would be on every channel. The girl was seen walking into the police station to file her grievance, and she glanced for a moment at the camera with big, gentle, sweet eyes. Dammit, she was photogenic!

The judge was doomed.

So was the state's attorney in Alabama and the governor of Oregon and the senator from Alaska and dammit, so was Lamble. Son of a bitch Lamble faked his doctorate from a nonexistent college. There were lots of ways to get yourself a degree that would stand up to scrutiny, and Lamble used an amateur's trick.

Whoever was gunning for them had penetrating resources and a knack for using them. The Truth-Be-Told Organization, or TU-TO, as the networks were calling it, could be none other than a branch of the government, and likely the same assassin's branch that had been harassing the White Hand for days.

Give him time, Flicker thought, and he could find out who they really were. He could expose them. He could propagandize those bastards out of existence.

He smiled ironically. It would be too late, just like the pedophile judge in Ohio proving the incriminating video was a fake.

"Mr. Orville Flicker," said his assistant darkly.

"What?" Flicker asked. He had never seen Kohd looking so stern. "What's wrong now?"

"What's wrong is you, sir," Kohd declared through gritted teeth. Kohd never gritted his teeth. "You are destroying yourself."

Flicker laughed, a bitter bark. "In case you weren't paying attention, Kohd, MAEBE is crumbling."

"Wrong, sir. MAEBE is you. MAEBE lives and dies with you. All those others are just the rungs in the ladder."

"The ladder is splitting up the middle, Kohd."

"But a strong man at the top can hold it together, sir, and stay upright. That is you, but all I see is a man who is giving up. I see you letting go and allowing yourself to slide down into the pool of cold mud. You are failing us all."

"You're an asshole!"

"Because I'm insulted by your weakness? Mr. Flicker, you are the greatest public-relations man ever. Nobody could have pulled this off except you. You're on the verge of being President."

"Kohd—"

"Orville, you still have the means to be President. We know how to make Senator Whiteslaw go away. We know how to exert control over the current President. The man at the top of the ladder, whether the ladder has rungs or not, stands just as tall as long as he keeps his balance. So I ask you sir, will you strive to remain erect, or will you allow yourself to topple?"

Flicker thought about it, then slowly sat up and spoke resolutely. "I choose to stay erect."

Kohd nodded and pulled out two mobile phones. "Good. Then I have calls to make."

Flicker got to his feet. "And I have a senator to assassinate."

39

"Hello, Robert, how are you these days?" Flicker shook the man's hands in both his own.

The redheaded guard was grinning. "Nice to see you, Mr. F. I'm sorry about all the trouble, losing Mr. Kriidelfisk and all."

Flicker nodded, appropriately somber. "It was a horrible turn of events."

"He was a good man," the guard said, saying the lines as perfectly as Flicker's press secretary had said them in interviews after the incident. Now a lot of people believed those words, even though none of them knew anything about the blackmailing, baskstabbing liar Kriidelfisk. "He was a living saint," the guard added. Another good line from the media spin.

Killing his running mate had been a cunningly successful political move, Flicker thought, his spirits improving all the time. "You bet he was, Robert."

Robert scanned Flicker with the metal-detection wand in a cursory manner. "So are you just visiting, Mr. F?"

"Seeing some old friends, Robert." Flicker said, lowering his hands and retrieving his keys and wallet from the basket.

"Gonna do some campaigning while you're at it, Mr. F?" Robert winked, waving one of his immensely bushy orange eyebrows.

"Maybe just little," Flicker said in a mock whisper. "Keep it under your hat."

The guard chuckled and Flicker received his VIP pass. His weapon undiscovered, Orville Flicker strolled into the private halls of the United States Senate as if he owned the place.

There were a number of senators who owed him favors on both sides of the aisle, and they'd assumed their debts were written off when Flicker left the White House. He had called them in today, and the indebted senators didn't dare refuse on the off chance, God forbid, the guy actually got the power he was seeking. Besides, what Flicker was asking for was benign enough. Flicker want to show he was still a Washington insider. All he needed was a pass into the Senate for some hand shaking and acquaintance renewing. It wasn't as if the man was a security risk.

The senators who got Flicker his pass, one from each party, came into the hall to greet him warmly, shaking his hand as they wove through the next security guards and escorted Flicker onto the floor of the U.S. Senate.

The Senate was not in session at the moment, but no member of that august body would have dared miss a special session intended to honor one of its own. They were talking in groups, networking, schmoozing, bartering votes like chits.

"What's going on?" asked a freshmen Republican senator from Arkansas as he watched the group in the aisle.

"It's that dumb-ass Flicker. What's he doing here, I wonder?" commented a famous heavy-drinking senator from one of the Carolinas, and the mentor to the young man from Arkansas.

"Sharp and Tosio are sure laying it on thick," the younger senator said. "Don't they know Flicker's star is falling fast? Least that's what I heard."

As he was thinking it over, the older man's cheeks ballooned with a belch that he expelled through his nose. His protégé, out of habit, held his breath until the lethal whiskey stench dissipated.

"I think you and me had better go do a little paw grabbin'," the wise old politician decided.

There was a joyous greeting between the elder senator and Flicker, and a boisterous "Good to meet you!" exchange between Flicker and the younger man.

Thirty feet away a small group watched with growing interest.

"What do the 'Publicans know that we don't know?" demanded "Rocky" Rutledge, D-New Mexico in a hastily called huddle. "There's three of them over there now with Flicker!"

"It's just glad-handing," said a Hawaiian senator dismissively. "Flicker's been on the down elevator since the bad news this afternoon."

"Maybe something more is going on," Rocky Rutledge countered. "Maybe he's turned it around in the polls again. Maybe he's got something going."

The Hawaiian shook his head. "I guarantee you, the only reason Flicker's here is to create some goodwill before we vote on the Whiteslaw bill."

"I heard there's gonna be opposition to the Whiteslaw bill," hissed the gaunt Montanan, Kartsotis. "I hear somebody's gonna air dirt on Whiteslaw."

"If Whiteslaw becomes untouchable, the bill won't pass and MAEBE could be on the ballot nationwide," Rutledge concluded. "That hack Flicker could be the next leader of the free world."

"Fat chance," commented the senator from Hawaii, only to find he was talking to himself. The huddle of Democrats had become a stampede of Democrats, bearing down on Orville Flicker. The Senator from Hawaii ran to join the herd.

"THE DEMOCRATS ARE getting in tight with Flicker!" said the top Republican. "I want to know why."

"Who knows with that S.O.B.," said the eternally disheveled senator from Nevada. "I can't keep track of that roller coaster of his. He was way up in the polls this morning, way down this afternoon. Who knows where he stands now?"

The senior Republican pursed his brows, a signal that his wisdom was about to issue forth.

"When in doubt, schmooz."

The knot of Republicans closed in on Flicker as if he were a brother coming home from the war.

ORVILLE FLICKER kept his dignity, didn't allow himself to get carried away, just took his time and kept shaking hands until he had shaken all of them—all except that of Herbert Whiteslaw, who entered in a wheelchair and was situated in the aisle near to the front of the great hall of the United States Senate.

Flicker felt the mobile phone in his pocket buzz twice, pause and buzz twice again. Kohd had come in through the rear and was in place, somewhere in the balcony above. Flicker had called in another favor to make that happen.

The senator who granted him that favor would never, ever admit to it, especially once he realized the consequences of his actions.

"Senator Tosio, are you prepared?" Flicker said quietly, returning to his longtime acquaintance after the reception line.

Tosio nodded with hooded eyes. "I'm ready. I'll come out against the Whiteslaw bill—but only after I see Whiteslaw go down."

"He's going down, even as we speak."

"It had better be. The special session starts in two minutes," Tosio said. Tosio nodded at the security guard who was coming to ask Flicker, very politely, to remove himself from the Senate floor.

"It will be delayed," Flicker promised.

A handful of aides unexpectedly entered, delivered

brief messages and left again. A buzz started among the senior senators, and then the junior senators began buzzing, as well, so they wouldn't look marginalized. The security guard was alert for trouble, wondering what all the hubbub was about, and didn't get around to ushering Flicker out. Senators started getting up and leaving in bigger numbers.

More buzzing. News of an unexpected recess. Most of them had no idea what was going on, and the wheelchair-bound Herbert Whiteslaw was like a trapped fish, searching for an explanation. Nobody got near him.

Tosio was a third-term senator, giving him enough seniority to get the news in the second batch of disturbed buzzing. He left with a group of ten senators, walking quickly, for an impromptu party conference.

Flicker waited, standing in the aisle, comfortable even amid so much uncertainty. This event had to be presented in just the right way, but Orville Flicker always knew the right way.

Step one, ruin the reputation of Senator Herbert Whiteslaw. Step two, eradicate Senator Herbert Whiteslaw. He'd never have the chance to make his humble-hero speech, and the dirty laundry that CNN was showing at this very moment would make it impossible for him to become a martyred hero. Senator Whiteslaw would be remembered as nothing more than a corrupt politician who got what he deserved.

Whiteslaw turned his wheelchair around, facing Flicker down the long aisle and smiling smugly, the bastard. Any minute now Flicker was going to have the rare opportunity of blasting that smile right off.

Whiteslaw crooked his finger, summoning Flicker. Bastard! Flicker couldn't ignore the cripple, not until the cripple was completely disgraced, and that would take a few minutes more. Flicker made the long, humiliating walk down the aisle to answer the call of his well-known adversary.

"Everybody's checking out the news," Whiteslaw said without a word of greeting. "Maybe you should have a look at it."

"Maybe you should, Senator," Flicker answered, viciously gleeful.

But Whiteslaw just sat back comfortably. "Already have."

Flicker knew then that something was wrong. He turned away from Whiteslaw, fast, before the man saw his doubts, then strolled up the long aisle again, into the narrow hall, joining a crowd outside a tiny office with a blaring TV.

On TV was the videotape of Senator Herbert Whiteslaw counting hundred-dollar bills and stuffing them into a bulging envelope. The man with him was the infamous foreign secretary of a now discredited and annihilated foreign dictatorship. When Whiteslaw was done counting the bills, he put the envelope in his jacket and withdrew another envelope, this one slim and sealed. He handed it to the foreign secretary, who grunted and left.

It was the most expensive piece of evidence Flicker

had ever purchased. Only his dire predicament had finally motivated him to spend the one million dollars the Saudi seller had demanded.

But something had changed, and it wasn't until the end of the tape that he knew what it was. Whiteslaw turned and walked toward the camera, but he wasn't Whiteslaw. The senator's face was replaced with the face of Orville Flicker.

"You bastard!" said somebody close by. It was one of the senators. And to think, not ten minutes ago the man had been shaking his hand as if they were best friends.

The taunting came.

"Benedict Arnold."

"Spy."

"Traitor."

"Stop it! That isn't me!"

"Sure, Flicker."

"Who let this criminal into the Senate building?" demanded Senator Tosio, who had, in fact, arranged the pass. "Security!"

"Tosio, this isn't how it is supposed to go," Flicker said, backing the senator up against the wall.

"What will you do, Mr. Flicker, buy us all off?" Tosio declared loudly for the gathering audience. "Looks like you pulled in a cool million on that deal."

"It wasn't me—it was Whiteslaw!"

"Get off it. Where's security?"

Flicker broke away and jogged to the Senate floor, slipped around the uniformed guard and ran at Whiteslaw, who sat in his wheelchair grinning like the devil.

Flicker was ruined, but he could still exact a little revenge. He could still get away with murder. He withdrew his phone and thumbed the speed-dial for Noah
Kohd. In the balcony, Noah responded.

"HERE HE COMES," Whiteslaw said aloud, craning his
neck, but couldn't find Remo.

Remo watched from behind a nearby desk. Flicker
was coming fast, his eyes wild. He wasn't trying to hide
his intentions. Smitty's little special-effects movie had
done the trick.

But Remo was very interested in seeing how he planned
to make this happen. Shoot down a senator, in cold blood,
on the floor of the Senate? That took some balls.

Flicker did something with his phone, put it back and
grabbed for the inside of his suit jacket again. He came
out with a pair of solid chrome glasses, which he
dragged over his eyes. The guy had sealed off his vision
completely. At that moment an ugly, lumpy woman
wearing the ID of a Senate intern came to the rail in the
balcony above and swung a small sack of grenades out
into the vast interior of the Senate.

Remo didn't watch. He hid his eyes in his arm, covered his ears, closing down all his highly tuned senses
as completely as he could.

The grenades went off when they were ten feet
above the ground, but this was no ordinary Army-
issue sound-and-light grenade. The sound was no
more than a quick hiss, and the light was so brilliant

and so brief that it had not been successfully measured, even by the munitions expert who developed the weapon.

Remo's eyes were squeezed shut and covered by his arm and still he saw the bones in his arm and the veins in his eyelids. The light diminished in a heartbeat, but that was when the panic started. Remo risked a glance, found it safe and blinked away the lingering red spots floating in front of his vision.

He was lucky. The Senate was full of blind people. Whiteslaw was rubbing at his eyes, trying to massage the functionality back into them, and all over were senators and staff who were doing the same thing. Some tried to stand and run, eventually crashing to the floor.

Only one man still had his vision. Orville Flicker pushed the chrome glasses onto his forehead and came at the wheelchair-bound senator wearing a sick smile. He extracted a yellow plastic device from a pocket high inside his jacket, just under the collar, and pointed it at Whiteslaw.

"Hi, what's that?" Remo asked, and took the device for himself as he emerged from hiding. "Is this a gun? Never seen one like this before."

Flicker stopped, shocked yet again. He knew whom he was looking at. "You ruined me," he said accusingly.

"Hey, whoa, you handled that one all by yourself. Did a damn good job of it, too."

"What's going on?" Whiteslaw demanded, squinting at them helplessly.

"Give me that," Flicker ordered, making a grab for the weapon, only to find it pulled just out of his reach.

"It's one of those disposable guns, right?" Remo asked. "All plastic, preloaded, fire it once and throw it away?"

"Give it to me!"

"You going to shoot the senator?" Remo asked. "Not a bad idea, actually."

"What?" Whiteslaw barked.

"Well, you did sell out the U.S.," Remo pointed out. "I, for one, know that it was you on the video. Orville here knows it, too. In my book, you're a slimebag who doesn't deserve to share my air."

Flicker saw a small glimmer of hope. "So give me the gun!"

"Yeah, okay," Remo said.

"No, don't do it," Whiteslaw blurted.

"Too late." Flicker laughed, then gripped the weapon in both hands and squeezed the trigger. There was a bang.

"Oops," Remo said.

"What happened?" Whiteslaw cried, then felt the limp body of Orville Flicker collapse heavily in his lap. "Get off me! What is this? I'm soaked."

"That would be blood," Remo explained helpfully.

The blind senator tried to get Flicker off him, and in the process he accidentally grabbed something strange. Soft human tissue. Spurting blood. Exposed bone. It was a wrist without a hand.

Flicker made disgusting sounds in his throat.

"Get away from me," Whiteslaw squealed and shoved at the wrist, only to find a second one. "For God's sake, get him off me."

"You know, Coleslaw, I think you two deserve each other."

Remo left them together.

On the balcony he found a hefty corpse sprawled alongside Chiun.

"You okay, Little Father?"

"Why would I not be okay?"

"There was this bright light, you might have noticed. See all the blind people around you?" He pointed out the stumbling, blinking interns.

Chiun nodded at the corpse. "From the booms this one activated."

"Yes."

"I closed my eyes," Chiun explained.

"I see."

"In truth, the flash was less intense here than below. See, these servants are not entirely blinded." He thrust a spread palm at the face of a stumbling young intern, who dodged it with a short sound and steered away, into a wall. She landed on all fours and found crawling was a safer option anyway.

"Who's the looker?" Remo asked, nudging at the blond wig. The face, behind the heavy makeup, was that of a middle-aged male. "Benny Hill looked more attractive in drag than this guy."

"As I said, he is the boom tosser. Unfortunately, he

did not reveal his presence until I was on the other side of the balcony. Otherwise I might have prevented the booms."

"Yeah. Well..." Remo shrugged. He stood at the rail. Below, Whiteslaw and Flicker were still tangled together, covered in blood. The Senate floor was filled with shouting and sobbing, blinded senators feeling one another's faces and tripping over one another.

"What a mess," Remo Williams said.

"Yes, it is."

"At the moment, I mean."

Chiun looked doubtful.

"It's not always a mess," Remo insisted. "Greatest country in the world and all that."

Chiun said, "The men with the sunglasses are arriving. We should go."

"Okay, but maybe we should come back sometime, you know, so we can see what it's like when it's running smoothly."

"Maybe you can come by yourself."

"Maybe I will."

"Fine."

40

"I'd say the Senate has some security leaks," Remo remarked. "Government by the people or not, you'd hope they could keep out visitors with grenades."

"They're plastic, just like Flicker's disposable handgun," Smith told them. "The metal detectors weren't set off. They were hermetically sealed, so the explosives didn't alert the dogs. Inside is a magnesium mixture with granularized high-pressure hydrogen canisters. It's an experimental flash grenade that burns very bright and very fast, and no one is quite sure what the lasting effects might be."

"My stars, what will they think of next?" Remo said.

"What happened to Flicker's gun, anyway?" Mark Howard asked from Smith's old sofa, although he was sure he already knew. Remo confirmed his assumption.

"I think I might have scratched the barrel and maybe accidentally pinched the muzzle a little and the thing blew back at him, took his hands right off," Remo said. "A shame, really."

"It is a shame he did not blow off his head," Chiun said.

"One way or another, Orville Flicker is no more," Smith said. "Bled to death. The Morals and Ethics Behavior Establishment collapsed and disintegrated in a matter of hours."

"Good riddance. Any mopping up required?"

Smith looked out from under his eyebrows. "Not by you. We disseminated our intelligence to several law-enforcement agencies and the FBI. They've already picked up members of the last two White Hand cells, which have also collapsed and dissipated. They had no reason to carry on once Flicker was out of the picture. He signed the paychecks. Flicker's housekeeper is proving to be a fount of intelligence."

"Did she provide an ID on the drag queen who tossed the grenades?" Remo asked.

"That was Flicker's personal assistant, Noah Kohd," explained Mark Howard from Smith's sofa.

"We all made spectacles of ourselves," Remo observed. "How much exposure did we suffer?"

"I've been monitoring all the video feeds coming out of the vicinity," Mark said. "There were no clear shots of your faces. Regardless, I sabotaged every electronic file I could trace. Very few people actually report seeing you, even in the Secret Service interviews so far. Remo seems to have gone entirely unnoticed."

"Meaning?" Chiun demanded.

"It was the kimono, Master Chiun," Smith explained. "A garment so truly distinctive, how could it go unno-

James Axler
Outlanders®

SUN LORD

In a fabled city of the ancient world, the neo-gods of Mexico are locked in a battle for domination. Harnessing the immutable power of alien technology and Earth's pre-Dark secrets, the high priests and whitecoats have hijacked Kane into the resurrected world of the Aztecs. Invested with the power of the great sun god, Kane is a pawn in the brutal struggle and must restore the legendary Quetzalcoatl to his rightful place—or become a human sacrifice....

Available May 2004 at your favorite retail outlet.

Or order your copy now by sending your name, address, zip or postal code, along with a check or money order (please do not send cash) for $6.50 for each book ordered ($7.99 in Canada), plus 75¢ postage and handling ($1.00 in Canada), payable to Gold Eagle Books, to:

In the U.S.	In Canada
Gold Eagle Books	Gold Eagle Books
3010 Walden Avenue	P.O. Box 636
P.O. Box 9077	Fort Erie, Ontario
Buffalo, NY 14269-9077	L2A 5X3

Please specify book title with your order.
Canadian residents add applicable federal and provincial taxes.

GOUT29

ticed with all those people around? I believe you may wish to retire that particular garment for a few years."

"The real problem comes from the people we were exposed to, namely Coleslaw," Remo insisted. "He saw what we did and he's not stupid."

"He saw nothing to lead him to believe he was in the hands of anything other than a personal security specialist," Smith said. "I'm not worried about the senator. And I believe we're wrapped up."

"No, we are not," Chiun protested. "You have not issued a decision regarding my marketing plan."

Smith became uneasy. "I have considered it, Master Chiun. I'm afraid we must continue with our long-term strategy. As MAEBE proved all too well, exposure could only mean complication for CURE."

"The right publicity could mean the Eagle Throne, Emperor Smith," Chiun countered.

"Which I do not desire."

Chiun sniffed. "I see."

Smith knew the matter wasn't settled. It would never be settled. If he was lucky, he had purchased a reprieve of a few months.

"I still think Humbert Coleslaw is an unresolved issue," said Remo. "What's his legal status?"

"Herbert Whiteslaw's status is pending," Smith said vaguely.

"Pending me visiting him?"

"No. You are not to assassinate Whiteslaw. He's cooperating with the CIA."

"He's going to do time, though, right? Like, centuries of time?"

"Yes."

Remo frowned. "I don't like the sound of that yes. Is it a yes, definitely or a yes, probably, we'll wait and see?"

"It's a yes, almost definitely."

Remo glared back. "I read you, loud and clear," he said sarcastically.

"Remo, do *not* assassinate Senator Whiteslaw."

"I won't, Smitty. Almost definitely."

There was an uncomfortable silence.

Remo got to his feet. "Well, this has been fun. Bye." Then he was gone. Dr. Smith and Mark Howard didn't see the door open and they didn't see it close, but the slam woke up sanitarium residents in the next wing.

Smith looked to the ancient Korean. "Master Chiun, as a favor to me, will you please try to prevent him from assassinating Senator Whiteslaw?"

Chiun opened his mouth, closed it and then said simply, "No."

"I see." Smith sat back, trying to come up with a persuasive argument, but then saw that both his chairs were now empty.

Chiun was gone, as well.

Stony Man is deployed against an armed
invasion on American soil...

TERMS OF CONTROL

Supertankers bound for the U.S. are being sabotaged,
and key foreign enterprises in America are coming under
attack. The message is loud and clear: someone wants the
U.S. to close its borders to outsiders—and Stony Man thinks
it knows who...a powerful senator bringing his own brand
of isolationism to the extreme. He's hired mercenaries to
do the dirty work, and the body toll is rising by the hour.
The outcome all boils down to luck, timing and the
combat skills of a few good men....

STONY MAN®

*Available
June 2004
at your favorite
retail outlet.*

DEATH LANDS.

Separation

Available June 2004
at your favorite retail outlet.

The group makes its way to a remote island in hopes of finding brief sanctuary. Instead, they are captured by an isolated tribe of descendants of African slaves from pre–Civil War days. When they declare Mildred Wyeth "free" from her white masters, it is a twist of fate that ultimately leads the battle-hardened medic to question where her true loyalties lie. Will she side with Ryan, J. B. Dix and those with whom she has forged a bond of trust and friendship…or with the people of her own blood?

TAKE 'EM FREE

2 action-packed novels plus a mystery bonus

NO RISK
NO OBLIGATION TO BUY

don't mind) want in such a very queer house as Number 20? It's altogether a very odd case, isn't it?"

"It is indeed, Austin; an extraordinary case. I didn't think, when I asked you about my old friend, I should strike on such strange metal. Well, I must be off; good-day."

Villiers went away, thinking of his own conceit of the Chinese boxes; here was quaint workmanship indeed.

IV   The Discovery in Paul Street

A few months after Villiers's meeting with Herbert, Mr. Clarke was sitting, as usual, by his after-dinner hearth, resolutely guarding his fancies from wandering in the direction of the bureau. For more than a week he had succeeded in keeping away from the "Memoirs," and he cherished hopes of a complete self-reformation; but in spite of his endeavours, he could not hush the wonder and the strange curiosity that that last case he had written down had excited within him. He had put the case, or rather the outline of it, conjecturally to a scientific friend, who shook his head, and thought Clarke getting queer, and on this particular evening Clarke was making an effort to rationalize the story, when a sudden knock at his door roused him from his meditations.

"Mr. Villiers to see you, sir."

"Dear me, Villiers, it is very kind of you to look me up; I have not seen you for many months; I should think nearly a year. Come in, come in. And how are you, Villiers: Want any advice about investments?"

"No, thanks, I fancy everything I have in that way is pretty safe. No, Clarke, I have really come to consult you about a rather curious matter that has been brought under my notice of late. I am afraid you will think it all rather absurd when I tell my tale. I sometimes think so myself, and that's just why I made up my mind to come to you, as I know you're a practical man."

Mr. Villiers was ignorant of the "Memoirs to Prove the Existence of the Devil."

"Well, Villiers, I shall be happy to give you my advice, to the best of my ability. What is the nature of the case?"

"It's an extraordinary thing altogether. You know my ways; I always keep my eyes open in the streets, and in my time I have chanced upon some queer customers, and queer cases too, but this, I think, beats all. I was coming out of a restaurant one nasty winter night about three months ago: I had had a capital dinner and a good bottle of Chianti, and I stood for a moment on the pavement, thinking what a mystery there is about London streets and the companies that pass along them. A bottle of red wine encourages these fancies, Clarke, and I dare say I should have thought a page of small type, but I was cut short by a beggar who had come behind me, and was making the usual appeals. Of course I looked round, and this beggar turned out to be what was left of an old friend of mine, a man named Herbert. I asked him how he had come to such a wretched pass, and he told me. We walked up and down one of those long dark Soho streets, and there I listened to his story. He said he had married a beautiful girl, some years younger than himself, and, as he put it, she had corrupted him body and soul. He wouldn't go into details; he said he dare not, that what he had seen and heard haunted him by night and day, and when I looked in his face I knew he was speaking the truth. There was something about the man that made me shiver. I don't know why, but it was there. I gave him a little money and sent him away, and I assure you that when he was gone I gasped for breath. His presence seemed to chill one's blood."

"Isn't all this just a little fanciful, Villiers? I suppose

the poor fellow had made an imprudent marriage, and, in plain English, gone to the bad."

"Well, listen to this." Villiers told Clarke the story he had heard from Austin.

"You see," he concluded, "there can be but little doubt that this Mr. Blank, whoever he was, died of sheer terror; he saw something so awful, so terrible, that it cut short his life. And what he saw, he most certainly saw in that house, which, somehow or other, had got a bad name in the neighbourhood. I had the curiosity to go and look at the place for myself. It's a saddening kind of street; the houses are old enough to be mean and dreary, but not old enough to be quaint. As far as I could see most of them are let in lodgings, furnished and unfurnished, and almost every door has three bells to it. Here and there the ground floors have been made into shops of the commonest kind; it's a dismal street in every way. I found Number 20 was to let, and I went to the agent's and got the key. Of course I should have heard nothing of the Herberts in that quarter, but I asked the man, fair and square, how long they had left the house, and whether there had been other tenants in the meanwhile. He looked at me queerly for a minute, and told me the Herberts had left immediately after the unpleasantness, as he called it, and since then the house had been empty."

Mr. Villiers paused for a moment.

"I have always been rather fond of going over empty houses; there's a sort of fascination about the desolate empty rooms, with the nails sticking in the walls, and the dust thick upon the window-sills. But I didn't enjoy going over Number 20, Paul Street. I had hardly put my foot inside the passage before I noticed a queer, heavy feeling about the air of the house. Of course all empty houses are stuffy, and so forth, but this was something quite different; I can't describe it to you, but it seemed to stop the breath. I went into the front room and the

back room, and the kitchens downstairs; they were all
dirty and dusty enough, as you would expect, but there
was something strange about them all. I couldn't define
it to you, I only know I felt queer. It was one of the
rooms on the first floor, though, that was the worst. It
was a largish room, and once on a time the paper must
have been cheerful enough, but when I saw it, paint,
paper, and everything were most doleful. But the room
was full of horror; I felt my teeth grinding as I put my
hand on the door, and when I went in, I thought I
should have fallen fainting to the floor. However, I
pulled myself together, and stood against the end wall,
wondering what on earth there could be about the room
to make my limbs tremble, and my heart beat as if I
were at the hour of death. In one corner there was a pile
of newspapers littered about on the floor, and I began
looking at them; they were papers of three or four years
ago, some of them half torn, and some crumpled as if
they had been used for packing. I turned the whole pile
over, and amongst them I found a curious drawing; I
will show it you presently. But I couldn't stay in the
room; I felt it was overpowering me. I was thankful to
come out, safe and sound, into the open air. People
stared at me as I walked along the street, and one man
said I was drunk. I was staggering about from one side
of the pavement to the other, and it was as much as I
could do to take the key back to the agent and get home.
I was in bed for a week, suffering from what my doctor
called nervous shock and exhaustion. One of those days
I was reading the evening paper, and happened to
notice a paragraph headed: 'Starved to Death.' It was
the usual style of thing; a model lodging-house in
Marylebone, a door locked for several days, and a dead
man in his chair when they broke in. 'The deceased,'
said the paragraph, 'was known as Charles Herbert,
and is believed to have been once a prosperous country

gentlemen. His name was familiar to the public three years ago in connection with the mysterious death in Paul Street, Tottenham Court Road, the deceased being the tenant of the house Number 20, in the area of which a gentleman of good position was found dead under circumstances not devoid of suspicion.' A tragic ending, wasn't it? But after all, if what he told me were true, which I am sure it was, the man's life was all a tragedy, and a tragedy of a stranger sort than they put on the boards."

"And that is the story, is it?" said Clarke musingly.

"Yes, that is the story."

"Well, really, Villiers, I scarcely know what to say about it. There are, no doubt, circumstances in the case which seem peculiar, the finding of the dead man in the area of Herbert's house, for instance, and the extraordinary opinion of the physician as to the cause of death; but, after all, it is conceivable that the facts may be explained in a straightforward manner. As to your own sensations, when you went to see the house, I would suggest that they were due to a vivid imagination; you must have been brooding, in a semi-conscious way, over what you had heard. I don't exactly see what more can be said or done in the matter; you evidently think there is a mystery of some kind, but Herbert is dead; where then do you propose to look?"

"I propose to look for the woman; the woman whom he married. *She* is the mystery."

The two men sat silent by the fireside; Clarke secretly congratulating himself on having successfully kept up the character of advocate of the commonplace, and Villiers wrapt in his gloomy fancies.

"I think I will have a cigarette," he said at last, and put his hand in his pocket to feel for the cigarette-case.

"Ah!" he said, starting slightly, "I forgot I had something to show you. You remember my saying that I had found a rather curious sketch amongst the pile of old newspapers at the house in Paul Street? Here it is."

Villiers drew out a small thin parcel from his pocket. It was covered with brown paper, and secured with string, and the knots were troublesome. In spite of himself Clarke felt inquisitive; he bent forward on his chair as Villiers painfully undid the string, and unfolded the outer covering. Inside was a second wrapping of tissue, and Villiers took it off and handed the small piece of paper to Clarke without a word.

There was dead silence in the room for five minutes or more; the two men sat so still that they could hear the ticking of the tall old-fashioned clock that stood outside in the hall, and in the mind of one of them the slow monotony of sound woke up a far, far memory. He was looking intently at the small pen-and-ink sketch of the woman's head; it had evidently been drawn with great care, and by a true artist, for the woman's soul looked out of the eyes, and the lips were parted with a strange smile. Clarke gazed still at the face; it brought to his memory one summer evening long ago; he saw again the long lovely valley, the river winding between the hills, the meadows and the cornfields, the dull red sun, and the cold white mist rising from the water. He heard a voice speaking to him across the waves of many years, and saying: "Clarke, Mary will see the God Pan!" and then he was standing in the grim room beside the doctor, listening to the heavy ticking of the clock, waiting and watching, watching the figure lying on the green chair beneath the lamp-light. Mary rose up, and he looked into her eyes, and his heart grew cold within him.

"Who is this woman?" he said at last. His voice was dry and hoarse.

"That is the woman whom Herbert married."

Clarke looked again at the sketch; it was not Mary

after all. There certainly was Mary's face, but there was something else, something he had not seen on Mary's features when the white-clad girl entered the laboratory with the doctor, nor at her terrible awakening, nor when she lay grinning on the bed. Whatever it was, the glance that came from those eyes, the smile on the full lips, or the expression of the whole face, Clarke shuddered before it in his inmost soul, and thought, unconsciously, of Dr. Phillip's words, "the most vivid presentment of evil I have ever seen." He turned the paper over mechanically in his hand and glanced at the back.

"Good God! Clarke, what is the matter? You are as white as death."

Villiers had started wildly from his chair, as Clarke fell back with a groan, and let the paper drop from his hands.

"I don't feel very well, Villiers, I am subject to these attacks. Pour me out a little wine; thanks, that will do. I shall feel better in a few minutes."

Villiers picked up the fallen sketch and turned it over as Clarke had done.

"You saw that?" he said. "That's how I identified it as being a portrait of Herbert's wife, or I should say his widow. How do you feel now?"

"Better, thanks, it was only a passing faintness. I don't think I quite catch your meaning. What did you say enabled you to identify the picture?"

"This word—'Helen'—written on the back. Didn't I tell you her name was Helen? Yes; Helen Vaughan."

Clarke groaned; there could be no shadow of doubt.

"Now, don't you agree with me," said Villiers, "that in the story I have told you tonight, and in the part this woman plays in it, there are some very strange points?"

"Yes, Villiers," Clarke muttered, "it is a strange story indeed; a strange story indeed. You must give me time to think it over; I may be able to help you or I may not. Must you be going now? Well, good-night, Villiers, good-night. Come and see me in the course of a week."

V   The Letter of Advice

"Do you know, Austin," said Villiers, as the two friends were pacing sedately along Picadilly one pleasant morning in May, "do you know I am convinced that what you told me about Paul Street and the Herberts is a mere episode in an extraordinary history? I may as well confess to you that when I asked you about Herbert a few months ago I had just seen him."

"You had seen him? Where?"

"He begged of me in the street one night. He was in the most pitiable plight, but I recognized the man, and I got him to tell me his history, or at least the outline of it. In brief, it amounted to this—he had been ruined by his wife."

"In what manner?"

"He would not tell me; he would only say that she had destroyed him, body and soul. The man is dead now."

"And what has become of his wife?"

"Ah, that's what I should like to know, and I mean to find her sooner or later. I know a man named Clarke, a dry fellow, in fact a man of business, but shrewd enough. You understand my meaning; not shrewd in the mere business sense of the word, but a man who really knows something about men and life. Well, I laid the case before him, and he was evidently impressed. He said it needed consideration, and asked me to come again in the course of a week. A few days later I received this extraordinary letter."

Austin took the envelope, drew out the letter, and read it curiously. It ran as follows:—

My dear Villiers,—I have thought over the matter on which you consulted me the other night, and my advice to you is this. Throw the portrait into the fire, blot out the story from your mind. Never give it another thought, Villiers, or you will be sorry. You will think, no doubt, that I am in possession of some secret information, and to a certain extent that is the case. But I only know a little; I am like a traveller who has peered over an abyss, and has drawn back in terror. What I know is strange enough and horrible enough, but beyond my knowledge there are depths and horrors more frightful still, more incredible than any tale told of winter nights about the fire. I have resolved, and nothing shall shake that resolve, to explore no whit farther, and if you value your happiness you will make the same determination.

Come and see me by all means; but we will talk on more cheerful topics than this.

Austin folded the letter methodically, and returned it to Villiers.

"It is certainly an extraordinary letter," he said; "what does he mean by the portrait?"

"Ah I forgot to tell you I have been to Paul Street and have made a discovery."

Villiers told his story as he had told it to Clarke, and Austin listened in silence. He seemed puzzled.

"How very curious that you should experience such an unpleasant sensation in that room!" he said at length. "I hardly gather that it was a mere matter of the imagination; a feeling of repulsion, in short."

"No, it was more physical than mental. It was as if I were inhaling at every breath some deadly fume, which seemed to penetrate to every nerve and bone and sinew of my body. I felt racked from head to foot, my eyes began to grow dim; it was like the entrance of death."

"Yes, yes, very strange, certainly. You see, your friend confesses that there is some very black story connected with this woman. Did you notice any particular emotion in him when you were telling your tale?"

"Yes, I did. He became very faint, but he assured me that it was a mere passing attack to which he was subject."

"Did you believe him?"

"I did at the time, but I don't now. He heard what I had to say with a good deal of indifference, till I showed him the portrait. It was then he was seized with the attack of which I spoke. He looked ghastly, I assure you."

"Then he must have seen the woman before. But there might be another explanation; it might have been the name, and not the face, which was familiar to him. What do you think?"

"I couldn't say. To the best of my belief it was after turning the portrait in his hands that he nearly dropped from his chair. The name, you know, was written on the back."

"Quite so. After all, it is impossible to come to any resolution in a case like this. I hate melodrama, and nothing strikes me as more commonplace and tedious than the ordinary ghost story of commerce; but really, Villiers, it looks as if there were something very queer at the bottom of all this."

The two men had, without noticing it, turned up Ashley Street, leading northward from Piccadilly. It was a long street, and rather a gloomy one, but here and there a brighter taste had illuminated the dark houses with flowers, and gay curtains, and a cheerful paint on the doors. Villiers glanced up as Austin stopped speaking, and looked at one of these houses; geraniums, red and white, drooped from every sill, and daffodil-coloured curtains were draped back from each window.

"It looks cheerful, doesn't it?" he said.

"Yes, and the inside is still more cheery. One of the pleasantest houses of the season, so I have heard. I haven't been there myself, but I've met several men who have, and they tell me it's uncommonly jovial."

"Whose house is it?"

"A Mrs. Beaumont's."

"And who is she?"

"I couldn't tell you. I have heard she comes from South America, but, after all, who she is is of little consequence. She is a very wealthy woman, there's no doubt of that, and some of the best people have taken her up. I heard she has some wonderful claret, really marvellous wine, which must have cost a fabulous sum. Lord Argentine was telling me about it; he was there last Sunday evening. He assures me he has never tasted such a wine, and Argentine, as you know, is an expert. By the way, that reminds me, she must be an oddish sort of woman, this Mrs. Beaumount. Argentine asked her how old the wine was, and what do you think she said? 'About a thousand years, I believe.' Lord Argentine thought she was chaffing him, you know, but when he laughed she said she was speaking quite seriously, and offered to show him the jar. Of course, he couldn't say anything more after that; but it seems rather antiquated for a beverage, doesn't it? Why, here we are at my rooms. Come in, won't you?"

"Thanks, I think I will. I haven't seen the curiosity-shop for some time."

It was a room furnished richly, yet oddly, where every chair and bookcase and table, and every rug and jar and ornament seemed to be a thing apart, preserving each its own individuality.

"Anything fresh lately?" said Villiers after a while.

"No; I think not; you saw those queer jugs, didn't you? I thought so. I don't think I have come across anything for the last few weeks."

Austin glanced round the room from cupboard to

cupboard, from shelf to shelf, in search of some new oddity. His eyes fell at last on an old chest, pleasantly and quaintly carved, which stood in a dark corner of the room.

"Ah," he said, "I was forgetting, I have got something to show you." Austin unlocked the chest, drew out a thick quarto volume, laid it on the table, and resumed the cigar he had put down.

"Did you know Arthur Meyrick the painter, Villiers?"

"A little; I met him two or three times at the house of a friend of mine. What has become of him? I haven't heard his name mentioned for some time."

"He's dead."

"You don't say so! Quite young, wasn't he?"

"Yes; only thirty when he died."

"What did he die of?"

"I don't know. He was an intimate friend of mine, and a thoroughly good fellow. He used to come here and talk to me for hours, and he was one of the best talkers I have met. He could even talk about painting, and that's more than can be said of most painters. About eighteen months ago he was feeling rather overworked, and partly at my suggestion he went off on a sort of roving expedition, with no very definite end or aim about it. I believe New York was to be his first port, but I never heard from him. Three months ago I got this book, with a very civil letter from an English doctor practising at Buenos Aires, stating that he had attended the late Mr. Meyrick during his illness, and that the deceased had expressed an earnest wish that the enclosed packet should be sent to me after his death. That was all."

"And haven't you written for further particulars?"

"I have been thinking of doing so. You would advise me to write to the doctor?"

"Certainly. And what about the book?"

"It was sealed up when I got it. I don't think the doctor had seen it."

"It is something very rare? Meyrick was a collector, perhaps?"

"No, I think not, hardly a collector. Now, what do you think of those Ainu jugs?"

"They are peculiar, but I like them. But aren't you going to show me poor Meyrick's legacy?"

"Yes, yes, to be sure. The fact is, it's rather a peculiar sort of thing, and I haven't shown it to anyone. I wouldn't say anything about it if I were you. There it is."

Villiers took the book, and opened it at haphazard.

"It isn't a printed volume then?" he said.

"No. It is a collection of drawings in black and white by my poor friend Meyrick."

Villiers turned to the first page, it was blank; the second bore a brief inscription, which he read:

> *Silet per diem universus, nec sine horrore secretus est; lucet nocturnis ignibus, chorus Aegipanum undique personatur: audiuntur et cantus tibiarum, et tinnitus cymbalorum per oram maritimam.*

On the third page was a design which made Villiers start and look up at Austin; he was gazing abstractedly out of the window. Villiers turned page after page, absorbed, in spite of himself, in the frightful Walpurgis-night of evil, strange monstrous evil, that the dead artist had set forth in hard black and white. The figures of fauns and satyrs and Aegipans danced before his eyes, the darkness of the thicket, the dance on the mountain-top, the scenes by lonely shores, in green vineyards, by rocks and desert places, passed before him: a world before which the human soul seemed to shrink back and shudder. Villiers whirled over the remaining pages; he had seen enough, but the picture on the last leaf caught his eye, as he almost closed the book.

"Austin!"

"Well, what is it?"

"Do you know who that is?"

It was a woman's face, alone on the white page.

"Know who it is? No, of course not."

"I do."

"Who is it?"

"It is Mrs. Herbert."

"Are you sure?"

"I am perfectly certain of it. Poor Meyrick! He is one more chapter in her history."

"But what do you think of the designs?"

"They are frightful. Lock the book up again, Austin. If I were you I would burn it; it must be a terrible companion even though it be in a chest."

"Yes, they are singular drawings. But I wonder what connection there could be between Meyrick and Mrs. Herbert, or what link between her and these designs?"

"Ah, who can say? It is possible that the matter may end here, and we shall never know, but in my own opinion this Helen Vaughan, or Mrs. Herbert, is only the beginning. She will come back to London, Austin; depend upon it, she will come back, and we shall hear more about her then. I don't think it will be very pleasant news."

VI　The Suicides

Lord Argentine was a great favourite in London society. At twenty he had been a poor man, decked with the surname of an illustrious family, but forced to earn a livelihood as best he could, and the most speculative of money-lenders would not have entrusted him with fifty pounds on the chance of his ever changing his name for a title, and his poverty for a great fortune. His father had been near enough to the fountain of good things to secure one of the family livings, but the son, even if he had taken orders, would scarcely have obtained so much as this, and moreover felt no vocation for the ecclesiastical estate. Thus he fronted the world with no better armour than the bachelor's gown and the wits of a younger son's grandson, with which equipment he contrived in some way to make a very tolerable fight of it. At twenty-five Mr. Charles Aubernoun saw himself still a man of struggles and of warfare with the world, but out of the seven who stood between him and the high places of his family three only remained. These three, however, were "good lives," but yet not proof against the Zulu assegais and typhoid fever, and so one morning Aubernoun woke up and found himself Lord Argentine, a man of thirty who had faced the difficulties of existence, and had conquered. The situation amused him immensely, and he resolved that riches should be as pleasant to him as poverty had always been. Argentine, after some little consideration, came to the conclusion that dining, regarded as a fine art, was perhaps the most amusing pursuit open to fallen humanity, and thus his dinners became famous in London, and an invitation to his table a thing covetously desired. After ten years of lordship and dinners Argentine still declined to be jaded, still persisted in enjoying life, and by a kind of infection had become recognized as the cause of joy in others, in short, as the best of company. His sudden and tragic death therefore caused a wide and deep sensation. People could scarce believe it, even though the newspaper was before their eyes, and the cry of "Mysterious Death of a Nobleman" came ringing up from the street. But there stood the brief paragraph: "Lord Argentine was found dead this morning by his valet under distressing circumstances.

It is stated that there can be no doubt that his lordship committed suicide, though no motive can be assigned for the act. The deceased nobleman was widely known in society, and much liked for his genial manner and sumptuous hospitality. He is succeeded by," etc., etc.

By slow degrees the details came to light, but the case still remained a mystery. The chief witness at the inquest was the dead nobleman's valet, who said that the night before his death Lord Argentine had dined with a lady of good position, whose name was suppressed in the newspaper reports. At about eleven o'clock Lord Argentine had returned, and informed his man that he should not require his services till the next morning. A little later the valet had occasion to cross the hall and was somewhat astonished to see his master quietly letting himself out at the front door. He had taken off his evening clothes, and was dressed in a Norfolk coat and knickerbockers, and wore a low brown hat. The valet had no reason to suppose that Lord Argentine had seen him, and though his master rarely kept late hours, thought little of the occurrence till the next morning, when he knocked at the bedroom door at a quarter to nine as usual. He received no answer, and, after knocking two or three times, entered the room, and saw Lord Argentine's body leaning forward at an angle from the bottom of the bed. He found that his master had tied a cord securely to one of the short bedposts, and, after making a running noose and slipping it round his neck, the unfortunate man must have resolutely fallen forward, to die by slow strangulation. He was dressed in the light suit in which the valet had seen him go out, and the doctor who was summoned pronounced that life had been extinct for more than four hours. All papers, letters, and so forth seemed in perfect order, and nothing was discovered which pointed in the most remote way to any scandal either great or small. Here the evidence ended; nothing more could be discovered. Several persons had been present at the dinner-party at which Lord Argentine had assisted, and to all these he seemed in his usual genial spirits. The valet, indeed, said he thought his master appeared a little excited when he came home, but he confessed that the alteration in his manner was very slight, hardly noticeable, indeed. It seemed hopeless to seek for any clue, and the suggestion that Lord Argentine had been suddenly attacked by acute suicidal mania was generally accepted.

It was otherwise, however, when within three weeks, three more gentlemen, one of them a nobleman, and the two others men of good position and ample means, perished miserably in almost precisely the same manner. Lord Swanleigh was found one morning in his dressing-room, hanging from a peg affixed to the wall, and Mr. Collier-Stuart and Mr. Herries had chosen to die as Lord Argentine. There was no explanation in either case; a few bald facts; a living man in the evening, and a dead body with a black swollen face in the morning. The police had been forced to confess themselves powerless to arrest or to explain the sordid murders of Whitechapel; but before the horrible suicides of Piccadilly and Mayfair they were dumbfounded, for not even the mere ferocity which did duty as an explanation of the crimes of the East End, could be of service in the West. Each of these men who had resolved to die a tortured shameful death was rich, prosperous, and to all appearances in love with the world, and not the acutest research could ferret out any shadow of a lurking motive in either case. There was a horror in the air, and men looked at one another's faces when they met, each wondering whether the other was to be the victim of the fifth nameless tragedy. Journalists sought in vain in their scrap-books for materials whereof to concoct reminiscent articles; and the morning paper was unfolded in many a house with a feeling of awe; no man knew when or where the blow would next light.

A short while after the last of these terrible events, Austin came to see Mr. Villiers. He was curious to know whether Villiers had succeeded in discovering any fresh traces of Mrs. Herbert, either through Clarke or by other sources, and he asked the question soon after he had sat down.

"No," said Villiers, "I wrote to Clarke, but he remains obdurate, and I have tried other channels, but without any result. I can't find out what became of Helen Vaughan after she left Paul Street, but I think she must have gone abroad. But to tell the truth, Austin, I haven't paid very much attention to the matter for the last few weeks; I knew poor Herries intimately, and his terrible death has been a great shock to me, a great shock."

"I can well believe it," answered Austin gravely; "you know Argentine was a friend of mine. If I remember rightly, we were speaking of him that day you came to my rooms."

"Yes; it was in connection with that house in Ashley Street, Mrs. Beaumont's house. You said something about Argentine's dining there."

"Quite so. Of course you know it was there Argentine dined the night before—before his death."

"No, I haven't heard that."

"Oh yes; the name was kept out of the papers to spare Mrs. Beaumont. Argentine was a great favourite of hers, and it is said she was in a terrible state for some time after."

A curious look came over Villiers's face; he seemed undecided whether to speak or not. Austin began again.

"I never experienced such a feeling of horror as when I read the account of Argentine's death. I didn't understand it at the time, and I don't now. I knew him well, and it completely passes my understanding for what possible cause he—or any of the others for the matter of that—could have resolved in cold blood to die in such an awful manner. You know how men babble away each other's characters in London, you may be sure any buried scandal or hidden skeleton would have been brought to light in such a case as this; but nothing of the sort has taken place. As for the theory of mania, that is very well, of course, for the coroner's jury, but everybody knows that it's all nonsense. Suicidal mania is not smallpox."

Austin relapsed into gloomy silence. Villiers sat silent also, watching his friend. The expression of indecision still fleeted across his face; he seemed as if weighing his thoughts in the balance, and the considerations he was revolving left him still silent. Austin tried to shake off the remembrance of tragedies as hopeless and perplexed as the labyrinth of Daedalus, and began to talk in an indifferent voice of the most pleasant incidents and adventures of the season.

"That Mrs. Beaumont," he said, "of whom we were speaking, is a great success; she has taken London almost by storm. I met her the other night at Fulham's; she is really a remarkable woman."

"You have met Mrs. Beaumont?"

"Yes; she had quite a court around her. She would be called very handsome, I suppose, and yet there is something about her face which I didn't like. The features are exquisite, but the expression is strange. And all the time I was looking at her, and afterwards, when I was going home, I had a curious feeling that that very expression was in some way or other familiar to me."

"You must have seen her in the Row."

"No, I am sure I never set eyes on the woman before; it is that which makes it puzzling. And to the best of my belief I have never seen anybody like her; what I felt was a kind of dim far-off memory, vague but persistent.

The only sensation I can compare it to, is that odd feeling one sometimes has in a dream, when fantastic cities and wondrous lands and phantom personages appear familiar and accustomed."

Villiers nodded and glanced aimlessly round the room, possibly in search of something on which to turn the conversation. His eyes fell on an old chest somewhat like that in which the artist's strange legacy lay hid beneath a Gothic scutcheon.

"Have you written to the doctor about poor Meyrick?" he asked.

"Yes; I wrote asking for full particulars as to his illness and death. I don't expect to have an answer for another three weeks or a month. I thought I might as well inquire whether Meyrick knew an Englishwoman named Herbert, and if so, whether the doctor could give me any information about her. But it's very possible that Meyrick fell in with her at New York, or Mexico, or San Francisco; I have no idea as to the extent or direction of his travels."

"Yes, and it's very possible that the woman may have more than one name."

"Exactly. I wish I had thought of asking you to lend me the portrait of her which you possess. I might have enclosed it in my letter to Dr. Matthews."

"So you might: that never occurred to me. We might send it now. Hark! what are those boys calling?"

While the two men had been talking together a confused noise of shouting had been gradually growing louder. The noise rose from the eastward and swelled down Piccadilly, drawing nearer and nearer, a very torrent of sound; surging up streets usually quiet, and making every window a frame for a face, curious or excited. The cries and voices came echoing up the silent street where Villiers lived, growing more distinct as they advanced, and, as Villiers spoke, an answer rang up from the pavement:

"THE WEST END HORRORS; ANOTHER AW-FUL SUICIDE; FULL DETAILS!"

Austin rushed down the stairs and bought a paper and read out the paragraph to Villiers as the uproar in the street rose and fell. The window was open and the air seemed full of noise and terror.

Another gentleman has fallen a victim to the terrible epidemic of suicide which for the last month has prevailed in the West End. Mr. Sidney Crashaw of Stoke House, Fulham, and King's Pomeroy, Devon, was found, after a prolonged search, hanging from the branch of a tree in his garden at one o'clock to-day. The deceased gentleman dined last night at the Carlton Club and seemed in his usual health and spirits. He left the Club at about ten o'clock, and was seen walking leisurely up St. James's Street a little later. Subsequent to this his movements cannot be traced. On the discovery of the body medical aid was at once summoned, but life had evidently been long extinct. So far as is known, Mr. Crashaw had no trouble or anxiety of any kind. This painful suicide, it will be remembered, is the fifth of the kind in the last month. The authorities at Scotland Yard are unable to suggest any explanation of these terrible occurrences.

Austin put down the paper in mute horror.

"I shall leave London tomorrow," he said, "it is a city of nightmares. How awful this is, Villiers!"

Mr. Villiers was sitting by the window quietly looking out into the street. He had listened to the newspaper report attentively, and the hint of indecision was no longer on his face.

"Wait a moment, Austin," he replied, "I have made up my mind to mention a little matter that occurred last night. It is stated, I think, that Crashaw was last seen alive in St. James's Street shortly after ten?"

"Yes, I think so. I will look again. Yes, you are quite right."

"Quite so. Well, I am in a position to contradict that statement at all events. Crashaw was seen after that; considerably later indeed."

"How do you know?"

"Because I happened to see Crashaw myself at about two o'clock this morning."

"You saw Crashaw? You, Villiers?"

"Yes, I saw him quite distinctly; indeed, there were but a few feet between us."

"Where, in Heaven's name, did you see him?"

"Not far from here. I saw him in Ashley Street. He was just leaving a house."

"Did you notice what house it was?"

"Yes. It was Mrs. Beaumont's."

"Villiers! Think what you are saying; there must be some mistake. How could Crashaw be in Mrs. Beaumont's house at two o'clock in the morning? Surely, surely, you must have been dreaming, Villiers, you were always rather fanciful."

"No; I was wide awake enough. Even if I had been dreaming as you say, what I saw would have roused me effectually."

"What you saw? What did you see? Was there anything strange about Crashaw? But I can't believe it; it is impossible."

"Well, if you like I will tell you what I saw, or if you please, what I think I saw, and you can judge for yourself."

"Very good, Villiers."

The noise and clamour of the street had died away, though now and then the sound of shouting still came from the distance, and the dull, leaden silence seemed like the quiet after an earthquake or a storm. Villiers turned from the window and began speaking.

"I was at a house near Regent's Park last night, and when I came away the fancy took me to walk home instead of taking a hansom. It was a clear pleasant night enough, and after a few minutes I had the streets pretty much to myself. It's a curious thing, Austin, to be alone in London at night, the gas-lamps stretching away in perspective, and the dead silence, and then perhaps the rush and clatter of a hansom on the stones, and the fire starting up under the horse's hoofs. I walked along pretty briskly, for I was feeling a little tired of being out in the night, and as the clocks were striking two I turned down Ashley Street, which, you know, is on my way. It was quieter than ever there, and the lamps were fewer; altogether, it looked as dark and gloomy as a forest in winter. I had done about half the length of the street when I heard a door closed very softly, and naturally I looked up to see who was abroad like myself at such an hour. As it happens, there is a street lamp close to the house in question, and I saw a man standing on the step. He had just shut the door and his face was towards me, and I recognized Crashaw directly. I never knew him to speak to, but I had often seen him, and I am positive that I was not mistaken in my man. I looked into his face for a moment, and then—I will confess the truth—I set off at a good run, and kept it up till I was within my own door."

"Why?"

"Why? Because it made my blood run cold to see that man's face. I could never have supposed that such an infernal medley of passions could have glared out of any human eyes; I almost fainted as I looked. I knew I had looked into the eyes of a lost soul, Austin, the man's outward form remained, but all hell was within it. Furious lust, and hate that was like fire, and the loss of all hope and horror that seemed to shriek aloud to the night, though his teeth were shut; and the utter blackness of despair. I am sure he did not see me; he saw nothing that you or I can see, but he saw what I hope we never shall. I do not know when he died; I suppose in an hour, or perhaps two, but when I passed down Ashley Street and heard the closing door, that man no longer belonged to this world; it was a devil's face I looked upon."

There was an interval of silence in the room when Villiers ceased speaking. The light was failing, and all the tumult of an hour ago was quite hushed. Austin had bent his head at the close of the story, and his hand covered his eyes.

"What can it mean?" he said at length.

"Who knows, Austin, who knows? It's a black business, but I think we had better keep it to ourselves, for the present at any rate. I will see if I cannot learn anything about that house through private channels of information, and if I do light upon anything I will let you know."

VII   The Encounter in Soho

Three weeks later Austin received a note from Villiers, asking him to call either that afternoon or the next. He chose the nearer date, and found Villiers sitting as usual by the window, apparently lost in meditation on the drowsy traffic of the street. There was a bamboo table by his side, a fantastic thing, enriched with gilding and queer painted scenes, and on it lay a little pile of papers arranged and docketed as neatly as anything in Mr. Clarke's office.

"Well, Villiers, have you made any discoveries in the last three weeks?"

"I think so; I have here one or two memoranda which

struck me as singular, and there is a statement to which I shall call your attention."

"And these documents relate to Mrs. Beaumont? It was really Crashaw whom you saw that night standing on the doorstep of the house in Ashley Street?"

"As to that matter my belief remains unchanged, but neither my inquiries nor their results have any special relation to Crashaw. But my investigations have had a strange issue. I have found out who Mrs. Beaumont is!"

"Who she is? In what way do you mean?"

"I mean that you and I know her better under another name."

"What name is that?"

"Herbert."

"Herbert!" Austin repeated the word, dazed with astonishment.

"Yes, Mrs. Herbert of Paul Street, Helen Vaughan of earlier adventures unknown to me. You had reason to recognize the expression of her face; when you go home look at the face in Meyrick's book of horrors, and you will know the sources of your recollection."

"And you have proof of this?"

"Yes, the best of proof; I have seen Mrs. Beaumont, or shall we say Mrs. Herbert?"

"Where did you see her?"

"Hardly in a place where you would expect to see a lady who lives in Ashley Street, Piccadilly. I saw her entering a house in one of the meanest and most disreputable streets in Soho. In fact, I had made an appointment, though not with her, and she was precise both to time and place."

"All this seems very wonderful, but I cannot call it incredible. You must remember, Villiers, that I have seen this woman, in the ordinary adventure of London society, talking and laughing, and sipping her coffee in a commonplace drawing-room with commonplace people. But you know what you are saying?"

"I do; I have not allowed myself to be led by surmises or fancies. It was with no thought of finding Helen Vaughan that I searched for Mrs. Beaumont in the dark waters of the life of London, but such has been the issue."

"You must have been in strange places, Villiers."

"Yes, I have been in very strange places. It would have been useless, you know, to go to Ashley Street, and ask Mrs. Beaumont to give me a short sketch of her previous history. No; assuming, as I had to assume, that her record was not of the cleanest, it would be pretty certain that at some previous time she must have moved in circles not quite so refined as her present ones. If you see mud on the top of a stream, you may be sure that it was once at the bottom. I went to the bottom. I have always been fond of diving into Queer Street for my amusement, and I found my knowledge of that locality and its inhabitants very useful. It is, perhaps, needless to say that my friends had never heard the name of Beaumont, and as I had never seen the lady, and was quite unable to describe her, I had to set to work in an indirect way. The people there know me; I have been able to do some of them a service now and again, so they made no difficulty about giving their information; they were aware I had no communication direct or indirect with Scotland Yard. I had to cast out a good many lines, though, before I got what I wanted, and when I landed the fish I did not for a moment suppose it was my fish. But I listened to what I was told out of a constitutional liking for useless information, and I found myself in possession of a very curious story, though, as I imagined, not the story I was looking for. It was to this effect. Some five or six years ago, a woman named Raymond suddenly made her appearance in the neighbourhood to which I am referring. She was described to me as being quite young, probably not more than seventeen or eighteen, very handsome, and looking as if she came from the country. I should be wrong in saying that she found her level in going to this particular quarter, or associating with these people, for from what I was told, I should think the worst den in London far too good for her. The person from whom I got my information, as you may suppose, no great Puritan, shuddered and grew sick in telling me of the nameless infamies which were laid to her charge. After living there for a year, or perhaps a little more, she disappeared as suddenly as she came, and they saw nothing of her till about the time of the Paul Street case. At first she came to her old haunts only occasionally, then more frequently, and finally took up her abode there as before, and remained for six or eight months. It's of no use my going into details as to the life that woman led; if you want particulars you can look at Meyrick's legacy. Those designs were not drawn from his imagination. She again disappeared, and the people of the place saw nothing of her till a few months ago. My informant told me that she had taken some rooms in a house which he pointed out, and these rooms she was in the habit of visiting two or three times a week and always at ten in the morning. I was led to expect that one of these visits would be paid on a certain day about a week ago, and I accordingly managed to be on the look-out in company with my cicerone at a quarter to ten, and the hour and the lady came with equal punctuality. My friend and I were standing under an archway, a little way back from the street, but she saw us, and gave me a glance that I shall be long in forgetting. That look was quite enough for me; I knew Miss Raymond to be Mrs. Herbert; as for Mrs. Beaumont she had quite gone out of my head. She went into the house, and I watched it till four o'clock, when she came out, and then I followed her. It was a long chase, and I had to be very careful to keep a long way in the background, and yet not lose sight of the woman. She took me down to the Strand, and then to Westminster, and then up St. James's Street, and along Piccadilly. I felt queerish when I saw her turn up Ashley Street; the thought that Mrs. Herbert was Mrs. Beaumont came into my mind, but it seemed too improbable to be true. I waited at the corner, keeping my eye on her all the time, and I took particular care to note the house at which she stopped. It was the house with the gay curtains, the house of flowers, the house out of which Crashaw came the night he hanged himself in his garden. I was just going away with my discovery, when I saw an empty carriage come round and draw up in front of the house, and I came to the conclusion that Mrs. Herbert was going out for a drive, and I was right. I took a hansom and followed the carriage into the Park. There, as it happened, I met a man I know, and we stood talking together a little distance from the carriage-way, to which I had my back. We had not been there for ten minutes when my friend took off his hat, and I glanced round and saw the lady I had been following all day. 'Who is that?' I said, and his answer was, 'Mrs. Beaumont; lives in Ashley Street.' Of course there could be no doubt after that. I don't know whether she saw me, but I don't think she did. I went home at once, and, on consideration, I thought that I had a sufficiently good case with which to go to Clarke."

"Why to Clarke?"

"Because I am sure that Clarke is in possession of facts about this woman, facts of which I know nothing."

"Well, what then?"

Mr. Villiers leaned back in his chair and looked reflectively at Austin for a moment before he answered:

"My idea was that Clarke and I should call on Mrs. Beaumont."

"You would never go into such a house as that? No,

no, Villiers, you cannot do it. Besides, consider; what result . . ."

"I will tell you soon. But I was going to say that my information does not end here; it has been completed in an extraordinary manner.

"Look at this neat little packet of manuscript; it is paginated, you see, and I have indulged in the civil coquetry of a ribbon of red tape. It has almost a legal air, hasn't it? Run your eye over it, Austin. It is an account of the entertainment Mrs. Beaumont provided for her choicer guests. The man who wrote this escaped with his life, but I do not think he will live many years. The doctors tell him he must have sustained some severe shock to the nerves."

Austin took the manuscript, but never read it. Opening the neat pages at haphazard his eye was caught by a word and a phrase that followed it; and, sick at heart, with white lips and a cold sweat pouring like water from his temples, he flung the paper down.

"Take it away, Villiers, never speak of this again. Are you made of stone, man? Why, the dread and horror of death itself, the thoughts of the man who stands in the keen morning air on the black platform, bound, the bell tolling in his ears, and waits for the harsh rattle of the bolt, are as nothing compared to this. I will not read it; I should never sleep again."

"Very good. I can fancy what you saw. Yes; it is horrible enough; but after all, it is an old story, an old mystery played in our day, and in dim London streets instead of amidst the vineyards and the olive gardens. We know what happened to those who chanced to meet the Great God Pan, and those who are wise know that all symbols are symbols of something, not of nothing. It was, indeed, an exquisite symbol beneath which men long ago veiled their knowledge of the most awful, most secret forces which lie at the heart of all things; forces

before which the souls of men must wither and die and
blacken, as their bodies blacken under the electric
current. Such forces cannot be named, cannot be
spoken, cannot be imagined except under a veil and a
symbol, a symbol to the most of us appearing a quaint,
poetic fancy, to some a foolish tale. But you and I, at all
events, have known something of the terror that may
dwell in the secret place of life, manifested under
human flesh; that which is without form taking to itself
a form. Oh, Austin, how can it be? How is it that the
very sunlight does not turn to blackness before this
thing, the hard earth melt and boil beneath such a
burden?"

Villiers was pacing up and down the room, and the
beads of sweat stood out on his forehead. Austin sat
silent for a while, but Villiers saw him make a sign upon
his breast.

"I say again, Villiers, you will surely never enter such
a house as that? You would never pass out alive."

"Yes, Austin, I shall go out alive—I, and Clarke with
me."

"What do you mean? You cannot, you would not
dare. . . ."

"Wait a moment. The air was very pleasant and fresh
this morning; there was a breeze blowing, even through
this dull street, and I thought I would take a walk.
Piccadilly stretched before me a clear, bright vista, and
the sun flashed on the carriages and on the quivering
leaves in the park. It was a joyous morning, and men
and women looked at the sky and smiled as they went
about their work or their pleasure, and the wind blew as
blithely as upon the meadows and the scented gorse.
But somehow or other I got out of the bustle and the
gaiety, and found myself walking slowly along a quiet,
dull street, where there seemed to be no sunshine and
no air, and where the few footpassengers loitered as

they walked, and hung indecisively about corners and archways. I walked along, hardly knowing where I was going or what I did there, but feeling impelled, as one sometimes is, to explore still further, with a vague idea of reaching some unknown goal. Thus I forged up the street, noting the small traffic of the milk-shop, and wondering at the incongruous medley of penny pipes, black tobacco, sweets, newspaper, and comic songs which here and there jostled one another in the short compass of a single window. I think it was a cold shudder that suddenly passed through me that first told me that I had found what I wanted. I looked up from the pavement and stopped before a dusty shop, above which the lettering had faded, where the red bricks of two hundred years ago had grimed to black; where the windows had gathered to themselves the fog and the dirt of winters innumerable. I saw what I required; but I think it was five minutes before I had steadied myself and could walk in and ask for it in a cool voice and with a calm face. I think there must even then have been a tremor in my words, for the old man who came out from his back parlour, and fumbled slowly amongst his goods, looked oddly at me as he tied the parcel. I paid what he asked, and stood leaning by the counter, with a strange reluctance to take up my goods and go. I asked about the business, and learnt that trade was bad and the profits cut down sadly; but then the street was not what it was before traffic had been diverted, but that was done forty years ago, 'just before my father died,' he said. I got away at last, and walked along sharply; it was a dismal street indeed, and I was glad to return to the bustle and the noise. Would you like to see my purchase?"

Austin said nothing, but nodded his head slightly; he still looked white and sick. Villiers pulled out a drawer in the bamboo table, and showed Austin a long coil of cord, hard and new; and at one end was a running noose.

"It is the best hempen cord," said Villiers, "just as it used to be made for the old trade, the man told me. Not an inch of jute from end to end."

Austin set his teeth hard, and stared at Villiers, growing whiter as he looked.

"You would not do it," he murmured at last. "You would not have blood on your hands, My God!" he exclaimed, with sudden vehemence, "you cannot mean this, Villiers, that you will make yourself a hangman?"

"No. I shall offer a choice, and leave Helen Vaughan alone with this cord in a locked room for fifteen minutes. If when we go in it is not done, I shall call the nearest policeman. That is all."

"I must go now. I cannot stay here any longer; I cannot bear this. Good-night."

"Good-night, Austin."

The door shut, but in a moment it was opened again, and Austin stood, white and ghastly, in the entrance.

"I was forgetting," he said, "that I too have something to tell. I have received a letter from Dr. Harding of Buenos Aires. He says that he attended Meyrick for three weeks before his death."

"And does he say what carried him off in the prime of life? It was not fever?"

"No, it was not fever. According to the doctor, it was an utter collapse of the whole system, probably caused by some severe shock. But hesitates that the patient would tell him nothing, and that he was consequently at some disadvantage in treating the case."

"Is there anything more?"

"Yes. Dr. Harding ends his letter by saying: 'I think this is all the information I can give you about your poor friend. He had not been long in Buenos Aires, and knew scarcely anyone, with the exception of a person who did not bear the best of characters, and has since left—a Mrs. Vaughan.'"

VIII   The Fragments

Amongst the papers of the well-known physician, Dr. Robert Matheson, of Ashley Street, Piccadilly, who died suddenly of apopletic seizure, at the beginning of 1892, a leaf of manuscript paper was found, covered with pencil jottings. These notes were in Latin, much abbreviated, and has evidently been made in great haste. The MS. was only deciphered with great difficulty, and some words have up to the present time evaded all the efforts of the expert employed. The date, "XXV Jul. 1888," is written on the right-hand corner of the MS. The following is a translation of Dr. Matheson's manuscript.

Whether science would benefit by these brief notes if they could be published, I do not know, but rather doubt. But certainly I shall never take the responsibility of publishing or divulging one word of what is here written, not only on account of my oath freely given to those two persons who were present, but also because the details are too abominable. It is probably that, upon mature consideration, and after weighing the good and evil, I shall one day destroy this paper, or at least leave it under seal to my friend D., trusting in his discretion, to use it or to burn it, as he may think fit.

As was befitting, I did all that my knowledge suggested to make sure that I was suffering under no delusion. At first astounded, I could hardly think, but in a minute's time I was sure that my pulse was steady and regular, and that I was in my real and true senses. I then fixed my eyes quietly on what was before me.

Though horror and revolting nausea rose up within me, and an odour of corruption choked my breath, I remained firm. I was then privileged or accursed, I dare not say which, to see that which was on the bed, lying there black like ink, transformed before my eyes. The skin, and the flesh, and the muscles, and the bones, and the firm structure of the human body that I had thought to be unchangeable, and permanent as adamant, began to melt and dissolve.

I knew that the body may be separated into its elements by external agencies, but I should have refused to believe what I saw. For here there was some internal force, of which I knew nothing, that caused dissolution and change.

Here too was all the work by which man had been made repeated before my eyes. I saw the form waver from sex to sex, dividing itself from itself, and then again reunited. Then I saw the body descend to the beasts whence it ascended, and that which was on the heights go down to the depths, even to the abyss of all being. The principle of life, which makes organism, always remained, while the outward form changed.

The light within the room had turned to blackness, not the darkness of night, in which objects are seen dimly, for I could see clearly and without difficulty. But it was the negation of light; objects were presented to my eyes, if I may say so, without any medium, in such a manner that if there had been a prism in the room I should have seen no colours represented in it.

I watched, and at last I saw nothing but a substance as jelly. Then the ladder was ascended again . . . [here the MS. is illegible] . . . for one instant I saw a Form, shaped in dimness before me, which I will not farther describe. But the symbol of this form may be seen in ancient sculptures, and in paintings which survived beneath the lava, too foul to be spoken of . . . as a horrible and unspeakable shape, neither man nor beast, was changed into human form, there came finally death.

I who saw all this, not without great horror and loathing of soul, here write my name, declaring all that I have set on this paper to be true.

Robert Matheson, Med. Dr.

. . . Such, Raymond, is the story of what I know and what I have seen. The burden of it was too heavy for me to bear alone, and yet I could tell it to none but you. Villiers, who was with me at the last, knows nothing of that awful secret of the wood, of how what we both saw die, lay upon the smooth, sweet turf amidst the summer flowers, half in sun and half in shadow, and holding the girl Rachel's hand, called and summoned those companions, and shaped in solid form, upon the earth we tread on, the horror which we can but hint at, which we can only name under a figure. I would not tell Villiers of this, nor of that resemblance, which struck me as with a blow upon my heart, when I saw the portrait, which filled the cup of terror at the end. What this can mean I dare not guess. I know that what I saw perish was not Mary, and yet in the last agony Mary's eyes looked into mine. Whether there be anyone who can show the last link in this chain of awful mystery, I do not know, but if there be anyone who can do this, you, Raymond, are the man. And if you know the secret, it rests with you to tell it or not, as you please.

I am writing this letter to you immediately on my getting back to town. I have been in the country for the last few days; perhaps you may be able to guess in what part. While the horror and wonder of London was at its height—for "Mrs. Beaumont," as I have told you, was well known in society—I wrote to my friend Dr. Phillips, giving some brief outline, or rather hint, of what had happened, and asking him to tell me the name of the village where the events he had related to me occurred. He gave me the name, as he said with the less hesitation, because Rachel's father and mother were dead, and the rest of the family had gone to a relative in the state of Washington six months before. The parents, he said, had undoubtedly died of grief and horror caused by the terrible death of their daughter, and by what had gone before that death. On the evening of the day on which I received Phillip's letter I was at Caermaen, and standing beneath the mouldering Roman walls, white with the winters of seventeen hundred years. I looked over the meadow where once had stood the older Temple of the "God of the Deeps," and saw a house gleaming in the sunlight. It was the house where Helen had lived. I stayed at Caermaen for several days. The people of the place, I found, knew little and had guessed less. Those whom I spoke to on the matter seemed surprised that an antiquarian (as I professed myself to be) should trouble about a village tragedy, of which they gave a very commonplace version, and, as you may imagine, I told nothing of what I knew. Most of my time was spent in the great wood that rises just above the village and climbs the hillside, and goes down to the river in the valley; such another long lovely valley, Raymond, as that on which we looked one summer night, walking to and fro before your house. For many an hour I strayed through the maze of the forest, turning now to right and now to left, pacing slowly down long alleys of undergrowth, shadowy and chill, even under the midday sun, and halting beneath great oaks; lying on the short turf of a clearing where the faint sweet scent of wild roses came to me on the wind and mixed with the heavy perfume of the elder, whose mingled odour is like the odour of the room of the dead, a vapour of incense and corruption. I stood at the edges of the wood, gazing at all the pomp and procession of the foxgloves towering amidst the bracken and shining red in the broad sunshine, and beyond them into deep thickets of close undergrowth where springs boil up from the rock and nourish the waterweeds, dank and evil. But in all my wanderings I avoided one part of the wood; it was not till yesterday that I climbed to the summit of the hill, and stood upon the ancient Roman road that threads the highest ridge of the wood. Here they had walked, Helen and Rachel, along this quiet causeway, upon the pavement of green turf, shut in on either side by high banks of red earth, and tall hedges of shining beech, and here I followed in their steps, looking out, now and again, through partings in the boughs, and seeing on one side the sweep of the wood stretching far to right and left, and sinking into the broad level, and beyond, the yellow sea, and the land over the sea. On the other side was the valley and the river and hill following hill as wave on wave, and wood and meadow, and cornfield, and white houses gleaming, and a great wall of mountain, and far blue peaks in the north. And so at last I came to the place. The track went up a gentle slope and widened out into an open space with a wall of thick undergrowth around it, and then, narrowing again, passed on into the distance and the faint blue mist of summer heat. And into this pleasant summer glade Rachel passed a girl, and left it, who shall say what? I did not stay long there.

In a small town near Caermaen there is a museum, containing for the most part Roman remains which have been found in the neighbourhood at various times. On the day after my arrival at Caermaen I walked over to the town in question, and took the opportunity of inspecting this museum. After I had seen most of the sculptured stones, the coffins, rings, coins, and fragments of tessellated pavement which the place contains, I was shown a small square pillar of white stone, which had been recently discovered in the wood of which I have been speaking, and, as I found on inquiry, in that open space where the Roman road broadens out. On one side of the pillar was an inscription, of which I took a note. Some of the letters have been defaced, but I do not think there can be any doubt as to those which I supply. The inscription is as follows:

> DEVOMNODENT*i*
> ELA*v*IVSSENILISPOSSV*it*
> PROPTERNVP*tias*
> *quas*VIDITSVBYMB*ra*

"To the great god Nodens (the god of the Great Deep or Abyss) Flavius Senilis has erected this pillar on account of the marriage which he saw beneath the shade."

The custodian of the museum informed me that local antiquaries were much puzzled, not by the inscription, or by any difficulty in translating it, but as to the circumstance or rite to which allusion is made.

. . . And now, my dear Clarke, as to what you tell me about Helen Vaughan, whom you say you saw die under circumstances of the utmost and almost incredible horror. I was interested in your account, but a good deal, nay all, of what you told me I knew already. I can understand the strange likeness you remarked both in the portrait and in the actual face; you have seen Helen's mother. You remember that still summer night so many years ago, when I talked to you of the world beyond the shadows, and of the god Pan. You remem-